PRAIS... ...OOKS

The Soul Hunter

"A bloody ax, a tragic victim, a persistent demon, a haunt... ...
a broken heart—all this and a bun... ...
supernatural mystery, Melanie V... ...
Hunter. A dash of romance and a... ...
soned with grace, makes this a t... ...

KATHRYN MACKEL, AU... ...IDDEN

"In *The Soul Hunter,* Melanie Wells demonstrates again her talent as a storyteller. Her lovably neurotic and intrepid narrator, Dr. Dylan Foster, is back, haunted once more by demonic Peter Terry, and terrified not only by the presence of a bloody ax on her doorstep but also by an invasion of rats in her home and an upcoming tenure review. Part mystery thriller, part comedy of manners, part novel of moral scrutiny, *The Soul Hunter* showcases Wells's gift for spinning an intricate tale filled with an edgy mix of humor, suspense, and spiritual intrigue. I swallowed the novel in one deliciously terrified gulp."

K. L. COOK, AUTHOR OF *LAST CALL* AND *THE GIRL FROM CHARNELLE*

"With deft humor and spiritual insight, Melanie Wells is creating one of the most memorable and likable heroines in mystery literature. This is spine-tingling storytelling. It's edgy. It's hip. And it's not to be missed!"

ERIC WILSON, AUTHOR OF *EXPIRATION DATE*

"Melanie Wells let me to see the world through a woman's eyes without getting grossed out or crying, "Cooties!" The Dylan Foster character was believable, relatable, and someone cool I'd like to be friends with. The fact that she's a demon-seeing curious professor who can't stay out of trouble is charming. It's great to "ride along" with a down-to-earth Christian who fits into her culture without apologies or overt preaching."

DOUG VAN PELT, EDITOR OF *HM MAGAZINE*

When the Day of Evil Comes

"*When the Day of Evil Comes* is a chilling story, blessedly short enough to be read over a weekend because you're not going to want to put it down until you've finished it."

"Melanie Wells has written a powerful first novel."

"*When the Day of Evil Comes* is a glimpse into the spiritual battle taking place not only for our hearts but also for our minds…a well-crafted novel with a compelling heroine and plot."

DAY OF EVIL
SERIES

BOOK
2

MELANIE WELLS

THE SOUL HUNTER

A NOVEL OF SUSPENSE

Multnomah® Publishers *Sisters, Oregon*

THE SOUL HUNTER

published by Multnomah Publishers, Inc.

© 2006 by Melanie Wells

International Standard Book Number: 1-59052-427-6

Interior typeset by Katherine Lloyd, The DESK

Multnomah is a trademark of Multnomah Publishers, Inc.,
and is registered in the U.S. Patent and Trademark Office.
The colophon is a trademark of Multnomah Publishers, Inc.

Printed in the United States of America

For information:

MULTNOMAH PUBLISHERS, INC.

601 North Larch Street

Sisters, Oregon 97759

Library of Congress Cataloging-in-Publication Data

Wells, Melanie.
    The soul hunter / Melanie Wells.
        p. cm. -- (Day of evil series ; bk. 2)
    ISBN 1-59052-427-6
    I. Title.
    PS3623.E476S67 2006
    813'.6--dc22

                                                        2006004900

06 07 08 09 10 11 12 — 10 9 8 7 6 5 4 3 2 1 0

~

For Dwight Huber,
who taught me always to speak my mind
and
For Vickie Kraft,
who taught me that perhaps *always* is not a good idea

"To us a human is primarily food; our aim is the absorption of its will into ours.… [But] one must face the fact that all the talk about [the Enemy's] love for men…is not (as one would gladly believe) mere propaganda, but an appalling truth."

SCREWTAPE TO WORMWOOD IN
THE SCREWTAPE LETTERS BY C.S. LEWIS

Acknowledgments

~

A magical transformation takes place when your first book gets published. Credibility, as it happens, opens a lot of doors. And waiting on the other side are articulate, accomplished professionals who are happy to help you with your research. Talking to these individuals, digging into their expertise, was the great joy of writing this book.

I'm indebted to the good folks of the Dallas Police Department Crimes Against Persons Division (CAPERS), Homicide Section, who do an impossible job under difficult circumstances, yet manage somehow to retain their decency and their humanity. Any authenticity in this story is theirs. Deliberate inaccuracies (the DPD does not keep prisoners handcuffed or chained during interrogation, for instance) are mine, kept for the sake of the story. Detectives Robert Quirk and Phil Harding, two of the finest and hardest working people I know, let me follow them around and made themselves available for all of my questions. Detective Dan Krieter gave me a fascinating explanation of fingerprint technology and helped me work out crucial details regarding physical evidence. Sergeant Eugene Reyes was generous in offering me access to his squad. And Gerry Meier, Senior District Judge, Dallas County (retired), who served as my entrée to the DPD, shared a pot of tea with me and helped me construct a criminal history for Gordon Pryne.

I'm grateful to Bruce Feldman for help with the Hebrew. And to my former colleague, Bob Pyne, Professor of Systematic Theology at Dallas Theological Seminary, for his help with theology, and for lending me a stack of his books for the better part of a year.

Pamela Lindsay Feagins, M.D., pitched in on medical issues, as did Drs. David Missimo and Bryan Forsythe. And a big thanks to Beverly Crittendon, the only female used car dealer in Dallas, for letting me use her car lot.

At Multnomah, Kevin Marks, fiction group publisher, and Sharon Znachko, group marketer for fiction, have been incredibly supportive, as have the rest of the folks up there in Sisters. And James Hall, the Multnomah artist who designed the cover for this book and for *When the Day of Evil Comes*, managed to capture the eerie character of both novels in a way that compels people to pick them up off the stack and take them home.

Rod Morris, my editor at Multnomah, waited patiently while I finished the draft—several months after deadline—and then managed, with his customary sharp eye, deft ear, and infallible tact, to excavate just the right words from the pile. What a pleasure to work with an editor who respects the writer's voice, yet knows exactly when to tone it down (by cutting the parentheticals, primarily).

Lisa Taylor, my publicist, is intrepid in her pursuit of reviews, interviews, press mentions, and speaking opportunities. My agent, Don Pape of Alive Communications, is a godsend, in the truest sense of the word. I'm humbled by his faith in me and grateful for his persistence on my behalf and his unflagging regard for my work.

Trish Murphy takes the solitude out of writing for me. I wrote much of this book parked at her kitchen table with my laptop while she tweaked song lyrics and made the tuna casserole. Dennis Ippolito read the manuscript several times, asking questions, offering suggestions, and helping me excise the mistakes.

His input has been invaluable. And Trish and Dennis both, champs that they are, sat around a swimming pool in Phoenix with me one hot weekend in September and read the entire manuscript out loud, laughing at all the right moments and helping me with nuances of tone, rhythm, plot, and dialogue.

Thanks to Elizabeth Emerson, Kim Coffin, and Christine Carberry, who combed the final draft for errors and picked them out, one by one.

A special thanks to the staff at LifeWorks, who fill in the gaps when I'm buried in book-related tasks. And to the Waah Waah Sisterhood for keeping me sane. Much love to Dot, Ron, Mike, Alissa, and Chance.

It takes a village to produce a novel. To those wonderful individuals who helped with this one, I offer my deepest thanks.

1
~

You'd think I'd have learned my lessons by now. Some people, it turns out, are not what they seem. Some secrets, it turns out, are better left untold. And some specters, it turns out, are better left unseen. And the answers, it turns out, don't always arrive in order. And when they do show up, they just might kick open a door you're better off leaving closed up tight.

I thought I'd gotten all the education I needed a year or so ago, starting with an innocuous decision I'd made to go to a cold spring pool on a hot summer day. I'd found myself standing in the gaze of the red-hot eyes of hell and discovered, quite by accident, that I'd caught the attention of the universe somehow. But not the kind of attention you want, if you get my meaning.

I'd looked evil in the eye that day and faced it down in the weeks that followed, more out of necessity than anything else. It certainly had nothing to do with bravery or spirituality or any quixotic sense of adventure I might have had. I'd just found myself in the target zone, so I'd fought when I had to, ducked when I could, and run when I couldn't think of anything else to do. And I'd eventually gotten out of the whole mess with a good-sized dose of grit, some help from the Almighty, and a couple of trips to Chicago.

It began this time, as some of my least intelligent moments do, in front of the mirror. It was the eve of my thirty-fifth birthday and

I was feeling the need for self-examination, I suppose. Some misguided ritual to mark the passageway to the other side of my thirties.

Magnifying mirrors were invented by Satan, I'm convinced. No human I've ever known could spend any time at all in front of a magnifying mirror examining pores and eyebrow hairs without coming away from there with a toxic sense of shame and self-doubt.

On this occasion, I committed the additional catastrophic error of looking at myself from behind. In a department store dressing room. Under fluorescent lights. While trying on bikinis. In winter.

To my dismay, stuck right there on the back of my formerly firm legs were my mother's thighs. My mother's Texas milkmaid thighs.

I work hard to stay in shape. Though I am an academic, and most of the professors I know are thoroughly slovenly in their personal habits, I have resolutely risen above the fray. I am non-lumpy. I have fitness goals. I have completed a triathlon.

And I absolutely refuse to let my rear end slide south toward my ankles.

So the dismay I felt at that moment under the lights was genuine. I could not have been more surprised.

Now, all women know the steps to combat body-image trauma. Men would do well to memorize the procedure too. This sort of handbook-type information, if utilized correctly, could cut the divorce rate by a third, I'm convinced.

The first step, of course, is to shop. Preferably for expensive fitness gear that will encourage you to work out with renewed vigor and dedication. Or, if you choose to punt on self-improvement, an alternative is to shop for a new and fetching outfit that disguises the body part in question.

I went for the fitness gear. I swim regularly, but those endless laps in the pool were not warding off the impending thigh disaster. Though I have to say, my arms looked pretty smokin'.

The answer here was shoes. I needed running shoes. Now.

The second step is to call a friend, or perhaps an evolved squeeze or spouse, and complain. Qualified and well-trained personnel will assure you that you look like a couple million bucks and that you're just in the middle of a psychotic break.

Let's go get double-hot-chocolate lattes, they'll say.

Which is step three.

Step four is to roll your sad little self out of bed the next morning, strap on your new gear, and get yourself to the gym. Most individuals hit the wall after steps one or three.

I intended to complete the entire process. I was not going down without a fight.

Since I was already at the mall, I abandoned my bikini search and marched myself straight to the sporting goods store, squaring my shoulders against the heady smell of chocolate chip cookies as I passed by Mrs. Fields.

I had momentum. I was feeling good. I was on it.

And then I ran into John Mulvaney.

John Mulvaney is a colleague of mine—a fellow psychology professor at Southern Methodist University. A full citizen in the sometimes moldy and pretentious world of academic clinical psychology. That is the entire extent of our common ground.

That, and the fact that we both believe deeply that he is a genuinely pathetic human being.

We'd crossed paths the year before in a bizarre incident that left me with a strange mix of pity and loathing toward the man. And a powerful urge to avoid him.

In this instance, avoiding him was impossible. I literally bumped right into him.

He was turning away from the cash register at Mrs. Fields, hands loaded with a half dozen greasy warm cookies, a soft drink, and a vanilla milkshake. He had a smear of chocolate on his upper lip.

I pasted on a fake smile. "Hello, John."

"Dr. Foster," he said back.

"You can call me Dylan, John."

"I prefer the title," he mumbled.

We went through this silly little ritual each time we spoke. He had never once gotten a "Dr. Mulvaney" out of me.

His eyes firmly fixed on the ground, he sucked hard on his milkshake straw, coaxing a thick clot of ice cream into his mouth. He chased it with an enormous bite of cookie.

I watched with raw disgust, fighting the urge to wipe the chocolate off his lip.

"Well," I said. "Nice seeing you, John. Have a good afternoon."

I turned to leave. I got a good twenty yards into my escape before he called out after me.

"I'm going shopping," he said. "I need a sweater."

I turned and stared at him. Was this merely a social-skills debacle on his part or had he gone insane?

Incredibly, he kept talking.

"And then I'm going to see a movie. The new art film. At the Inwood."

"Okay, John. Have a good time."

Why do academics love art films? And why was John Mulvaney telling me about his afternoon plans?

I shot him a little wave and walked away. Rapidly. I made it this time. A clean exit.

I bought myself some nifty high-tech running shoes, after a fairly intriguing ritual of rolling up my jeans and walking barefoot in front of the sales person so she could see what my feet do when I walk. I pronate, apparently.

And then I initiated step two and called my evolved boyfriend.

"David Shykovsky," he said.

"I hope you know the correct answer to this question.."

"What question is that, Sugar Pea?"

"What do you think of my legs?"

"Ah. Let's see. Many men would fail this test. But not me."
Darling man.

"The correct answer," he said, "if I recall from years of answering this sort of question miserably in other, less crucial circumstances with other, less fabulous women, is that your legs, like the rest of you, are perfect. Wonderful. Sublime."

"Flabby?"

"Absolutely not."

"Good man."

"Why?"

"No reason. Want to meet me for a double-hot-chocolate latte?"

"I'm working, babe."

Rats. So much for step three.

"Funeral today?"

"Nope. Body coming in."

"I don't know how you do that job."

"I don't know how you do yours either, Professor. At least my patients are mentally stable."

"Your patients are dead."

"Exactly. I don't talk to them. I don't worry about them. I don't listen to their problems. I just drain 'em and dress 'em."

"That's so gross."

"I prefer to think of it as a necessary art."

"How do you figure?"

"You try to make a ninety-seven-year-old dead person with no teeth look like they're forty years younger and in deep, peaceful repose. It's not easy."

"I could see that. Are you still taking me out tonight for a surprise birthday supper?"

"Check."

"Italian food?"

"Check."

"White tablecloths?"

"Check."

"Expensive wine?"

"Midlist, I'd say."

"Death business been slow?"

"Check."

"How about six thirty?"

"You'll be late."

"Seven?" I said.

"Check. See you at seven thirty."

"Check."

We hung up. David Shykovsky is an enigma to me. Delightful man. Smart. Charming. Good-looking. Adores me.

Owns a funeral home in Hillsboro.

I can't quite get past that last part.

I spent the rest of the afternoon, a rare sunny Saturday in January, embarking on my new Thigh Recovery Program. Lunges, squats, weights, and a three-mile run. Take that, milkmaid.

I'd be lucky if I could walk the next day.

After my workout, I showered, stared at my thighs some more—I swear they looked better—and then spent a good half hour primping for my dress-up, pre-birthday date with David. All in all, a pretty high-end day for me.

I was smack in mid-primp when I heard something at the front door. It was a knock of sorts. More of a thump, actually. Or a clunk.

I heard a car pulling away from the house. Maybe I'd missed UPS or something. Maybe it was a pre-birthday present!

Twinkling with anticipation, I threw on a robe and scooted to the front door, checking the peephole.

I unlocked the deadbolt and opened the door.

Something slid across the wood and smacked heavily onto the floor of the entryway, catching my baby toe under its end.

I let out a little scream—a mixture of pain and indignation—and looked down to see what had fallen into my house and onto my foot.

It was an ax.

I couldn't see it clearly against the hardwood, so I reached down and picked it up, then flipped on the light.

My hands were red. Why were my hands red?

I turned the ax over in my hands.

The ax was red. Had it just been painted?

I looked over at the light switch. A handprint was smeared in red on my wall. My handprint.

I squinted at the blade.

There was hair on the blade.

I dropped the ax, my eyes widening as it thwacked heavily to the floor.

I slid to the floor, my back against the wall.

That ax was covered in blood.

And that, of course, was the moment I knew I'd made my first mistake.

2

~

The first of many, it turned out. I do believe, looking back on it, that the entire episode just struck me dumb—dumb as a stump, to be exact. I just sat there, rooted to that floor, my front door standing wide open, the cold night air rushing in around me.

Eventually, I did manage to lean over and stare at the ax, this time being careful not to touch anything. I could see my handprints on the handle, perfectly imprinted where I'd grabbed it.

I peered at the blade again, squinting at the little tangle of hair. The hairs were short—maybe four inches long—mangled like Brillo and stuck to the jagged edge of the blade. The hair looked to be a bright auburn red. A white chip of something clung to the blade. A rush of nausea hit me.

The slam of a car door and footsteps on the sidewalk shook me out of my stupor. I scrambled to my feet, bracing myself against the wall as I stood, leaving another angry smear on the pale yellow paint. I slammed the door shut, locked it, and slapped the light switch off.

I leaned against the door, breathing hard, my heart knocking against my ribs, my brain screaming at me. *Idiot,* it screamed. *Run.*

The footsteps stopped on my front porch.

I held my breath.

"Dylan?"

I squeezed my eyes shut.

The doorknob rattled.

"Dylan!" he said again, sharply this time.

I reached down and grabbed the ax, stepping slowly away from the door.

He knocked. Loudly. "I know you're in there. Open the door."

I finally recognized the voice. *Idiot,* my brain said to me again.

"David?" I said out loud.

"Dylan?"

"Is that you?"

"Of course it's me. Let me in." He rattled the doorknob again.

"Is anyone out there?"

"I am. I'm out here. Let me in."

"Are you alone?"

"Of course I'm alone. What do you think, I brought a date? I'm here to pick you up."

"Is anyone in the yard?"

"I am. I'm in the yard. Let me in."

"I'm not opening the door—not until you check."

"No one is out here, Dylan. It's just me. Open the door. It's, like, ten degrees out."

"Go look on the sides of the house. And in the back. And check behind the Burkes' bushes."

I waited while he walked around and searched the yard.

"All clear, Sugar Pea. Come on, babe. Open the door. I'm freezing out here."

I shifted the ax to my left hand and opened the door.

David stepped in and flipped on the light, sucking in a quick breath as he got a look at me.

"Sweet Moses," he said, and began to move toward me.

I backed up and raised the ax with both hands, stupid and wild with fear. I must have made a strange apparition. My white bathrobe was smeared with blood. My hands were smeared with blood. My wall and light switch were smeared with blood.

He stopped and held his hands up.

"Dylan. Come on, Sugar Pea. Settle down. It's me."

"It's you," I repeated.

"It's me. Everything's okay. Put the ax down, honey." He spoke as though talking to a child. Or to a frightened pet.

I dropped the ax, the handle slapping to the floor.

I held out my arms. He stepped into them, holding me as I started to cry.

He had the good sense not to say anything. He just let me leak tears all over his nicely pressed shirt. When I finally pulled away, he had a little spider of a mascara stain on his chest.

"What happened, Dylan? Are you hurt?"

"No, no. I'm not hurt. I don't know why I got so scared."

He pulled back and looked at me, then passed his eyes around the hallway, taking in the scene. The scene of some vicarious carnage.

"What happened?" he asked again.

"Nothing. I don't know."

"Whose blood is this? It's not yours? I thought you were hurt."

"No, I'm not hurt. I don't know whose blood it is."

"Well how did it get all over you?" He looked around at the blood-swiped walls, then back at me, reaching for my hands and turning them over, inspecting my sticky red palms.

"Someone left this ax on my porch. I thought it was a present. From UPS."

"Dylan, you're not making any sense."

"I heard something at the door. I thought maybe it was UPS or something. Bringing a birthday present, maybe. I opened the door and there was this ax. I picked it up before I knew it was—"

"Bloody? Someone left a bloody ax on your front porch? Whose ax is it?"

"I don't go around taking inventory of other people's gardening tools, David."

He held his hands up again. "Okay, okay. Sorry. I just meant…what did I mean?" He took a breath. "It's not your ax, I take it."

"It could be mine, I guess. I don't even know if I own an ax. Maybe someone took it out of my garage. Was the garage door open?"

"No. It's closed."

We both stood there for a minute, dumbstruck. That dumbness was contagious, it seemed.

"Maybe it's animal blood," he offered. "Maybe someone killed a dog or something…"

I recoiled.

"…and left the ax as some sort of sick prank. To scare you."

"It worked."

"I can see that." He looked around again.

"What should we do?" I asked. "Call the police?"

"Probably. This is not the sort of thing you don't report."

"There's hair on the blade," I said.

He squatted down and peered at the blade, careful not to touch it.

"It looks like human hair to me," he said. "A woman's hair."

"How can you tell?"

"It's too long to be a dog's. Or a man's. Most men, anyway. And it's too red. It looks dyed."

I knelt down beside him. It did look dyed. The roots were black.

"Do you want me to call?" he said.

"Please."

He turned and went to the kitchen.

I heard him dial 911, wait a moment, and then start the conversation. "I have something a little odd to report…"

I went to my bedroom and kicked the door shut behind me. Surely it would take the police a while to get here. This was the Dallas Police Department, after all. In a city of over a million people, they must have real, actual crimes in progress to take care of.

I stepped into the bathroom and caught sight of myself in the mirror. My third ghastly encounter with a mirror that day.

The wave of nausea returned, almost doubling me over. I retched into the sink, keeping my head down for a minute, letting the cold water run. I straightened back up and faced myself.

I looked like I'd been assaulted. Violently. My face was drained of color, and my eye makeup was smudged into little black rivers on my cheeks. My hair was wrecked. Blood was smeared in little hieroglyphs all over me and all over my fluffy white robe. My hands were sticky, almost brown now as the blood dried.

I peeled the robe off and let it drop onto the floor in a heap, vowing to myself that I would burn it at the first opportunity. I stepped into the tub and pulled the shower curtain closed. I felt like I could scrub forever and never get that blood off. Some red-headed woman's blood.

I couldn't even stand to think about it, whose blood that might be.

I worked up a good, thick lather, soaping myself generously and watching as the water went from pink to clear and circled into the drain. I was just starting to settle down when someone banged on the bathroom door, scaring me half out of my skin again.

"Dylan?"

"David? Is that you?"

He shouted through the door. "The police are here, Dylan. They want you to get out of the shower immediately."

"Why?"

"I don't know, babe, but they don't look to me like they're

going to take no for an answer. Finish up and come on out, okay?"

I rinsed off quickly and toweled off, hoping they weren't waiting in the bedroom. I had nothing in here but my bathrobe and I wasn't about to put that thing on.

Steam curled through the doorway as I cracked the door and peered into my bedroom. It was uninhabited. The door was closed. I grabbed some jeans and a sweatshirt, threw them on quickly and went out to face the DPD.

Two uniformed policemen were with David on the front porch. The front door was open, a police cruiser parked in front of my house, red and blue lights blazing. A white DPD van pulled up to the curb as I stepped into the hall.

"Hello," I said.

Everyone turned to look at me.

"Miss Foster?" one of the men said.

"Doctor," David said.

"Dylan," I said, extending my hand.

The officer did not offer his in return. I dropped my hand back to my side, strangely hurt. I checked their name tags. Hernandez and Jones.

"Step outside, please," Hernandez said.

"Can I just…?" I reached for the hall closet to grab a jacket.

Hernandez stopped me. "Step outside, ma'am."

I obeyed—a rare instance of compliance on my part.

"Can you tell me what happened, ma'am?" Jones asked.

"Sure. I was in the bathroom getting ready for a date. A date with David." I nodded at him. "And I heard something at the door."

"What time was this?" Hernandez asked.

"I guess around ten after seven. Maybe seven fifteen? He was supposed to pick me up at seven thirty."

"Okay. Go on."

"So. I came to the door and opened it and this ax fell in."

"It just…fell in?" Jones said.

I nodded. "And it was dark, because I hadn't turned the porch light on and I couldn't see what it was. So I picked it up and turned the light on." I nodded at the light switch just inside the doorway.

Everyone looked at the switch and then back at me.

Officers Jones and Hernandez didn't look like they were buying my story. My absolutely true story. It hadn't dawned on me that anyone wouldn't believe me. Why would I make something like that up?

"Do you own an ax?" Hernandez asked me.

"I don't think so."

"But you don't know?" He raised his eyebrows at me.

I smiled weakly. "Apparently ax ownership is something most people document more carefully than I do."

Hernandez scowled. "It's not your ax, ma'am?"

"I'm not sure. I mean, I don't think it's my ax. If it is, I don't know how it got onto the porch."

"What happened after that?" Jones said.

"Well. So. Then, I realized it had something on it. I thought it might be paint. And then I looked at the blade and saw those—" I looked down at the blade, "—hairs." I could barely say the word. "And I sort of freaked out."

"And then I walked up," David said. "Right, honey?"

He never called me honey. It sounded fake and sing-songy, like he was coaching me. We all glared at him to shut up.

"That's right," I said. "I didn't know it was him, though. I thought it might be the ax guy. So I slammed the door shut and locked it and turned off the light."

Hernandez walked over, stepping carefully around what I now realized was evidence and inspected the inside of the door. The story was there. Written in red handprints and streaks.

"And I couldn't get her to open the door," David said. "She was really scared. I had to convince her it was me, and she wanted me to walk around and make sure no one was out there. And even when I finally did get her to open the door, she was still scared. When I walked in, she raised the ax up, like she was going to hit me. Like a reflex or something. She was really traumatized."

I think he was trying, bless his heart, to help me. But it was coming out like I'd been a participant in something. Or the victim of something.

"Who was in the yard, Dr. Foster? Did someone attack you tonight?" Jones asked.

"Nobody attacked me. I swear. I mean, take a look. I'm not injured or anything." I held out my hands and rolled up my sleeves.

"We'll get all that downtown. Photos and swabs," Jones said.

"Photos and swabs?"

"You're a crime scene, Miss Foster," Hernandez said. "And your house is a crime scene." He turned to Jones. "Who's coming?"

"Jackson. He'll bring the waiver."

"Waiver?"

"Consent to search," Hernandez said.

"Search? What for? I found the ax." I pointed at the floor. "Lying right there on the floor. I told you. I picked it up, and then when David came, I just got scared and sort of freaked out. It was a reflex, just like he said, but then I realized everything was fine and no one was out there, and I put the ax down and hugged him and that's why he has the mascara on his shirt."

I hadn't used a sentence that long since I was fourteen and talking on the phone about boys. I sounded like an idiot. A defensive, guilty idiot.

"And the shower?" Hernandez asked.

"Well…I wanted to get the blood off. I mean, it's pretty gross. Don't you think?"

It hadn't occurred to me until then that the shower was another mistake. I could see it now, though. It made me look guilty of something.

Moron, my brain said.

Officer Jones nodded at the squad car. "If you'll have a seat in the car, Dr. Foster, we'll talk to Mr...."

"Shykovsky," I said.

"Mr. Shykovsky," he said. "We'll get your statements while PES gets to work."

"PES?"

"Physical Evidence Section." Jones nodded toward the white van. "Baggers and taggers. And then we can get out of your hair."

I winced. Don't say *hair.*

Hernandez walked me to the squad car. Jones stayed on the porch and grilled David as the evidence team filed into my house. Officers Hernandez and Jones conferred for a minute and came out to talk to me again. Finally, they parked David in the backseat of the squad car next to me and locked us in.

I nodded at the growing knot of DPD personnel in my hallway. "They don't believe me, do they?"

"Sure they do. They just have to ask all the questions, you know, be thorough. It's their job."

"You're lying. They think I'm a nut."

"No," he said, looking at me with his beautiful, clear green eyes. Eyes which, in that tender moment, offered up enormous sobriety and compassion.

"What is it, then?" I asked, hoping he wouldn't say it.

"They think you whacked someone with that ax tonight."

We looked at each other for a moment, the dreadful thought just hanging there, almost blocking the view between us.

"You were in jail last year, weren't you?"

He was referring to an unfortunate incident in which I was wrongly accused of, well, trespassing and assault. None of which was my fault, might I add.

I nodded ruefully. "Check."

"How was it?"

"Wonderful."

"White tablecloths?" he asked, grinning.

"Check."

"Expensive wine?"

"Midlist."

"The presumption of innocence?"

"Check."

He put his arm around me. "Sugar Pea, I love you, but you have the worst luck of anyone I know."

I leaned my head back on his shoulder and settled in to await my fate.

3

There are no white tablecloths in jail. Or white sheets for that matter. Or white towels. Everything is gray. And old. And stained. The food, such as it is, is also gray. And old. Not to mention cold and greasy. Served on paper plates and plastic trays with plastic utensils and little crummy foil packs of generic ketchup and those tiny, ridged paper packets of salt and pepper that scatter their contents when you open them. The beds are hard, the toilets squalid, the walls sticky and defiled with graffiti and other things you'd rather not know about, and the entire place smells like a sickening mix of disinfectant, vomit, and urine.

Fortunately, I did not enjoy a repeat visit to the pokey that night. Maybe Jesus took pity on me, knowing (since so many of His followers have done jail time) the apocalyptic impact such an experience would have on my fragile mental health that evening.

It was a long night anyway, though. Jones and Hernandez were joined by Jackson, Skank (I'm not kidding), and Brueheimer. Jackson was the detective. Skank and Brueheimer—who, taken together, sounded to me like Hitler's law firm or something—were the evidence team. Baggers and taggers, Jones had called them.

I watched from the squad car as the five of them, the Jackson Five of the DPD as they quickly became in my mind, tiptoed through the rosy patches of evidence in my foyer, wearing white

Mickey Mouse gloves and muttering gravely to one another. They took prints from every surface in the hallway. They bagged up the ax—in a brown paper bag, if you can believe that—like something they picked up at the grocery store. They searched my yard. They photographed everything. The whole bit.

Then they hauled David and me downtown, stuck us in separate rooms, asked us invasive, suspicious questions, and got our statements. I'd signed the consent form, so they swabbed the inside of my mouth for DNA. They photographed my bare arms and legs. They documented every second of my Saturday. Every phone call. Every conversation. Every encounter.

Between the two of us, we gave a solid performance. Truth was on our side, of course, but it seemed obvious to me that the Jackson Five did not believe us for one red-hot second.

Jackson was the toughest nut to crack. He was a solid six-foot barrel of a man and looked as though he could pull a tree down with his bare hands. He was black and gravelly as the asphalt street in front of my house. By the time he was finished with me, I was wracked with tension, and he was convinced I was a pathological liar.

Finally, he warned me not to leave town anytime soon and sent us both home in a squad car. The cop dropped us off, and David walked me to the front door, which was blocked off with yellow crime scene tape.

David, lovely man that he is, was a sport. A true blue, all-American, homegrown sport. He offered to stay the night on my couch, but I sent him home. I locked the door behind him, tippie-toed my way through the dried blood, which I absolutely could not deal with tonight, and took a long bath.

The night called for bubbles. Lots of bubbles. I loaded up the bath water with my most expensive milky bubble bath and popped a can of Dr Pepper.

I drank the soda while soaking in suds up to my ears, then

toweled off and reached for my bathrobe. It wasn't there, of course. The Jackson Five had confiscated it, standing in my foyer and folding it solemnly, like white-gloved marines folding the flag at a military funeral. They carted it away in a big brown paper grocery bag. To save for later. In case they needed it to incriminate me.

I wrapped a towel around myself and dug in my closet for my oldest, softest flannel jammies, and then finally snuggled myself under the covers.

I thought about doing something spiritual like praying, as any decent Christian would do. But though I am a Christian person, I can't claim, much of the time, to be anywhere near decent at it. Sometimes I am downright terrible at it, in fact. I stared at my Bible from under my quilt. It just sat there, its covers firmly closed like lips withholding wisdom. Another mistake on my already teetering stack. As though shunning God would somehow be a productive, helpful idea.

The clear day had left no warm blanket of clouds for the city, and I shivered through that bitter night. My quilt and my electric blanket—meager defense against an inadequate heating system in an old, drafty house—could not keep the cold at bay.

So I slept in shallow dreams, whipped around by snow and howling wind. White, swirling cold bit at my extremities. My toes were icy, my nose a little sniffly block of ice.

Somewhere around three thirty—a witching hour for me, for many terrible and frightening things have happened to me at three thirty in the morning—I heard another thump.

My house is tiny. It's just six rooms, arranged in sort of a strange jigsaw. Just inside the front porch is a living room with a small, adjacent dining room. Behind that is the kitchen, and beside the kitchen is the bedroom with an attached bath. The garage is attached to the bedroom, straight at the back of the house. To get to the garage from anywhere in the house, then, a person must go through my bedroom.

The thump that woke me that night came from the door that leads from my bedroom to the kitchen. I'd closed that door, wanting to shut myself into the smallest corner of the house.

After the thump, I swear I heard footsteps on my creaky wood floor, coming from the kitchen and striding through the bedroom. The footsteps stopped at the garage door.

Careful not to move, I slowly opened my eyes, my heart in my throat, fully expecting to see an ax murderer standing at the foot of my bed.

No one was there. I moved my eyes around the room. The bedroom door was still closed.

I had just about convinced myself I'd dreamed the whole thing when the door to the garage burst open, letting in a silvery blast of icy air.

I flew out of bed and slammed myself against the garage door. I bolted the door and reached for the bedside table, fumbling for the light, and then stared, panting, at the empty room.

I did the requisite search—checked the bathroom, the closet, the garage, and under the bed—and then stalked to the kitchen and snatched the phone out of its cradle. To call whom? The police? David? Just exactly who did I think was going to rescue me? And from what? A draft?

I replaced the phone slowly, feeling the cold settle in on me as I sat down, quiet and still, on a barstool.

And then I remembered. I'd been dreaming when I'd heard the thump. About a lumberjack. A lumberjack standing in my bedroom doorway.

He was tall and thin, clad in chinos and a plaid flannel shirt and boots. The one incongruous thing about him, other than the lumberjack part—we don't have many of those in Dallas—and that he was standing in my bedroom at 3:30 a.m., was that he was sickly white and bone thin. Not a Paul Bunyan sort of lumberjack, all hearty and lively and powerful. He was more of a drug-addict-with-a-terminal-disease sort of lumberjack. Puny. Sickly. Weak. And he was bald. Bald as a naked mountain peak in the dead of winter. And just as white. I didn't have to see him without his hat to know it.

The lumberjack's name is Peter Terry. At least that's how he'd introduced himself to me the year before, though he probably had used dozens of names, maybe hundreds, over the centuries of his work. He'd been wearing bathing trunks that day last summer, his white, pasty skin taking on a surreal sheen in the Texas sunshine. I knew that the plaid lumberjack shirt he wore tonight concealed a horizontal slash on his back that ran between his shoulder blades. A slash representing, I believe, the confiscation of his wings at the moment of judgment, millennia before.

Peter Terry is bad news. I hold both a healthy fear of him and a steely resolve toward him. I know him to be capricious, deceitful, and thoroughly malevolent. He is capable of both patient planning and violent fits of impulsive, pernicious rage. He is wildly immature and at the same time sagacious and shrewd. He is a raw nerve—petulant, churlish, childish, vengeful, dangerous.

Peter Terry is evil. Evil as the viper of Eden.

Had he just walked through my bedroom and into my garage? Or had I dreamed the whole thing?

But the door. The door had burst open.

I wasn't sure which was worse. That Peter Terry had trespassed in my house or in my mind. Both possibilities terrified me.

I sat there in my kitchen, shivering from cold, knowing somehow that he would not breach either barrier again tonight. It would be unlike him. He was more of a skulker than one to attack directly. He would content himself with the scare, with his twisted little lumberjack joke. And he'd spend his night—if time divides into days and nights for such beings—satisfied that he'd reminded me of his presence.

I filled the teakettle and lit the gas stove, then padded back into the bedroom and slipped a sweatshirt over my head and found myself some warm socks. Naturally, I developed a sudden, desperate interest in God again, now that I felt threatened by the other side. I sat in my kitchen and thumbed through my Bible, drinking hot tea with milk and sugar, until the sun came up.

I was looking for an obscure passage that I'd remembered finding a year before—something about God allowing one of those assorted kings or Old Testament characters, whose names I could never remember, to see the angels around him.

I never found the passage, but I longed to see the angels. I'd seen the enemy. It seemed only fair to me that I should get to see the allies too.

No angels appeared for me that morning. And I didn't waste any time asking why this was happening to me, either. I could wonder all I wanted. There would be no answer forthcoming. God's ways are not my ways. He'd made that little fact perfectly plain to me the year before.

Somehow, I'd gotten caught up in the swirl of battle again. Like the citizens of those little French towns after D-Day, those unlucky natives who learned to duck, to run, to fight, to hide.

They had watched their monuments shatter, their archives burn, their loved ones die. They endured the cacophony, the chaos, the carnage. All with the firm and undeniable certainty that the battle had nothing to do with them. It was a clash of ideologies, of powers exponentially larger and more powerful than they. A raging thunderclap of conflict between two mighty forces.

They just happened to be in the way.

The bravest among them had learned that it was possible, even necessary, to participate. To do their part. To join the resistance. Courage comes in the moment, it turns out. God has a way of doling it out at the very second we need it most.

God would win this battle, I knew, with or without me. The war had raged, after all, since the beginning of time. Faithfulness to the task, for those of us who find ourselves in the crossfire, is utterly necessary. God has designed it that way. But I did not look forward to the wounds I knew I was about to receive.

My contribution to the war effort would be small. Miniscule. But I intended to gear up and show up anyway. I would never, ever go down without a fight. Peter Terry should know that about me by now.

As the sun rose that morning, bringing with it the hope of a new day, my bones hurt, I was so cold. If I was going into battle, I wanted a hot shower first.

I lit a match in the bathroom, turning on the little hiss of gas in the heater on the wall and enjoying the small whoosh as the blue flame leapt to life and did its job. I shut the door and the bathroom began to warm. I held my hands out and toasted them in front of the flame.

After some of the circulation returned to my fingers, I turned around and twisted the faucet handle in the tub, letting the water run onto the icy porcelain, holding my hand under the stream, waiting for the heat.

The water stayed cold, my fingers bluing as I held them there. I turned the faucet off. The *H* was right there, staring at me. *H* for hot. I turned the knob again and waited, thinking maybe the pipes were so cold the hot water would take longer to heat up. Still nothing.

It finally dawned on me that the footsteps had come through the kitchen last night.

The water heater was in the kitchen.

Feeling the rage rise up inside me, I moved to the kitchen and yanked open the water heater closet and touched the skin of the water heater. It was ice cold. I knelt down, eye level now with the base of the unit and the little wads of dust and foul mysterious clumps of nastiness that accumulate in such places. I listened for the pilot light. Absolute dead silence.

I found some matches, pried off the metal screen that obscured the pilot light (another invention of Satan, I'm certain), and spent half an hour trying unsuccessfully to light that stupid little blue flame. (Why can't they make it easy to light these things?)

The procedure involved a bizarre gymnastic twist in which my left index finger held the gas button down while, with my right hand, I reached up inside the belly of the water heater to a little nib that was impossible to see from any angle. The flame had to be held on that nib for several long, awkward, painful seconds while a weak little stream of gas snaked its way up the tube. Any interruption on any link of this delicate chain would ensure that the flame would not light. And that's exactly what happened.

I got it lit once and experienced a quick rush of ecstasy, only to hear the flame sputter and die as I held my ear to the water heater and prayed for success.

I ended up taking an arctic shower, my skin purple and goose-bumped when I was done, and shampoo still tangled in my long, auburn hair.

My mood at that point was beyond foul. And all nine of the fruits of the Spirit evaded me. I had no love, joy, or peace. And don't even talk to me about patience and all that other nonsense.

I was bitter. And angry. And cold. The fruits of a dead pilot light and a long, disastrous night.

I dried my hair and got myself ready for the day, throwing on my oldest pair of jeans and my warmest sweater. I clicked the lock behind me as I stepped into the shivery chill of my garage. More cold air rushed into the garage as I pushed the button to raise the door.

My truck started, to my great relief. I made it halfway down my street before I realized what day it was.

Happy birthday to me.

4
~

I don't know where I was planning on going at 7:45 in the morning. I'd really just wanted to get out of the house. I drove around aimlessly for a few minutes, then on impulse, I turned onto the SMU campus.

The North American college student is a nocturnal creature. Daytime activities for this species are characterized by a dull, sloth-like sluggishness, which wears off slowly as the day progresses. Hunting, frolicking, and mating activities generally take place after sunset, on a seven-day cycle, peaking in activity sometime between Thursday afternoon happy hour and Saturday night when the bars close.

Early Sunday morning, these creatures return to their dens and hibernate their hangovers away.

Which meant the parking lots this morning were full. Completely.

Southern Methodist University is a private university. An expensive private university. When I drive onto the campus, I'm always struck by the vast gap between my income level and those of my students. I work there, but I could not afford to attend my own classes. I have more in common financially with the janitors, in point of fact.

The cars I was passing were late model BMWs, Land Rovers, Mercedes. I drive a pickup. A crummy 1972 Ford pickup that I bought for seven hundred dollars. It needs a new muffler, so it has all the delicate engine whir of a dump truck. The bench seat is cracked, patched with duct tape, and lets out a mighty squeak every time I hit a bump in the road. The paint is a nondescript shade that used to be brown, I think. And there is nothing automatic about it. Not the windows, the locks, or the transmission. It's three-on-the-tree, stiff clutch and all.

I love my truck. I have sort of a twisted sense of pride in that truck.

I cruised the lot, circling several times before I finally found a spot as far away from the pool as it could possibly be, between a Mercedes convertible and a bright yellow Hummer, the largest street-legal passenger vehicle known to man. Why a college student would have need for such a behemoth, I could not imagine.

I had about six inches on either side after I parked. I squeezed myself out the door and scooted out from between the cars, grabbing my swim bag from the back of the truck.

My breath hung in the air as I walked, and I could see steam rising from the surface of the outdoor pool in big, white, cloudy puffs. Normally I'd swim inside on a day as cold as today, but the indoor pool was only twenty-five yards long and I needed the full fifty meters of the outdoor pool. I wanted to put some distance between myself and the wall behind me before I hit another one.

I changed clothes quickly. The locker rooms were chilly, but not nearly as bad as my house had been this morning. The pool, at eighty-two degrees, would feel positively balmy after the shower I'd just had. I shouldn't have even taken that stupid shower. I should have just come straight to the pool. Even if I hadn't decided to swim, I could have taken a hot shower here.

Moron, my brain said to me.

Wearing my favorite tank suit with the peace sign on it, groovy purple goggles, and my swim cap—I always feel like a Q-Tip in that thing—I ran the distance between the locker room and the pool. I threw my towel onto the starting block and dove into the middle lane, knifed cleanly into the water, holding a long streamline and taking my first stroke about a quarter of the way down the pool.

The rhythm of swimming calms me, steadies my mind.

I took long, slow strokes, getting used to the water, enjoying the way it felt on my skin, watching the billows of steam move around me as I looked to my right for each breath. Stroke, stroke, breathe. Stroke, stroke, breathe.

I had the pool to myself. No one else was foolish enough to be swimming in the outdoor pool at 7:45 in the morning when it was twenty-five degrees out. I let my mind go.

Peter Terry's reappearance confused me. I'd had one direct encounter with him a year before, a few distant glimpses, and lots of indirect warfare. He'd trashed my house and my life. At least I blamed it on him. I'd never quite figured out how much of it had been his doing.

But I hadn't seen hide nor hair—or scalp, I should say—since then. Not in a year. A year and a half, nearly.

I'd started to wonder if I'd imagined him somehow.

I thought of that thing in Hebrews. About being hospitable to strangers because you never knew when one might be an angel. It stood to reason, I figured, that demons wandered around like that too. In the flesh, so to speak. Posing as people.

Interesting that the arrival of Peter Terry in a dream bothered me more than finding a bloody ax in my entryway. The ax was a problem, mind you. I wasn't diminishing that disaster for one slim second. But that problem seemed more solvable to me. I was innocent. I hadn't done anything except open my door and pick up the ax. And in spite of all I'd been through recently, I maintained an optimistic, if naïve, view of the American justice system. I was certain I wouldn't be held responsible for something I didn't do.

Peter Terry, on the other hand, was not a solvable problem.

I hadn't imagined the door slamming open, the burst of cold wind from a closed garage, the blown pilot light. I wasn't positive about the footsteps, but I was as sure as I could be without a recording or something. Peter Terry was coming around again. And something important was happening that I did not want to be a part of.

I took a breath, glided into the wall and did a flip turn, pushing off the wall, feeling the stiffness in my legs from my thigh workout the day before. How many laps was that? Five or so, I thought. Five hundred meters. Fifteen hundred was a mile, give or take. I wanted to get in at least that today. Maybe a little more. I was a third of the way there.

I felt someone dive in behind me. Maybe in the next lane. I felt a little resentful about sharing my pool. I had been downright serene swimming alone, despite the tumble of thoughts churning around in my head.

Another wall. Breathe, duck, flip, push, glide…stroke, stroke, breathe. My arms slapped against the water in rhythm.

The other swimmer must have been only a few yards behind me, because by the time I took my first stroke, I was alone in front again. I hadn't caught sight of anyone at the turn. Whoever it was, he was swimming in my blind spot.

I glanced back over my shoulder, but couldn't see anyone behind me through the steam. The turbulence of two swimmers was roiling the air and the water, producing a thick layer of steam. I could only see a few feet around me, lane ropes on either side and still water in front.

I forgot about the other swimmer and settled back into my rhythm, my thoughts returning quickly to the night before. The ax. Who had left the ax? Was Peter Terry responsible for that? He had to be. It was too much of a coincidence that he'd shown up the same night. He had a history, with me anyway, of leaving tantalizing little trails for me to follow. Which I tended to do, just as blind and oblivious as a puppy running into traffic after a ball.

Had I walked into a trap by picking up the ax? Was he trying to frame me for something? Had someone been murdered with that ax the night before? Horrible thought. And if so, what could that possibly have to do with me?

I did another flip turn, hoping again to catch a glimpse of the other swimmer. We must have turned seconds apart. I could sense the turbulence in the water behind me, see the steam billowing, but couldn't catch sight of anyone.

I switched sides, breathing to my left, thinking I might get a glimpse over the other shoulder. I still couldn't see anything, but I could tell the other swimmer was keeping up with me.

Kicking hard to give myself some speed, I increased the length and turnover of my strokes, pulling all the way through, brushing my hand against my thigh at the end of each stroke. Another wall. Another turn, another streamline. Coming up for my first stroke, pulling a hard breath of cold air. Kicking faster. Six beat kick.

The other swimmer was racing me, it seemed. Or chasing me.

I took a breath, put my head down, kicked hard, and threw my shoulders into my stroke, sprinting to the wall. I grabbed the gutter and stopped, sucking wind and turning to look behind me.

No one was there.

My wake was still coming into the wall, rolling little waves of clean blue water. But no one glided to the wall beside me. I ducked back under the water, looking for another pair of legs. Nothing. Underwater, I could see about halfway down the pool, though not all the way to the other side. As far as I could tell, the pool was empty.

I pushed off the wall again, and switched to breaststroke, popping my head up and looking around at each breath. A full

fifty meters, back to the other end of the pool. And no sign of the
other swimmer. I took a breath and let myself sink to the bottom
of the pool, looking around again.

I pulled myself out of the water and sat on the icy tile on
the edge of the pool, steam rising off my wet body. I yanked my
goggles off and squinted into the fog. I could see only a few
yards ahead, but the pool was silent. I couldn't hear anyone
else in the water.

I pulled my feet out of the water and stood up on the deck,
my arms crossed tightly. I couldn't see anyone else on the pool
deck. I couldn't see into the water through the steam.

By that time, my hands and feet were blue with cold. I'd be
better off back in the pool. But the chill I felt had little to do with
the freezing air. I was not getting back in that pool.

I grabbed my towel and wrapped it around me, running on
tiptoe the full length of the pool deck and down the steps and
into the natatorium, grateful for the warm, humid air that hugged
me as I stepped inside.

I was ridiculously relieved to see other swimmers in the
indoor pool. The slap, slap of their arms against the water com-
forted me.

I turned around and looked through the door at the sidewalk
outside. I could see my wet footsteps leading from the pool, down
the steps, and into the natatorium. The rest of the view was uninhabited. Downright barren of life. Even the grass was dead.

I sat and watched the swimmers a while, analyzing their
strokes. A couple of them were good swimmers. Better than me.
I made a mental note to add stroke drills to my workout in addition to my new Thigh Recovery Program. I didn't know anyone
in the pool, so decided to hit the shower. The locker room was
empty, though one locker was open and had a swim bag sitting
beside it. Even the presence of the bag—evidence of human life—
felt better to me than nothing.

I peeled off my suit, my skin goose-bumped and cold, grabbed my shampoo, and headed for the shower. I almost sang with joy as I stepped under the hot stream. I could feel myself calming down, my mind clearing as I experienced my first real warmth in twelve hours.

I was losing my mind. That, at least, was obvious. Someone else got in and out of the pool without my seeing them. That's what happened, probably. It's perfectly logical and ordinary. You, on the other hand, I told myself firmly, are a lunatic. A fruit loop, wacko, nut-ball.

Whoever had been in that pool, I was not going to let them ruin this perfectly sublime shower. I soaped, I rinsed, I soaped again. I warmed myself up and rinsed myself off, thrilled at the simple luxury of hot water as it ran through my hair and over my sore, grateful muscles.

No more outdoor swims for me until spring.

I finished my shower, my skin glowing red, and got myself made up and blow-dried. I didn't look too dreadful, considering I'd had no sleep. Not bad for my first day as a thirty-five-year-old. I threw my sweater over my head and pulled on my jeans.

On my way out of the locker room I ran into Duke, the pool manager. Duke is a large and intimidating Cajun with fewer than the normal allotment of teeth. He is territorial, a bulldog of a man who likes to kick people out of his pools for the tiniest little violation. He randomly invents violations.

For some reason, Duke had taken an early liking to me. I am proud to say the SMU pool is one of the few things I have never been kicked out of. A rare streak of non-rule-breaking behavior on my part.

"Morning, Dr. Foster," he said. "You up bright and early this Sunday. Morning." His speech had an odd limp to it. Must be a Louisiana thing.

We exchanged pleasantries for a minute. I always ask about

his wife. He always pats his enormous stomach and tells me she's trying to kill him with her fried chicken.

"Not working, though," he said. "She can try. But she gonna have to use more than an old yard bird to get rid of me. No sir. Not rid of me." He laughed, cracking himself up with a joke he'd told a thousand times.

"Listen, Duke. Did you happen to see anyone in the pool with me this morning?"

"Outside? No, no, honey. No one else dumb enough to swim outside on a day like today. You done lost your mind doing that."

"Are you sure? I'm positive someone was swimming behind me."

"Not like I watched you the whole time. But I'm telling you, no one else dumb enough to swim outside today. You the only one."

"Thanks, Duke. That's quite a compliment."

"You a professor, Doc, but you might not be too smart."

"I couldn't agree more." I turned to leave. "Say hi to Mrs. Duke for me."

I decided to take another look at the pool on the way back to my truck. I walked back up the steps and onto the pool deck, wondering what I'd been thinking to swim outside today. Duke was right. I'm a professor. But I might not be too smart.

The steam covered the surface of the water, but it was still and the air was silent. The pool was clearly empty.

I walked the entire circle around the pool. As I passed the starting blocks, I noticed something.

Footprints.

Wet footprints leading from the pool toward the back gate. There were only a few, diminishing in clarity as they got farther from the pool.

I leaned down to look at them. They looked like ordinary footprints. No claws or hooves or extra toes or anything.

They must have been made just moments before. They were still puddly.

I straightened and looked around. Still, I saw no one. There was no movement in the parking lot. No cars starting themselves ominously. I squinted at the back gate. It was padlocked.

"Hey!" The voice behind me nearly frightened me out of my sneakers.

I turned to see Duke walking across the deck toward me.

"You not thinking of jumping back in, now, Doc, are you?" he said.

"No, I was just looking at these footprints." I pointed down.

They were gone. The blasted prints were gone. They could not possibly have dried that fast.

"There were wet footprints here a minute ago," I said.

Duke stopped beside me and looked down. "Don't see any prints, Dr. Foster. I'm telling you, no one else swimming outside today. No one but you. And you might need a little rest. Or something, maybe."

"Yeah. I might need a little rest," I said. "This time I'm really leaving. Have a good Sunday, Duke."

"And a good Sunday to you, Dr. Foster. Good Sunday."

I stalked out to my truck, freezing the whole way and berating myself for failing to bring a coat with me. I threw my bag into the back and squeezed in past that stupid Hummer. My truck started with a glorious rumble.

I didn't know whether to be scared, angry, or confused. All three were appropriate, I suppose. Was it Peter Terry again? Or was it just my imagination sneaking up on me?

My cell phone rang somewhere in the muffled darkness of my purse. I fished for it and said hello.

"Good morning, Sugar Pea." It was David.

"Am I glad to hear your voice."

"Been missing my wit, charm, and fantastic personality?"

"That, and I've had a strange morning."

"Couldn't have been weirder than last night."

"Nothing could be weirder than last night."

"Well, whatever's happened, it's about to get worse."

"Why?" I said, dread creeping into my voice.

"Have you seen the paper?"

"No. Why?"

I heard him rattle the newspaper.

"Page two, Metro. Co-ed Discovered in Car," he read.

"What was she doing in a car that got her in the paper?"

Even as I asked it, I knew what he was going to say. I could hear it in his voice. I closed my eyes.

"She's dead, Dylan," he said. "And it looks like she was killed with an ax."

5

~

Her name was Drew. Drew Sturdivant. She was nineteen years old.

"Is there a picture?" I asked.

"Short hair. Maybe four to six inches long. Cut kind of choppy. Darker at the roots."

"Can you tell what color it is?"

"It's a black and white photo. Probably brown or red. It's her, Dylan."

"What else does it say?" I asked.

He read me the article.

Drew's body was found inside the trunk of a car, which was parked at a used car lot on Harry Hines Boulevard. She was identified as a local exotic dancer, employed by Caligula, a men's club, also on Harry Hines Boulevard. In her daytime life, she was a student at El Centro College, which is part of the local community college system. A preliminary report from the Dallas County medical examiner's office suggested manner of death to be murder, cause of death to be "blunt force trauma with a sharp ax-like instrument. Multiple blows."

I felt my stomachache return.

The police were investigating leads, David was saying. The paper listed a number for a tip line.

"Do you think I'm one of the leads?" I asked. It was a

rhetorical question. Of course I was one of the leads.

"Have you heard from the DPD?" he asked.

"The Jackson Five? Not yet, but they're probably waiting for me at my house."

"Yeah. I tried your home number first. Where are you, so early on a cold Sunday morning?"

I told him my swimming story with the wet footprints, finishing with the weird garage door lumberjack incident from the night before.

He whistled. "You win the contest for the worst twenty-four hours."

"Drew won that one, I think."

"Yeah. Some prize."

We were silent for a minute, sharing an odd, intimate connection to this real-life girl, a living, breathing human person who had gotten up yesterday morning like she did any other day. And had died at the business end of an ax.

I fought to keep the image out of my brain. I didn't want it there. But my mind, attracted by some sort of morbid magnetic field, would not cooperate. I could see it happening in front of me, playing out in vivid, full-blown, Fujifilm detail.

I felt the most profound sadness for her.

"You must be exhausted," David was saying. "Want to come out here?" He lived about an hour south of town. "Hide from the posse and get a little rest? I could make you tomato soup and Cheetos. Served up with a cold Dr Pepper. Cold milk and Oreos for dessert. Your favorite."

A nap on David's couch and a babysitter lunch sounded absurdly luxurious to me.

"I'd love to, but I couldn't sleep on a bet, I don't think. I'm too wound up."

"How about dinner then? We need do-overs for last night. I owe you midlist wine and a white tablecloth."

The white tablecloth jarred my memory. I groaned. "I'm supposed to have lunch with my dad today. And his horrible new wife Kellee with two *e*'s."

"They're in town?"

"They flew in for lunch. Their version of a birthday present."

"Happy birthday. Sorry. I should have said it when you picked up the phone. I was focused on the paper."

"No, no, it's fine. Happy birthday, cha cha cha. My birthday's the last thing on my mind."

"I didn't get to give you your present. I was going to give it to you at dinner last night."

I brightened. "What did you get me?"

"Do you really want to know? Or do you want it to be a surprise?"

"Hm. I think I'll take the surprise. I'm going to need some cheering up later. I can tell from here."

"Do they let you bring wrapped gifts into Lew Sterrett Justice Center?"

"Very funny. Hey. Maybe I need a lawyer. Do you think?"

"I'd get one, if I were you."

"I don't know any lawyers. I've always been so proud of that fact."

"What about the Pink Ice Queen Lawyer from last year?"

"She works for the university, I think. SMU is going to fire me if I keep getting accused of crimes…" I mused, almost to myself. "I gotta get myself out of this."

"What time is lunch?"

"Twelve thirty. After church."

"Your dad goes to church?"

"No, me. I go to church."

"Are you still going?" he asked.

"To church or lunch?"

"Either."

I looked at my watch. It was almost nine thirty. I could make the early service. At the very least, I'd have somewhere to hide from the Jackson Five for a few hours.

"I really can't get out of lunch. And I probably need a Holy Spirit spanking before I spend any time with Dad and Kellee."

"Want to leave dinner open?"

"That'll leave you in limbo all day."

"Don't mind."

"Pining for me, I hope."

"Pining. Yes. Absolutely. And worrying," he promised. "Lots of worrying."

"Good. That makes me feel better, actually. I'm needy today."

"Understandable. Call me if anything comes up."

I threw the phone in my purse, and then remembered how I was dressed. I looked like a homeless person. My jeans were ripped, my sweater old and pilled, and I had on my favorite ratty pair of thrift shop Converse All Stars. The red canvas ones. From, like, 1977. When Jimmy Carter was president.

Jesus didn't mind, I'm sure, but I think the people around me were a little taken aback. My church is pretty casual, but I was stretching even those limits today. I tried to cover up the hole in the knee of my jeans with my purse at first—a fringed leather version of a fig leaf, I guess—then gave up and focused on the service. It was about truth, handily enough, which it turns out is your best defense against evil. Nifty little fact to know. At least I had truth on my side.

Church ended at ten thirty. Time to face the DPD. I headed home.

No cruisers were waiting there for me. Detective Jackson had left a message on my machine, however. He wanted me to call when I got in.

Stalling seemed good. I erased the message and threw my purse on the bar stool, then tossed my swim bag into the bedroom and emptied it out onto the bed. I could see my breath almost, it was so cold in my house. I kicked the on-switch on my space heater, then lit the gas heater in the bathroom, holding my hands over the blue flame for warmth. I hung my wet bathing suit on the shower curtain. It would probably freeze stiff hanging there.

My house is almost a hundred years old. Built when the only central heat in Texas was the kind that came from the sun. Other than my state-of-the-art oil-filled space heater, the ancient gas wall unit was the only source of heat in this part of the house. Between the two of them, they did a fairly passable job most of the time.

Striking the match reminded me of my hot water situation. Fighting off a level of rage completely disproportional to the problem at hand, I took my matches into the kitchen and stared at the water heater. I leaned in and listened hard for that annoying knocking sound it makes when it's doing its job. All I heard was dead, stubborn silence.

"Light," I said, as though that would help.

I held out my hands, rattling the matchbox and waving my fingers at the Whirlpool insignia. "In the name of Jeeeeesus," I said in my best TV evangelist voice, "I command thee to light. Give thine heat to mine water."

I waggled my fingers some more, entertaining myself with the absurdity of it all. Still, if Peter Terry could blow the blasted thing out, why couldn't God show up just this one teeny-weeny time and cut me a break?

Whatever His reasons, He wasn't saying. I was going to have to do it the old-fashioned way. I assumed the position and struck a match. As I reached inside the skin of the beast, I noticed for the first time the drippy rust stains that ran down the sides.

It is a rule in the universe that one should never look at an appliance too closely. Especially an artifact generations removed from the moment of examination. Layers of sticky filth concealed what I suspected was formerly white paint. Or porcelain. Or whatever they made water heaters out of in the Stone Age. Maybe it was like a tree. A ring of filth for each year. I could probably saw it in half and find out how old it was.

I blew out my match, unfolded myself, and retrieved my giant, industrial-sized bottle of Zep Orange Industrial Degreaser— invented by God, by the way, not Satan. I cracked open a brand new roll of Dawg Blue Mastiff Industrial Strength paper towels. I was armed and dangerous.

In military terms, what happened next is known as "mission creep"—starting off with one discrete task and allowing it to expand exponentially into an amorphous monster of a project. This is what happens on Saturdays when I run errands. Running out and getting some milk turns into throwing an impromptu dinner party because the produce at the grocery store looks so fabulously fresh, and besides, they have the most wonderful organic, grain-fed beef tenderloin, and wouldn't it be nice with some roasted potatoes and a mango salad? And, of course, I'll need new placemats, but I like chargers instead of placemats, and I think Pier One is having a sale…

This is mission creep. It is generally a bad idea.

Ignoring my better instincts, I hosed down the sides of the water heater with Zep and tried to swipe my paper towel over the surface. The paper towel stuck in the goo. I resisted the urge to vomit. I squirted it down again and went to get the vacuum cleaner.

Since I am obsessively tidy—I prefer the term *obsessive compulsive "inclination"* to *obsessive compulsive "disorder"* (much less damning)—I have a state-of-the-art vacuum cleaner. It has hoses. It has attachments. It has brushes and nozzles and a tiny little needle-nose device for use in corners. I can practically do surgery with my vacuum cleaner. Or pick up a bowling ball. Whichever the situation calls for.

I wrestled the python tubing, assembled my weapon, and plugged it in, peering under the water heater and plotting the demise of the filthy little archaeological site under there. And then I saw something even more alarming.

A hole in my wall. Behind the water heater. Leading into the poorly insulated space behind the closet.

And pellets. Little brown pellets. Lots of little brown pellets.

Nowhere in the Bible, that I'm aware of, are rodents mentioned as minions of spiritual scourge. But I am convinced that had there been an eleventh plague in Egypt, if the flies, frogs, and boils had failed to convince, God would have sent mice. Hoards of nasty little crawling filthy gnawing mice. And rats. To chew into grain sacks and nest there, leaving their foul little droppings behind as presents. That would have been the fatal blow.

Maybe Pharaoh knew the mice were next. Maybe that's why he caved after the whole Passover-death thing.

I dropped my vacuum hose with a clatter and yanked open the pantry door. Labels stood at attention on my shelves, spices alphabetized, soup cans grouped into categories by ingredients and use (broth or cream-based, for meals or for cooking).

My pantry was immaculate.

And it had mice. There was the evidence, right down there in the corner. Mouse droppings.

At this point, my obsessive inclinations may have bordered on a disorder. I admit that. I should probably have dropped the entire matter and gone to a Twelve-Step group.

Instead, I started flinging things out of my pantry, letting out little shrieks of indignation each time I spied evidence of the beasts. A chewed hole in my brand new box of Premium Saltines. A rip in the cellophane around my spaghetti. Little brown pellets behind my carton of Hefty Handle-Tie garbage bags. Gnaw marks in my neatly folded environmentally correct, brown, recycled-paper grocery bags.

I broke off periodically to scour the water heater and squirt more Zep Degreaser on it.

In the midst of this madness, I lost all track of time. When the phone rang, I was on my knees, with my can of Comet and my antibacterial cellulose sponge with the green scrubby thingy on it, disinfecting the pantry floor.

I whipped my head around and stared at the phone, then peeled off my rubber gloves and picked up the receiver.

"Hello?"

"Where are you?"

I looked at my watch. It was one fifteen.

"I sort of lost track of time, Dad," I said.

"Well that's just rich, Dylan. Here Kellee and I fly all the way up here to honor you on your birthday, taking time out of our very busy schedules. On our one day in the week to be together. Kellee is sitting here with this beautiful gift that she wrapped herself…"

What is she, a five-year-old? She wants a parade for wrapping a gift?

"What do you want to do, Dad? Reschedule? Or I can be there in twenty minutes."

"We flew up from Houston, Dylan. We're here. We have a table. We're waiting for you."

My dad is a heart surgeon. Possibly in need of his own services. He sounded like he was about to blow a valve or something.

"So you want me to go ahead and come?"

"Isn't that what I just said?"

"I'll be right there."

I hung up without saying good-bye and looked around the kitchen. It was as if an explosive device had gone off in the pantry. Cans, boxes, and bags lay in piles where they'd landed. A package of spaghetti had broken when I tossed it, scattering pasta pick-up sticks on the kitchen floor.

And over there, on the other side of the kitchen, the water heater was gleaming white and spotless, the closet completely devoid of even microscopic traces of dust. The mouse droppings were gone, the hole covered with a plastic Cool Whip lid and duct tape.

The water heater still didn't work, mind you, but it was clean.

This is the problem with mission creep. All that work and still no hot water.

I stepped over the pantry debris and went to the bedroom and picked out an outfit. Frayed bellbottom jeans, an orange turtleneck, and my purple Doc Martens, which I know my father hates. That's how mature I am. On my thirty-fifth birthday.

Could be time to go back to therapy.

6

~

I was backing out of my garage when Detective Jackson pulled his navy blue Impala into the driveway behind me.

He got out of his car and walked over to the truck. I cranked my window down.

"Morning, Dr. Foster," he said, in the same deadpan voice he might have used to say, "Stand against that wall over there and place this hood over your head."

"Good morning, Detective Jackson." I faked a smile. "Fancy seeing you here."

"On your way out?"

No. I like to sit in my driveway with my truck running and my reverse lights on.

I put a crowbar in my personality and tried to be cordial. "I'm meeting my father for lunch," I said sweetly.

"I need a minute of your time."

"I'm forty-five minutes late already."

"I need a minute of your time." He wasn't asking.

I turned off the ignition, and my truck engine sputtered to a stop.

He followed me to the house and stepped into the foyer with me. I hadn't realized until that moment that the blood was still there. In my zest to eradicate the mouse plague and sterilize the outside of my water heater, I'd forgotten to scrub the streaked traces of murder off my walls.

Mission creep strikes again.

I stepped past the stains without acknowledging them and led him into the living room.

"I really only have a minute," I said.

"Have a seat." He motioned to the couch and set a three-ring notebook on the coffee table in front of me.

"We found a body last night," he said. Still no emotion at all from the man. He might as well have been reciting his grocery list.

"I know."

He waited for me to explain.

"It was in the paper this morning. Drew Sturdivant."

"I have some photographs for you to look at," he said.

Surely he wasn't going to show me pictures of the murder scene. I started to protest as he opened the notebook, but was surprised to see six mug shots instead.

"I'd like you to tell me if you recognize any of these men," he said. "Take your time."

A row of faces stared up at me from my coffee table. Pale, angry faces, with stubble beards, greasy unkempt hair, and hate in their eyes.

I studied them, peering at their dead expressions, wondering what their stories were. How had these men, these human beings, one by one, made their way from the promise of fresh-born, bright-eyed infancy to the pages of a mug-shot book? At what point on their journeys did they lose their way?

Out of the corner of my eye, I watched Detective Jackson watching me. I closed the cover and looked up at him.

"Not a one," I said. "I've never seen any of them before. Why?"

He ignored my question and opened the book again.

"No one on this page?"

I looked again. "Nope."

"You're positive?"

"I told you. I don't recognize any of them."

He closed the book. "We've accounted for your activities at the time of the murder."

"I was home. I told you that."

"We verified your activities."

"How?"

"Cell phone records."

"So I'm not a suspect?"

"That is correct."

I tried to feel relieved instead of invaded. "You have a suspect, then? Is that what the pictures are for?"

"I'd rather not say at this time."

"I found the ax on my front porch, Detective. I think I have a right to know what's going on. This guy could be coming after me."

His face softened, almost imperceptibly. Just a tiny bit around the corners of his mouth.

"We are following some promising leads. And, yes, that is what the pictures are for. I believe we'll make an arrest by the end of the day."

My expression must have changed, because he worked quickly to douse any relief I might have felt.

"I'd like to know how that ax ended up on your front porch, Dr. Foster," he said, the softness gone from his expression, his voice hard. "I'll encourage you once again to come forward with any information you may have."

I stood up, the universal therapist signal that the session is over. "I've told you everything I know, Detective. I have nothing to hide and no reason to hide it."

He picked up his notebook and stood, an enormous oak of a man sprouting from my living room floor. He folded his arms over the notebook and stared at me without budging.

"Will there be anything else?" I asked.

"No. This is just a friendly visit."

In a friendly manner, I said, "Then please get out of my house. I'm late meeting my father."

He turned to leave, and I followed him to the door, closing it behind him and quickly cramming my face against the peephole as he knelt to examine the porch and the front door. He knew I was watching him. After a few minutes, he straightened and walked slowly to his car, finally driving away at dogtrot speed. A stray with mange could have overtaken that car. The man was letting me know he wouldn't be pushed around.

I didn't see his car as I left, but I figured he was parked down the street watching me.

Dad and Kellee were waiting for me at the Landmark Restaurant in the Melrose Hotel. It's about four minutes from my house. I got there at 1:39. An hour and nine minutes late.

Neither of them stood to greet me. My dad looked me up and down, his distaste for my outfit plainly registered on his face, and said, "Glad you could make it."

"Sorry I'm late."

I leaned down and fake-kissed Kellee, who lifted her perfect self-tanned cheek to accept the gesture.

I pulled out my own chair and seated myself, settling my napkin in my lap. "What are we ordering?"

They both opened their menus. A third menu sat unopened on the table between them, out of my reach. I waited for someone to hand it to me.

Our waiter's arrival cracked the silence. "Another drink for you, sir?" he asked my father.

My dad examined his glass, shook the ice around, and threw back the last sip. "Tanqueray martini. On the rocks. With a twist."

"Certainly, sir. And you, ma'am?" He turned to Kellee.

"Another club soda, please," she said, tilting her head and

smiling at him with cosmetically altered, blazing white teeth. A new feature in the perpetual evolution of Kellee.

The waiter didn't even glance in my direction.

"Pardon me," I asked, as he turned to leave. "I'd like to order. Hot tea. Please?"

"Certainly, ma'am."

"English breakfast?" I continued. "Cream and sugar?" I pointed across the table. "And could you hand me that menu, please?"

He picked up the menu and served it up to me, along with a healthy dose of contempt. I couldn't blame him for his attitude, really. The Landmark was packed on Sundays. If I hadn't been so late, he would have turned this table over by now. I made a mental note to leave him an extra tip. I have a soft spot for grumpy, overworked people.

We all studied our menus, waiting to see who would elbow through the tension and speak up first.

I finally caved, looking up and smiling brightly. "I think I'll go with the French dip sandwich. It's supposed to be really good here."

"Eggs Benedict," my father said, slapping his menu shut.

My heart sank. I pictured runny egg yolk clinging to gelatinous half-cooked egg white, all smeared together onto a soggy English muffin. My father knows I loathe eggs. Just the smell of them makes me nauseous. It was a spite order.

Kellee looked at him as though he'd just announced he was planning on ingesting a live frog.

"What's the matter?" he asked, throwing his hands up in the air.

"Do you have to get eggs?" she said.

For a lightning fraction of a second, I thought maybe Kellee was taking my side. My hatred of eggs is lifelong and well documented. Even Kellee, new to our family, knew better than to cook or eat eggs in my presence. I realized instantly that this was a wildly misguided flash of optimism. But I never thought to anticipate what was coming next.

"I won't subject myself to it, knowing I have to get back on a plane this afternoon," she said prissily. "I won't. I just won't."

"When did that start? I thought we were on tuna still," my father said.

"Eggs and tuna. And cantaloupe."

What sort of diet would prohibit cantaloupe?

"And shrimp," she was saying. "In fact, please don't order any seafood of any kind." She turned to me. "A French dip is fine."

"Thank you," I said, before I could help it.

My father rolled his eyes and studied his menu again. "How about an omelet? I want a ham and cheese omelet."

"Absolutely not," she said.

My father lobbed one food selection after another in her direction, only to have Kellee shake her head and swat it right back at him. I watched several rounds of this game before I realized with horror what was unfolding before me. It was the smoked salmon that elicited the crucial clue.

"I can't tolerate the smell," she said. "You always want pungent food. Pick something…ordinary. Something that smells…nice."

"Someone want to tell me what's going on?" I was already dreading the answer.

Kellee stopped swinging at my father's menu choices and beamed at him. My dad turned to me and delivered the bad news. "You're going to be an aunt," he said, thrusting his chin up and his chest out.

"Guthrie and Cleo are expecting?" I asked. My brother and his wife had been married for over six years and so far had parented only cats.

"Not Guthrie," my father said, exasperated. "Me. And Kellee." He reached across the table and grasped one of her perfectly manicured hands. "We're pregnant."

I turned to Kellee, who continued to beam, but had turned

the glaring, white-happy spotlight on me now.

"You're kidding," I said.

"Do I look like I'm kidding?" my father asked.

I looked back at him. Lord save me, he didn't.

I tried to allow the disastrous news to sink in. "That would make me a sister," I said. "Not an aunt."

Kellee handed me the present she had wrapped herself, thrusting it joyfully in my direction. "Open it," she commanded.

I ripped the paper, opened the box, and revealed a pink T-shirt with the words "World's Greatest Aunt" silk-screened on the front in pale blue ink.

I looked at both of them helplessly. "But I'll be a sister, not an aunt." I don't know why I was jabbing at this point. What could it possibly matter?

My father should never have reproduced in the first place. Guthrie and I agreed on this when we were very small. We both held childhood fantasies that we'd been adopted, though our mother's features were watermarked on our own. We both had her green eyes, her auburn hair. And now, of course, I'd inherited her thighs.

If not adoption, then perhaps there was a mystery in our past, we fantasized. Perhaps our father, so indifferent to us, was not our father at all. Maybe we were royalty! Maybe our mother had a dalliance with a passing prince while she and our "imposter" father were in Italy!

Childhood imaginings had long been abandoned. My father, for better or worse, was my father. My brother and I both shared his best and his worst qualities: his quick mind, his ambition, his fanatical attention to detail, and most horribly, his stunning capacity for selfishness. It was this last trait that had kept me from marrying and Guthrie from parenting. Neither of us had much optimism about purging this bit of sewage from our DNA.

And now here was my father with a thirty-year-old, silicone-enhanced wife, the two of them with the combined maturity of a thirteen-year-old—not that I was in any position to talk, I suppose—and they had decided to procreate. I could not imagine what they were thinking. Why they felt it necessary to do so would remain, for me probably, one of life's stubborn mysteries.

I had endured my father's affair with his scrub nurse Kellee, an affair that began long before he and my mother divorced, with barely concealed hostility. I had skipped their wedding—a Disneyesque affair complete with matching white horses—without bothering to make up an excuse.

Unbelievably, the possibility that they would have children had never occurred to me. But Kellee was only thirty. And my father was handsome, successful, and wealthy. Of course she would want to have his babies.

I was too horrified to speak.

"Well?" my father asked.

"Well what?" I said.

"Congratulate us."

"Oh. Congratulations." I turned to Kellee. "Thanks for the shirt. It's really a sweet gesture. When are you due?"

"July 27." She began prattling about the intricacies of calculating ovulation and due dates. I tuned her out and did the math. July 27. This was January. I had seven months to wrench my attitude into place and get ready to be an aunt. I mean, a sister.

"Well," I said at last, raising my water glass. "Congratulations." What else was there to do?

They raised their glasses and we clinked. I asked some obligatory baby questions—Do you want a girl or a boy? Have you thought about names?—until the waiter brought our drinks and stood over us, refusing to leave the table until we'd ordered. The two of them returned to their menus, oblivious to my distress.

My father's self-absorption can be a blessing sometimes.

My dad finally ordered a steak, which seemed to meet with Kellee's approval. She spent five minutes ordering a broiled chicken breast, specifying in intricate detail the cooking instructions and side dishes she wanted, apparently subjecting every item and procedure to the smell test she'd applied to my father's order.

We ate our meal and, as usual, I made it through the entire affair without anyone at the table asking me anything about myself. Which was just as well.

What was there to say? Someone left a bloody ax on my porch last night? Some poor girl named Drew was found dead in the trunk of a car? The guy could be coming after me? I'm being chased by a demonic lumberjack? I'll be a sister, not an aunt?

Sometimes it's better just to keep your mouth shut.

7

~

God is in the details, someone once said. An architect, I think it was. Le Corbusier? Or Van der Rohe, maybe. I get them mixed up. It's an apt observation coming from one who creates secure, carefully structured space. I spent the rest of my birthday trying to restore structure and security to my space. Paying attention to the details that might summon peace to my house and my mind.

First order of business was to clean the blood off the walls and floor of my entryway. I believe in the sanctifying power of Pine Sol. Just the smell of it gives me a wonderful (if false) sense of security, a comforting sense of denial. I smiled serenely as the familiar fragrance wafted off my mop. By the time I was done scrubbing, I could almost pretend the blood had never been there in the first place.

I swept up the pantry-bomb debris in my kitchen, reorganizing cans and boxes on my shelves with meticulous, Dewey-decimal exactitude. And after a few more attempts to light the water heater and a couple of fits of wildly creative cussing, I repented, conceded defeat, and called a plumber.

When I heard his Sunday rates, we agreed he'd come first thing Monday and take a look at it. If I had any shot whatsoever of regaining my sanctification, I was going to need hot water. I was not capable of maintaining even a passable attitude without it.

I put off supper with David. Celebration seemed inappropriate to me that night. Instead, I ate alone in my newly disinfected and de-moused kitchen, and lit a single birthday candle for myself, poking it into a toasted, chocolate fudge Pop-Tart, cracking the icing just enough to perch the candle upright. It was a nice evening, actually. I spent the solitude trying to come to terms with the last twenty-four hours of my life.

Strangely, my father's news had trumped everything else, at least for the moment. It was selfish and immature of me, I know, to focus on what was truly a trivial personal issue. *Selfish* and *immature*—both adjectives I routinely applied to my father and to Kellee. The irony didn't escape me. If anything, it amplified my distress.

But when I teased away my petty little resentments and tuned out my own whining, it boiled down to this for me. It seemed almost sacrilegious, a puerile affront to my mother's memory and to that of our ragged little family, such as it was, that my father would so blithely create a second family. It was almost as if he'd simply opened up a new kit, complete with steps and procedures and shiny, new interchangeable parts.

Kellee was Other-Woman Scrub Nurse Barbie, my dad was Handsome-but-Unfaithful Doctor Ken, and now they were going to produce a little duplicate of themselves. Beautiful Midlife-Crisis Baby. As though my mother, my brother, and I were replaceable. Or maybe even disposable. We were just the old dolls, tossed under the bed and forgotten, hair uncombed and legs askew.

Not that I got the feeling, through the entire excruciating lunch, that my father cared two hoots about having more children. It was clearly Kellee's agenda, not his. My father went along to get along, shoveling out to Kellee whatever little bauble or indulgence she wanted.

Kellee, with her manufactured beauty, her petulant bossiness, and her enormous wedding ring—a ring that would choke a farm horse, the jeweler had said to me—raked it all in. Any of my father's scant available affection, any microscopic drop of other-ness he possessed, he doled out to her. And she snatched it up and gobbled it with a sense of entitlement that sent me reeling.

Why did he care more about Kellee than he had my mother? Or—and this was the muddy bottom of it for me—why did he care more about Kellee than he did about me? This was a man whose chief interactions with me had always seemed to be after-thoughts. My father's leviathan ego—at once immense and primitive and insatiable—had consumed our relationship for most of my life.

Why did I care so much? Why, at thirty-five years old—a speed-limit birthday, my mother would have said, always a mile-stone—why at thirty-five did I still chafe in the face of my father's apathy?

The more I thought about it, the more ashamed I felt. Ashamed of being a reject and ashamed of caring. Both.

As I contemplated my father's defection, I was flattened by an old, unappeasable deficiency, a nagging urge I've spent my life try-ing to overcome—not for my dad, for I was determined to finally outgrow my girlish need for him. But for Father, for God. For someone to sign up to care about me and to promise not to leave me alone in the world.

God as Father—now there's a concept that continues to baffle me. I've wondered often why God chose to introduce Himself as Father. It's a uniquely New Testament idea. The idea shows up only a few times in the Old Testament, faint traces of foreshadow-ing. Which must have been why Jesus' contemporaries were shocked at such an ambitious claim. Son of God indeed. Yahweh had sure ratcheted up the intimacy level with that one.

In spite of my better knowledge, I tend to conduct myself in my relationship with God as I do in my relationship with my own dad. Independently.

I am secretly convinced that God thinks, as I know my father does, that I am fine on my own. Or had better learn to be. I am certain, in that lonely place in some dusty corner of my soul, that help is indeed NOT on the way, and that, generally speaking, I am not on God's to-do list. That He, like my father the heart surgeon, has other people to attend to, people who need Him more than I ever should.

People whose hearts are far more important to Him than mine.

This is absurd theology, of course. I went to seminary. I studied the Bible. In the original languages. I majored in systematic theology. I graduated with a 4.0. I should be a spiritual genius.

After all that study, I know the drill. All about how God sees me as His child. All about how I am, though not divine like Jesus, nevertheless a fellow-heir, a sister of the King. Yep, that's me and Jesus, sitting in the way back of the station wagon while God points out the historical markers on the highway.

Unfortunately for me, there's a primal tie, psychologically speaking, between one's experience of God and one's experience of an earthly father. And I just cannot seem to pick that knot out of my stubborn, twisted brain. The God I know, often, is not a product of theology, but one of biology. I look at heaven and I see my dad.

Indifferent.

Powerfully, thoroughly, immutably indifferent.

The Peter Terry incident the year before had forced me out of this posture for a while. I'd had no choice but to ask for help. Desperation does that. Flattens me out and sends me begging. And now again, spiritual forces more malicious than I could contemplate were invading my life. So, how about it, God? Father, Abba, Eloi…*Eloi, Eloi, lama sabachthani*? Or more appropriately, in my case, my God, my God, don't bail out on me.

God was driving me to my knees. And he was using my narcissistic father, his vapid wife, a bloody ax, and a demon dressed as a lumberjack to do it.

Whoever said the Lord Almighty didn't have a sense of humor?

I cracked my Bible again that night, poking around in Isaiah. Isaiah must have had a crummy father too. He seems to spend a lot of time reminding himself that God gives a hoot.

It was ten o'clock before I finally washed my supper dishes. My house was meat-locker cold, my water practically coming out in cubes.

Rarely in my life have I gone to bed at night without a hot bath first. I've been doing the bubble bath thing since I was three. Bath, jammies, bed, read, sleep. That's the ritual. Leaving out the bath part threw me off completely. Instead of getting to sink into a warm tub of bubbly water, I sank quickly back into cranky self-pity. I switched on my electric blanket, brushed my teeth, warming my flannel jammies and socks over the flame in the bathroom before I put them on. I read with mittens on to keep my hands from turning blue.

Tired as I was, I was edgy and couldn't concentrate on my book. My mind wandered, flitting first to Peter Terry, then to my father, then to Drew Sturdivant and the ax. But exhaustion won out, eventually, and I turned out the light and slept hard.

Until 3:30 a.m.

At three thirty, right on schedule, I was jolted out of my dreams and sat bolt upright in bed.

By my stereo. Which came on full blast. By itself.

I threw back the covers and stomped into the living room, more furious than afraid. I checked the locks and looked in all the closets to make sure no one was in the house. But I knew the whole time I wouldn't find anyone. No one had broken in.

I popped the CD out just to double-check my theory, but it wasn't really necessary. I knew what was in there. I'd recognized the song immediately, even at stentorian volume.

Peter Terry had selected a CD I hadn't listened to in maybe

ten years—a leftover from a reject boyfriend who was into metal music. The CD was an old one, released in 1991. *Use Your Illusion* by Guns N' Roses. The first cut on the record, the one Peter Terry chose to wake me with, is called "Right Next Door to Hell."

Guns N' Roses' lead singer is a man named William Bailey, a choir-boy turned criminal turned rock-star with an astonishing vocal range, passable guitar technique, and a powerful ability to claim an audience.

His stage name is Axl Rose.

I turned off the stereo and unplugged it.

"Very funny," I said out loud.

I snapped off the light and went back to bed.

8

~

Monday morning came early, on the heels of two nights of demon-visitation insomnia. But this is not the sort of thing you complain about out loud. Normal civilian people do not have problems like that. And they think you're batty if you do. So I painted a smile on my face and greeted the plumber as though I were fresh-as-a-daisy rested and happy to see him.

His name was Paulie. Of Paulie's Pretty-Quick Plumbing Repair. When I opened the water heater closet, he let out a whistle of admiration.

"I never seen one so clean before." He reached out and touched it gingerly, as though it were a rare work of art. "You just buy this or something?" He squinted at the Whirlpool emblem. "But it looks pretty old."

I pictured myself at Twelve-Step group. *Hi. My name is Dylan. I spent an hour and a half cleaning my water heater yesterday.*

"It came with the house," I said. "I don't know how old it is."

He hiked his pants up and squatted down. "Let's take a look," he said, "see what the problem is."

He shined his flashlight into the hole and reached up in there while I busied myself making tea.

"Can you tell what's wrong with it?" I asked.

He was fully prone now, in the water-heater worship position, his hand way up inside its belly.

"The line's pinched off," he said at last. "It can't get no gas."

"That would explain why the pilot won't light," I said, nodding.

He looked up at me, puzzled. "You try to move it or something?"

"The water heater? No. Why?"

"The line's pinched off," he said again.

I pictured a length of rubber tubing with a kink in it. "Can't you just straighten it out?"

"Line's copper. It don't pinch by itself. Looks like it got pinched off moving it. Or something."

"It's a metal line?" I asked.

"Copper. And it's pinched off. Like someone took pliers to it."

"I doubt pliers were necessary."

"Pardon?"

"Nothing. Can you fix it?"

"Have to replace it."

"The whole thing?" I tried not to panic as I calculated the cost of a new water heater.

"Naw, just the line. Take ten minutes." He scooted himself upright and went out to his truck, returning with tubing and a blowtorch and a box of tools.

A blowtorch and a gas line didn't seem like a safe combination to me, so I went into the bedroom to pack for my day. I had office hours in the morning and a senior seminar to teach from two to five. A brutal day in the salt mines for an academic. We try not to work more than an hour or two a day if we can possibly help it.

I got my books together and twisted my hair into an emergency up-do. There was no way I was taking another goose-bumping, toe-bluing shower. I grabbed my swim bag and returned to the kitchen just as Paulie was dusting himself off.

He handed me a business card. "Might want to give my brother a call."

I looked at the card. Randy's Right-Now Rodent Removal.

"I think I got rid of them," I said.

"Take a look." He shined the flashlight under the water heater and, sure enough, there were the little brown pellets again. I peered behind the water heater. The monsters had chewed through my Cool Whip top.

"They love plastic," Paulie said. "Best favor you could've done 'em. They use it in their nests." He picked up his clipboard and began writing my invoice.

He tore the sheet off and handed it to me. Eighty-five dollars. For twenty minutes of work. I was in the wrong business.

"Rats are like roaches. You see one, he's got a whole bunch of buddies," he said.

"You think it's rats? Or mice?"

"What difference does it make? You got 'em living in your kitchen."

I took the card.

"Good point."

The campus was buzzing when I arrived. Students crisscrossed in front of me as I lugged my stuff up the stairs to my office. I dumped it all in a heap in the hallway while I jammed my key in the lock. Someone had taped a note to my door. I grabbed it and stuck it in my mouth, gathering my stuff again to lug it across the threshold.

I threw it all down and reached for my tea mug, then headed out to the kitchen area. First things first. On the way, I opened the note.

My boss wanted to see me. Immediately.

I stuck my head in her office as I passed by.

Helene Levine glared at me over black, half-moon glasses. "Come in and shut the door."

"I was on my way for tea."

"Coffee for me," she said. "Black."

Helene is very bossy. Everyone is terrified of her. I adore her.

I fetched our refreshments and settled myself into an ancient armchair, crossing my feet on her desk.

"What's up?" I asked.

"The police were here this morning."

I tried not to look too alarmed.

"And?"

"And they were asking about you." She raised her eyebrows at me. "Is there anything you'd like to tell me?"

"Was it Detective Jackson?"

She checked her notes. "And someone named McKnight. Charming, delightful conversationalists, both of them."

"I haven't met McKnight. But Jackson," I gestured with my tea mug. "That dude has all the warmth and charisma of a box of rocks."

"You're avoiding my question."

"What do you want to know?"

"What do I need to know?"

"What did they ask you?"

"They wanted to know how long you've been here, how well I knew you. What I thought of you. Whether you were well liked on campus. Things of that nature."

I took a sip of my tea. "What did you tell them?"

"I answered everything in your favor, if that's what you're wondering. I painted you the saint."

"Doesn't sainthood usually involve flaying? Or being burned alive? It's always some dreadful, medieval way to die. Slowly."

"Stop stalling. Are you in trouble again?"

My problems last year had involved a patient of mine, Eric Zocci, a student who'd come for therapy at the school's clinic, and who had later flown off a twelfth-floor balcony to his death. The entire mess had landed squarely in Helene's lap. Though I'd been cleared of any wrongdoing, I still don't think Helene has forgiven me. She runs the place like a general. She does not like surprises. Especially surprises that involve lawsuits and police departments and indictments. Things of that nature.

"I don't know," I said. "I don't think so. In danger, maybe."

She waited.

I braced myself and told her about the ax. I left out the lumberjack part and the swimming and the wet footsteps. And the water heater line with the kink in it. And Axl Rose. I didn't see any reason to make myself out to be completely unbalanced. The ax was bad enough.

"Is it your ax?" she asked.

"I don't think so."

"You don't know?"

"Why is everyone obsessed with this point? Do you own an ax, Helene?"

"I own two. One belonged to my grandfather."

"Was he an outdoorsy type?" I asked.

"Who ever heard of a Jewish outdoorsy type? He was an accountant."

"Why do you have his ax?"

"Why not? The point is, I know whether or not I own an ax."

"You live in a high-rise. When do you chop wood?"

She took a sip of coffee and gave me a withering look. "Why would anyone leave a bloody ax on your doorstep?"

"How would I know, Helene?"

"Was this the ax that killed the girl in the paper? The one they found in the car?"

"I think so."

"And your fingerprints are all over it."

"Yes."

"Do they think you did it?"

"I don't think so. They said they have a suspect. Someone

besides me. Jackson came by with a bunch of mug shots yesterday. He said they'd have an arrest by the end of the day. He didn't
mention that to you?"

"He didn't say anything about arresting anyone else. He just
asked questions about you."

"That must have been disquieting."

"I'm getting used to it."

"I think he believes I know who did it."

"Well, do you?" She folded her hands and looked squarely
at me.

"Of course not. I do not personally know any ax murderers.
And if I did, I would have said so by now. Do you really think I'm
going to keep something like that to myself? Come on, Helene."

"Well," she waved her hand dismissively, "I had to ask. I
thought maybe it was a patient of yours or something."

Hey. That hadn't dawned on me.

"Your luck hasn't been too good lately," she was saying. "You
seem to have a knack for attracting problem cases."

I smiled a sardonic thanks.

"Did you know the girl? What was her name?"

"Drew," I said. "Drew Sturdivant. I didn't know her."

"Wasn't she a student?"

I nodded. "But not here. She goes to El Centro. Went to El
Centro."

I drank some tea.

"Did you tell them anything about last year?" I asked, hoping
she hadn't. "Jackson and…what was the other guy's name?"

"McKnight. Of course not. I'm on your side, remember?"

"I forget sometimes."

"Oh, don't be absurd. What are you going to do?"

"About what?"

"About the girl? And the ax? Aren't you going to try to find
out how that ax ended up on your front porch?"

I stirred my tea. "I was hoping the police would do that."

"They probably will. But unlike me, they're not on your side. And they don't share your motivation. If it was one of your patients, you're liable."

I shrugged. "Maybe they've already arrested the guy."

"Have you called Jackson today?" she asked.

"I'm avoiding Jackson. Why would I call him?"

"He's got your fate in his hands. I wouldn't make an enemy out of him if I were you. I'd become the man's best friend."

She had a point.

"Or try McKnight," she said. "He seemed nice."

"Nice? A DPD detective?"

"They're just doing their jobs, Dylan."

I nodded, conceding the point.

"His first name is Mike. He left me his number."

She wrote it down for me.

"Mike McKnight," I said. "Okay. I'll call him after class."

"And look through your client files," she said as I left. "That would make the most sense."

She was right. The first thing I'd learned from Helene, years ago in our first clinical supervision session, had become a slogan, almost, over the years. "Never forget," she'd said, "that you're working with unstable people. Unstable people do unpredictable things."

I put in a message for Mike McKnight and left to teach my class.

Unstable people do unpredictable things. Indeed.

9

~

In the SMU counseling clinic, the catalog of unstable people runs the gamut. And I'm not talking about the patients. Aside from me—with my obsessive-compulsive inclinations and possible auditory and visual hallucinations—there is Marci, the office manager, whose savage mood swings hold us all in quaking fear of committing even the tiniest paperwork transgression; John Mulvaney, whose profound personality limitations finally disqualified him from seeing patients at all; and Kay-Ann, our eating disorder specialist, who lives on bagels and cream cheese and never, ever goes anywhere without a bag of peanut M&Ms, a pack of cigarettes, and a generous supply of chewing gum. Sugarless, of course.

I could go on. Suffice it to say, we are not an impressive bunch.

Our patient diagnoses are typical of a college population. Boyfriend problems, girlfriend problems, loads of anxiety, panic disorder, bipolar disorder, depression ranging from mild to severe to psychotic, the full list of eating disorders (anorexia, bulimia, binge-eating, purging, laxative abuse, and any other noxious way to disrupt the simple act of dining), abuse of and addiction to a wild variety of substances—everything from beer to prescription drugs to Elmer's glue. And good old-fashioned homesickness. Lots to choose from.

I started with my active files. There were about thirty of them in my drawer at the moment.

A close inspection, word by word, of every single one of my files yielded exactly zippo. I had no patients with homicidal ideation, no patients who were experiencing angry outbursts or violent fantasies. No patients who had mentioned Drew Sturdivant or anyone like her, or who had any known connections to El Centro College. I'd have to find out the name of her hometown. Maybe someone went to high school with her or something. In my previous year's trouble, I'd run across two students who were having recurrent Peter Terry dreams. But he had apparently stayed away from this group of kids so far. I saw no hint of him in the files.

My next step was to move to my archived files, which were stored electronically as well as warehoused in boxes somewhere. State regulations require that counseling records be kept for seven years. Which is a lot of files in a clinic the size of ours.

To get to my archived files I had to get past Marci. I crossed my fingers and prayed for a depressed phase. She was much easier to deal with in that incarnation. Downright limp, in point of fact. Her manic swing was the dangerous one.

One glimpse of Marci and I knew I was in luck. She wore no makeup, and her hair was pulled back in a messy, greasy bun. Her sweater was wrong-side out, and she wore tube socks and Birkenstocks with her dress instead of her regulation L'eggs panty hose and navy, round-toed pumps.

She was sitting at her desk staring into space.

"Morning, Marci," I said brightly.

She looked up, her eyes vague. "Is it still morning?"

"Actually, no. My mistake. It's twelve thirty." I plunged ahead. "Listen, I need to take a look at my archived files. Mind if I squeeze past you and log in?"

The archive computer was kept under lock and key in a tiny office behind Marci's. Officially, she was the only one with the password. Which was Sinatra, by the way, the name of her choleric gray cat. I had cracked that code with about fifteen seconds of thought a few years ago.

"Did you talk to John?" she asked.

"John who?"

"Dr. Mulvaney. He asked about you today."

"Terrific. What did he want?"

"Whether you were in today. He wanted to know if you had patients today."

"I don't work in the clinic on Mondays."

"What is today? I thought it was Tuesday."

"No, Marci. It's Monday. All day long. So how about it? Can I take a look?"

"You should stop in and say hello to him. I think he's lonely." She began to cry, long drippy tears sliding down her face. Someone needed to medicate the woman.

"I'll do that on my way out," I said. "Now how about logging me in back there?"

She blew her nose and turned wordlessly, slumping her way into the back office and typing in the super-secret password.

I squeezed past her and scooted into the chair, turning my back as quickly as possible to let her know our dynamic little conversation was over.

There were about two hundred archived files logged under my name. I'd never get through them all today. But I was hoping a name, at least, would jog my memory. They were sorted by name and by date, so I started with the most recent ones first.

I was a few files into my scan when my cell phone rang.

"Dylan Foster," I said.

"Dr. Foster. Mike McKnight. Returning your call."

I shut the door and tried to speak quietly. "Detective. Thanks so much for calling me back."

"No sweat. What can I do for you?"

He sounded like a pretty regular guy. Not too hostile.

"I'm wondering if you've made an arrest in the Sturdivant case. Detective Jackson said yesterday you had a suspect."

"We do have a suspect. But we have not yet apprehended him."

"Can you tell me his name?"

"Actually, no."

"Can you tell me why not?" I was trying to muster some reasonable facsimile of politeness, but I was coming at this with no sleep and a terrible attitude. So it was a stretch.

"We're trying to preserve the chain of evidence, Dr. Foster."

"Meaning?"

"Meaning, we're working to establish connections in this case."

"As in, connections to me."

"Among others, yes."

"Can you tell me why he hasn't been arrested yet?"

"His location is yet to be ascertained."

I wondered if they taught classes at the police academy about answering questions while conveying essentially no information. Obtuse Conversation 101.

"You mean, you don't know where he is," I said.

"That is correct."

"So this nut job is still on the loose."

"That is correct."

"Listen, Detective, I understand your situation. I really do. But I am a little worried about my own safety here. I really feel I need to know what's going on."

"Tell you what." I heard him tapping on his desk. "I can do this for you. Let me speak with Detective Jackson. If he's cool we'll meet with you and explain the status of the case. Maybe that will jar your memory. How's two thirty sound?"

"I'm in class until five. How about five thirty?"

"Your office?" he asked.

Absolutely not. "How about I come to you?"

He gave me directions. We hung up and I returned to my files.

Another hour of looking turned up little. I culled a few names of patients with anger problems. One boy had talked about violent dreams involving bludgeoning his girlfriend to death. That could be something. I checked his intake sheet again. He was a sophomore now. A psych major, naturally.

I called the registrar's office and asked about his schedule. He'd been in John Mulvaney's lab this morning.

The stars were aligning against me. Like it or not, I was going to have to have a conversation with Mulvaney.

When dealing with a socially inappropriate misfit, it's very important to project an air of thorough unavailability. The absolute last thing I wanted to do was encourage any weird little fantasy John Mulvaney might be having about the two of us. I'd cut him off a year ago, effectively shutting that problem down before it took root. Last weekend's conversation at the mall, though, seemed way off to me, like something had watered that weed and it had somehow sprung back to life.

I'd rather have set my face on fire than seek the man out, especially if he'd been sniffing around about me already today, but there it was.

I checked my watch. It was a quarter to two. I had time to stop by his office on my way to class.

John's office is in the clinic rather than in Hyer Hall with most of the rest of the faculty, which was one reason we rarely ran into one another. His office days tended to coincide with my teaching days.

His door was closed. I was tempted to take this as a sign from the Lord Himself that I was off the hook. But I knew it was just wishful thinking. I knocked before giving myself a chance to slip away.

I heard the violent slide of a chair against linoleum as he

pushed away from his desk. The noise came almost immediately after my knock, as if I'd startled him or something, and was followed by a hasty shuffling. A few seconds later, John opened his door a crack and looked out at me. His face was flushed and he was sucking wind like he'd just lugged a block of concrete across the floor.

"Hi, John. Sorry to interrupt you."

As usual, he looked at my chin and said, "Okay."

"Can I come in for a minute?"

He turned and looked back into his office, then back at my chin. "Okay." He opened the door.

I walked in and was reminded immediately of the other reason I never come near this office.

In John's lab space were a dozen or so open-top aquariums housing a variety of rodents—rats, mice, and guinea pigs, mainly—nesting in mounded bedding. Bags of Purina Mouse Chow, sacks of cedar shavings, bottles of distilled water—all the necessary provisions—were stacked on dusty Formica shelving.

John is a research psychologist, part of that mutant strain of humans who are interested enough in human behavior to study psychology but who do not know how to interact with their own kind. John has all the social skills of a sack of potatoes. (And the physique to match, by the way. Twenty pounds of potatoes in a ten-pound sack.)

Which was why he'd been such an abject failure in his early forays into clinical work. I can't remember who it was that decided that the entire psychology faculty needed to rotate through the clinic—probably Helene—but this optimistic little experiment had not worked out in John's case. He hadn't gotten past the first session with any patient in an entire semester of clinical work. He'd run them off, one by one, with his colossal ineptitude.

John was sweating through his shirt. His office was freezing, though. I guess the rats liked it that way.

He paced the room for a second, finally stopping to stand uncomfortably behind his desk, a nice safe stretch of desk between us.

"I just wanted to ask a quick question," I said. "Was Lance Richardson in class this morning?"

"Lance," he repeated. "Richardson? I don't know."

"He's in your eight o'clock lab, John. There can't be more than six people in there."

"What does he look like?"

"Don't you know?"

"I don't know their names." He shifted his weight from one foot to the other, glanced at his computer screen, and then looked down at his desk. "He could have been there."

I looked around the room. Each glass enclosure had a laminated label on it with the rodents' names. The one next to me housed Ozzie and Harriet.

"Don't you take roll?" I asked.

"Usually."

"Did you take roll this morning?"

"I don't think so."

Jesus provides patience for His followers during moments like these. I, of course, was too irritated to wait for mine to arrive.

"Well, if you remember one way or another, could you send me an e-mail and let me know? And if he was there, I'd like to know how he seemed to you."

"How he seemed?"

"You know, his manner. Did he seem normal? Anything out of the ordinary? Were his clothes neat? Did he look rested or tired? Things like that."

"Okay."

"Right." I turned to leave, smiling a fake, hostile smile I reserve for such occasions. "Thanks, John. I'll let myself out."

I was almost out the door when he did another last-minute verbal tackle.

"How was your weekend?" he asked.

I turned and stared at him.

"Mine was pretty good," he said.

I watched his face get red. He'd panicked himself by starting an ordinary conversation.

"Normal. Just like any normal weekend."

"How was the movie?" I asked.

I didn't really care, of course, but the poor guy was just so pitiful. Watching him try to participate in a simple dialogue was like watching an insect impaled by a pin. You just want to stomp the poor thing and put it out of its misery.

"Movie?"

"You said you were going to see an art film, right? At the Inwood?"

"Oh. The movie. Yeah, it was good. Very artistic."

"That's great, John." I turned to leave again. "Okay. Thanks again."

I shut the door and put some yardage between myself and John. Between the rodents and John Mulvaney, I was completely creeped out.

I made it to class on time, taught a reasonably coherent seminar on differential diagnosis, and then beat it for DPD headquarters to meet with Jackson and McKnight.

10

~

Detective Jackson met me in the huge, sparkling lobby of the new DPD headquarters downtown. He seemed almost lifelike in his natural setting. He walked me past the metal detectors and down the hall to the elevators, greeting cops by name as we passed them, using actual facial expressions and conversing in normal inflections with multi-syllable words.

The baseboard was stripped away from the wall in the corridor. I pointed at it. "What happened?"

"Flooding." He pushed the button for the fifth floor. "Water main. Flooded the whole first floor. Place smelled like mold for a week." We took a right out of the elevator and walked into a door marked "CAPERS, Homicide."

"CAPERS?"

"Crimes Against Persons." He opened the squad-room door for me, led me to his desk, and found me a chair, which I took to mean I'd graduated from suspect to normal human being. I looked at the pictures on his desk. Three kids. All girls.

"Dr. Foster, Detective McKnight." He nodded toward a tow-headed man in an expensive tie whose skin looked as though it had recently been sandblasted. McKnight looked to be about thirty. Jackson was clearly senior to him.

"Coffee?" Jackson said.

"No. Thanks, though." I shook McKnight's hand. "Detective."

I took a seat and opened my mouth to speak, but Jackson beat me to it.

"Our suspect's name is Gordon Pryne."

They both watched for my reaction, but of course there wasn't one. I'd never heard of the man.

"Ring a bell?" McKnight asked me.

"Nope." I watched them try to figure out if I was lying. "Sounds like a folk singer."

"He ain't folks," Jackson said. "And the only singing he's ever done is as a jailbird. Man's bad. All the way through."

"What can you tell me about him?"

"Rap sheet as long as my arm," McKnight said. He opened a file. "Started out stealing drugs and boosting cars when he was fifteen, then moved up to armed robbery and assault. Always with a knife of some kind. This is still as a juvenile. When he aged out of juvie, he moved on to sexual assault of a child, manslaughter, aggravated sexual assault. Man's an artist. What we call a serial violent offender. He was born a criminal."

"No one is born a criminal," I said.

They looked at me, surprised, I think, that I'd challenged them. We sat there in a face-off, mutually suspicious, our expressions showing the wear of so many years of looking inside people's sad, secret lives.

"Why do you think it's him?" I asked at last.

"His last offense," Jackson said. "Broke into an apartment in Arlington. Two white females, nineteen and twenty-two. Girls had just finished their fall semester at UT–Arlington. Got 'em in the middle of the night. Smacked each of them in the back of the head, tied them up, and then started raping them. In front of each other."

"Nice," I said.

"Yeah, real prince of a guy," McKnight said.

Jackson nodded. "Real prince. Waved a hatchet at 'em while

he was assaulting them. Said he was going to chop 'em when he was done."

"Why isn't he in prison?" I asked.

"He didn't finish the job," Jackson said. "He got the hatchet from a fire extinguisher cabinet. Fire alarm went off when he broke the glass. He fled the scene when the Arlington FD arrived. Girls ID'd him out of a photo lineup."

"And you're sure it was him," I said.

"No doubt whatsoever," McKnight said. "We got the two eye-witnesses. And physical evidence at the scene which links the suspect to the crime."

"The crime in Arlington," I said.

"That is correct," McKnight said.

"How long ago was this?" I asked.

"December," Jackson said.

"And what happened after that? He just disappeared?"

"The suspect remains at large," Jackson said. "But he didn't go far. He's around. We have no doubt about that."

"A hatchet isn't an ax, detectives. What makes you think he killed Drew Sturdivant?"

"The suspect is known to frequent Caligula," McKnight said.

"Where she worked," I said. "Did he know her?"

"Must have," Jackson said. "Twelve dancers," he said the word with contempt, "working there. No way she never ran into Pryne. Probably gave him a lap dance."

"So he was there that night? The night Drew was killed?"

"We're looking into that," McKnight said.

"But you don't know. Not for sure."

"No," Jackson said bluntly. "We don't."

"Where was she killed?" I asked. "The other girls were attacked in their apartment, right?"

"In the alley behind Critter Cars, on Harry Hines Boulevard," McKnight said. "Lots of nice, clear footprints on the pavement. Head wounds leave a lot of blood."

I winced. "Is that the car lot where they found her?"

McKnight nodded. "One of those pay-cash-by-the-week places. Interest is highway robbery. The body was found in the trunk of a 2001 Honda sedan. He dumped it in there to buy himself some time."

It. Drew Sturdivant had become an "it."

"We've tied him to the M.O. and to the complainant. We're still collecting physical evidence," McKnight said. "But he's the guy."

"Complainant?"

"The victim. When your complainant is acquainted with a known serial offender who used the same type weapon in his last offense—that's no coincidence. Once we get him, you should be safe."

"Were his fingerprints on the ax or anything?"

Jackson shook his head. "Wood doesn't pick up fingerprints. Blood does. Only fingerprints on the ax belong to you. Dr. Dylan Foster." He recited my address, my phone number, my social security number, my driver's license number.

"How do you account for that?" I asked. "Not my fingerprints. I mean, that there weren't any others?"

"Gloves," Jackson said simply. "There were wool fibers on the ax suggesting that the perp wore gloves during the assault. Leather, we think. With wool lining."

I nodded. "It was a cold night."

"Eighteen degrees," Jackson said. "Coldest night of the year."

"She probably never knew what hit her," McKnight was saying. "No defense wounds or anything. All the blows were to the head. First blow or two killed her."

I could feel the color draining from my face. I felt cold suddenly. "I guess that's a mercy of sorts."

"With an ax, that's all you get," Jackson said.

"And why do you think he left the ax on my porch? Do you think it was just random?"

"That's what we'd like to know, Dr. Foster," McKnight said. "You say you don't know him?"

"I don't."

"So we have a little problem," Jackson said. "Either you're holding something back, or…"

"Or maybe he's after me next?" I asked.

"Could be," McKnight said.

"Can I see a picture of him?"

Jackson reached for a three-ring notebook, flipped it open to a tab divider, and pointed at an image.

I laid eyes on Gordon Pryne for the first time. His hair was wild, brown, curly, shoulder length. His skin was mottled with acne scars, his lips full and petulant, his eyes an empty brownish-green. The color of a polluted pond.

His stats and his record were detailed below the photo. Gordon Weldon Pryne, age forty-six. Five foot ten, one hundred fifty-five pounds. His offenses were listed in order, a catalog of violence, itemized. He'd escaped nine months ago.

"He escaped?" I asked.

Jackson nodded. "He was in the middle of ten years flat in Huntsville. Aggravated sexual assault. Guess he decided he'd done enough time. Faked a seizure. Escaped during transport to the medical facility. Switched wristbands with another prisoner. Medical personnel thought he was a non-violent."

"What makes you think he's in Dallas?" I asked.

"Got a kid here," Jackson said.

I looked at the photo again. "He's a father?"

"He's got the necessary equipment," McKnight said. "That's all it takes."

"And he keeps in touch with this child?"

"Showed up once," Jackson said. "In five years."

"When was—?"

"Day of the murder. Around 5:30 p.m. Stoned. Crazy. Brought the kid a teddy bear. Scared the babysitter half to death. Mom gets home from her job at Parkland and calls 911. Pryne was gone by the time they got there."

I sighed. "So. What does this mean for me?"

"Keep your eyes and ears open, Dr. Foster," McKnight said. "And call us if you notice anything out of the ordinary."

"Any strange cars parked in front of your house. Anyone following you home. Any strange phone calls or hang-ups," Jackson said.

"Any chance of a distant connection with this guy?" McKnight asked. "Through a patient of yours or something?"

"Not that I know of. But I started going through my old files today, thinking maybe someone back there was unstable enough to be responsible for this. I do work with unstable people, obviously." I thought a minute. "Could you write down his biographical information for me? Full name, hometown, and so on?"

"We'd like to get a look at those files," McKnight said.

I'd been waiting for this. "I never release files, on principle," I said. "Patients have a right to their privacy."

"Not in the state of Texas they don't," McKnight said. "It's confidentiality, not privilege."

He was right. In Texas, only lawyers have privilege, which means that their records are untouchable. Physicians and psychologists have confidentiality, which means records are confidential, with a few exceptions. If Jackson and McKnight wanted my files, all they had to do was subpoena them. I could fight it, but eventually I'd have to turn them over.

"I realize that," I said, "but I've got over two hundred files. I don't want to jeopardize confidentiality of all those patients on a fishing expedition."

"Fair enough," McKnight said.

"But I will finish my search and give you a list of any possible connections. Anything at all." I held up my hand. "Promise. And if you want those, I'll sign the release and copy them for you myself."

"I think we can start with that," McKnight said.

"You live alone," Jackson said.

"Yes."

"Might want to think about a roommate for a while."

"Or a dog," McKnight suggested.

"I'll think about it," I said. "Thanks for talking to me today. I really do appreciate the information."

"I'm sorry we couldn't be more forthcoming earlier," McKnight said, looking sideways at Jackson. I couldn't tell if they'd disagreed about this, or if he was just acknowledging that Jackson had made the call. "We didn't feel it was appropriate until we'd fully investigated your involvement."

"And now you believe I wasn't involved?"

"I think you're telling the truth," McKnight said.

"That doesn't mean you're not involved," Jackson added. "You just may not know it yet."

That was an unsettling thought.

I looked at my watch. It was six thirty. A long day. It would be dark by now.

They must have known what I was thinking, because McKnight said, "Would you like an escort to your vehicle?"

"Sure. But if this guy is the artist you say he is, I doubt he's hanging around the police station waiting for me to come out. I'm probably safer here than I have been in a while."

"We can have a squad car follow you home," Jackson offered.

I nodded and thanked him. "What do I do if I hear or see anything?"

"Call 911," McKnight said. "Immediately."

"And then call us." Jackson handed me a card. "My cell number. Detective McKnight's cell number. Anytime, day or night, twenty-four/seven. We never close."

"Thank you." I took the cards and stood to leave, once again offering my hand to Jackson. This time he accepted it. "They breaking your heart yet?" I asked, pointing at the photos on his desk.

He shook his head and smiled for the first time. "Any minute now."

I drove home in a daze, a cruiser following closely behind me. My head was filled with images of Gordon Pryne and of Drew Sturdivant and of axes and blood and alleyways. The thin veneer had once again been stripped off the ugliness of the world for me. I knew it would return (the veneer, I mean), filmy and comforting and deceptively opaque, offering up the attractive illusion that life on this earth is safe and reasonably tidy and involves mainly nice people and generally good behavior. But then you walk into a filthy public restroom, or watch local television news, or cross paths with someone who dwells on the underside—some bottom-feeder—and the seamy sin seeps out of the cracks. The stench, the sticky oozing mess, is noxious.

I wonder how God stands it.

I felt like crying. Or sleeping for a week. But mainly I felt like taking a hot shower and having supper at an Italian restaurant with white tablecloths and sharing a bottle of wine with my handsome, well-behaved boyfriend, whose worst offense was probably a traffic violation in the sleepy town of Hillsboro.

I called him on my way home. We agreed he'd pick me up at eight thirty. Give this date one more shot.

My house was dark when I got there. And cold, as usual. The cop followed me in, and I flipped on lights as he checked the house. When I shut the door behind him, I felt the safety of home wrap around me. Okay, so I had mice. Or maybe rats. And Peter Terry was back, dressed as a lumberjack. And I could be the next victim of an ax murderer. But I was home. And my water heater was fixed.

Sometimes, you have to take the small victories.

I dumped my stuff, kicked my space heater on, and checked the water to make sure it was hot, which it was. I started myself a pot of water for tea and went to the front door to get the mail, leafing through it, tossing out a couple of credit card offers and a reminder from my dentist that it was time to have my teeth cleaned.

Mixed into the stack was a sealed, unmarked envelope. I opened it and stopped mid-stride.

The note was written in child-scrawl, in red felt-tip pen.

"Did you like the gift I left on your porch?"

11

~

Jackson and McKnight were there within minutes. They gloved their hands and picked up the note with a pair of tweezers, sealing it into a baggie and labeling the bag with a felt-tip pen.

"If we're lucky, Pryne's sloppy. We can get prints off the paper," McKnight said to me. "And DNA from the saliva."

"Saliva?"

McKnight pointed at the envelope.

"Oh. Right."

"You have any place to stay tonight?" Jackson asked me.

"Do you think it's necessary?"

"Second visit from this nut in a week," McKnight said.

"No time and no reason to be a hero," Jackson said. "Be smart. You might live."

"He's enjoying this," I said, the thought sickening me as I said it.

"You want to sit around and enjoy it with him, it's up to you," McKnight said. "But if I were you, I'd find myself somewhere to stay. Do you have a gun?"

"No. Should I?"

"Wouldn't hurt. Pryne's a blade man. Gun beats a blade every time."

"I wouldn't know how to shoot it," I said.

"You get yourself a gun," McKnight said, "and I'll teach you how to shoot it myself. Get a revolver. Ruger makes a good one, and Winchester. Five-shot. With a small grip for a woman's hand."

"I'll think about it," I said. "Thanks again for coming so quickly."

I was touched by their concern for my safety. They were rough men, all starched shirts and neckties and sturdy shoes, bound up with the bailing wire of regulation and procedure. They were suspicious by trade, guarded by nature, and probably more socialized to deal with criminals and victims than with any sort of regular type of human individual. I wondered what their home lives were like. Did they watch cop shows after work? Did they have pets? How did they shake off their dark, oppressive days?

I showed them out, locked the door behind them, and headed for my bedroom, fantasizing about the hot shower I knew was waiting for me. I needed to cleanse myself of Gordon Pryne and all this talk of guns and knives and axes.

In reality, few fantasies live up to expectations, but this one did. I didn't even have *Psycho* shower paranoia, which you'd think I would. No visions of a knife slicing through my shower curtain, or of Janet Leigh's lifeless legs hanging over the tub. The shower was hot and thoroughly satisfying. I was completely unconflicted about it.

David picked me up at eight thirty, sharp. The man is a gem. Charming, good-looking. And punctual. What more could a woman want?

He took me to our favorite restaurant, an Italian place we're convinced is owned by the mob. Since we're boring, white-bread voting citizens, the two of us, we find it sort of exotic to watch the mobsters congregate at the corner tables. We cook up wild stories about what they're talking about and who they're going to whack next, fantasizing in a semi-sick way about ordering hits on various people we don't like. Tonight, though, the game had no appeal, for obvious reasons.

We contented ourselves with a nice New Zealand sauvignon blanc (midlist, but beautifully dry with hints of tart citrus), an antipasti plate, and two orders of the special.

When the wine came, David placed a small, wrapped box in the center of my plate.

I love small gifts. Small is almost always good news.

He raised his glass. "To the birthday girl, whose life can only get better."

"Is that your version of optimism?" I asked, grinning.

"I try to look on the bright side."

I ripped the paper and cracked the lid of the jewelry box. It was a necklace. A black leather cord with a moonstone drop, set in silver.

"It's by that designer you like," he said. "Rosa Guevera."

I took it out of the box. It was gorgeous, a luminous moonstone—transparent and opaque at the same time—hugged in by a clean thin line of silver. I turned it over, and there was Rosa's stamp in the silver: RG with a tiny symbol next to it. I leaned over and gave him a kiss. "It's beautiful. Perfect. Thank you."

"I had a hard time finding it," he said. "Only one shop in town sells her stuff. Down on Cedar Springs."

"Did I ever tell you my mom helped her start her business?" I fought back an unexpected rush of tears. "It should be against the rules of the universe or something for a mother to die before you're finished needing her."

He nodded. "I know."

"My mother should be here where she belongs having a birthday supper with me. We should be contemplating cake, bemoaning milkmaid thighs, and discussing the significance of speed-limit birthdays."

David reached across the table and wiped my cheek. He smiled and didn't say anything. That's one of his great gifts. He knows what not to say.

I found a tissue in my purse and blew my nose. "You know the trusts I manage? My mother's estate? One of her donations before she died was to a women's co-op in Guatemala—Rosa Guevera and her friends starting their businesses. I think it was like five hundred bucks to each woman. Something tiny like that." I took a sip of wine and dabbed my eyes. "Amazing what such a small amount of money can do. She changed that woman's life."

"You know anything about her?" he asked. "I mean other than the jewelry? Does she have kids or anything?"

"I don't have any idea. I never thought to find out. Funny. Maybe I'll see if I can learn more about her. I think the grant application is still in the files somewhere." I raised my glass. "To Rosa. And her new life."

He clinked his glass with mine. "And to your mother. Who is responsible for two creations at this table. That necklace. And you."

The antipasti came, which we lingered over. I can't remember when anything tasted so good to me. I hadn't realized how hungry I was. Being stalked by an ax murderer can help you work up an appetite, I guess.

"What was her name again?" David asked, spearing a slice of salami.

"Whose?"

"Your mother's."

"Mary Nell," I said. "Everyone always called her Nell. She hated it. My brother and I had all sorts of variations on it. Mary Nelly, Mary Nelly Jelly, Mary Nelly Jelly Belly."

He laughed. "I bet she loved that one."

"She hated them all. She thought Nell was a more appropriate name for a bovine than a woman. She claimed she was named after a little red heifer."

"Was it true?" he asked.

"Her dad raised cattle. Outside Hillsboro, actually. She spent her whole childhood milking cows, cleaning stalls, and kicking bales of hay out the back of her dad's pickup."

"Ah. The origin of the Texas milkmaid image."

"Yep," I said. "Pass the garlic bread, please."

"Have you suspended your new thigh fitness program?" he asked, adding quickly, "Not that I think you need one in the first place."

"Thigh *Recovery* Program. They used to be there. I just want them back." I took a bite of bread. "I have a greater need for garlic bread and gnocchi than for firm thighs at the moment. It's been a rough week."

"Any new developments?"

I told him about Gordon Pryne. And the weird, murderer-stalker note.

"I might have to rescind my toast," he said. "I didn't think your life could get any worse."

"Well it is."

"You have a knack."

"Thank you."

"Pardon my provincial, controlling male attitude, but I don't think I can let you stay at that house by yourself."

"*Let*?" I raised my eyebrows. "Did I just hear you say *let*? Surely you didn't say *let*."

He nodded. "*Let* is exactly what I said. Don't even start with me."

"I don't think it's really up to you, David. But I appreciate your concern. I really do."

"You are the most impossibly stubborn woman I have ever met in my life."

I smiled sweetly. "Thank you." I held out my glass for more wine. "Truth is, I don't have anywhere else to stay. It occurs to me that I have no friends. Which is pathetic because I have lived in this city pretty much forever. I work too much."

"No kidding."

I glared at him.

"And even if I did have someone to stay with, I'd just be leading an ax murderer to their house. The man's attacked two women at once before."

"A hotel," he said. "What about that?"

"A hotel wouldn't do me any good. I wouldn't be any safer there."

"Stay with me," he said.

"I'm not commuting from Hillsboro, David. And besides, it's a small town. People would talk."

"People talk anyway. The women of that town have had me married, divorced, and gay all in the same week."

"You're fast. And adaptable, apparently."

He feigned modesty. "I do what I can."

"McKnight suggested I buy a gun. Or get a dog."

"How about both? I'll pick out the gun, you pick out the dog."

"We'll see."

I was tired of talking about Gordon Pryne and worrying about getting whacked with an ax. I wanted to enjoy my birthday supper. So I raised my glass and changed the subject, and we finished our dinner talking about regulation boyfriend-girlfriend stuff. I had my first taste of normalcy in days. Not to mention the gnocchi. Which was lovely.

Somehow the effort of conducting ourselves in a nonemergency manner wore us both out. I asked him to take me home after supper. David checked the house for me before he left, and then I sent him away with a good-night kiss, faking bravery but secretly wanting to be protected and rescued and saved from the bogeyman and the bogey-demon.

After he left, I paced the house for a while, unable to settle myself down. I finally landed at the dining room table I'd inherited from my mother, perching myself on a needlepoint chair cushion with a yellow legal pad in my hand. I wrote down everything that was on my mind.

Most of the scribbles were about Drew Sturdivant, Gordon Pryne, and Peter Terry. Were the three of them somehow connected? Or was Peter Terry simply acting on impulse, taking advantage of a bizarre crack in the normally serene routine of my days to insert himself back into my life?

There was no way to know at this point, but I did know one thing. I needed a plan. If for no other reason than to manage my own anxiety. Helene was right. I could not sit on my hands and wait for the police to tie this mess up. I wanted my own answers, in my own time.

I made a list of the things I knew.

I started with Drew Sturdivant. Nineteen years old, a student at El Centro College. She was supporting herself by stripping at Caligula, a nasty men's club for nasty men, in my opinion, on Harry Hines. She dyed her black hair a sort of bright orangy red. And she was dead. Murdered Saturday night, in an alley behind a Harry Hines car lot, by someone wielding an ax. The blows had been from behind and directed at her head, intended to kill her instantly.

Okay. Gordon Pryne.

Forty-six years old, career criminal. White. A hundred and fifty-five pounds. Five foot something. Five foot nine? Or ten?

I wondered how tall Drew was. And whether her height and his matched up in any way. Maybe there was something forensically important about the angle of the ax wound that would be illuminating.

Back to Pryne. He had wild brown hair and bad skin, at least in his mug shot. His criminal career ran the gamut. Theft, robbery, assault, sexual assault, and one manslaughter conviction. He'd escaped from prison by switching wristbands with a nonviolent criminal and faking a seizure. Pretty wily.

He'd tied up and raped two female college students this past winter, threatening them with a hatchet. His other assaults had involved a knife of some kind. He was a blade man, McKnight had said.

Pryne had a child. I wasn't sure how old the kid was or whether it was a boy or a girl. I didn't know whether he'd ever been married to the mother. And I didn't know the mother's name. I was pretty sure Jackson and McKnight had said she worked at Parkland Hospital.

On to Peter Terry. Demon with a sick sense of humor. Liked to bother me in annoying, disgusting ways. Had infested my house last year with flies (could he be responsible for the rodents?) and infused my home with the horrible, sulfuric smell of deviled eggs. Seemed to enjoy devil references, in fact. And puns. Axl Rose indeed.

Oh. I had forgotten about this. A year and a half ago, Peter Terry had introduced himself to me the same day I received two anonymous gifts—my mother's wedding ring, which had been buried with her two years before, and a necklace made by Rosa Guevera. John Mulvaney had received an identically wrapped gift that same day, which led to a series of bizarre misunderstandings and almost got me fired. I had never been certain that Peter Terry had sent the gifts. But it seemed the logical conclusion.

Peter Terry had haunted Eric Zocci, the patient who had died last year. And had also targeted another student of mine named Gavin, who had attempted suicide and landed in the psych unit, and who had later become a Christian. Gavin was a sophomore at SMU now. I hadn't seen him in a while.

I put down my pen, went to the kitchen, and made myself some hot chocolate. I sat there in my cold kitchen, in the dark, drinking my hot chocolate, thinking about my list, and listening to the rodents crawl around behind my water heater.

12

~

Tuesday is a clinic day for me, so I was up and in by nine, stirring my tea and listening to a nineteen-year-old girl complain about her boyfriend problems and obsess about her half-pound weight gain. Which is exactly what nineteen-year-old girls should have the luxury of worrying about.

Why was Drew Sturdivant, at nineteen, stripping for a living instead of waiting tables or mooching off her parents? At a dump like Caligula, I imagined the money was terrible. I was inexperienced in such matters, though, so was purely guessing.

I had a break after my first session. Marci, the bipolar office manager, had taken the day off to see her shrink, which meant she'd be fully medicated and back on the warpath in no time. I took advantage of her absence to continue searching my archived files.

Since I didn't really know what I was looking for, the search was directionless and ultimately fruitless. None of my patients seemed like ax-murderer types. Some of them were angry. And entitled. And one or two had been violent or had violent fantasies. Lots of them were into pornography and strip clubs, but they were college-age boys. Though I didn't find these to be particularly palatable habits, I'd hardly call an interest in naked women aberrant behavior at that age. None of the boys had mentioned Caligula specifically. No one had transferred from El Centro College. And none of them had mentioned Drew Sturdivant.

I printed out a few files anyway, just in case, but I was convinced they would lead nowhere.

I shifted gears and fired up the Internet, searching for Parkland Hospital. Maybe there was some way to track down Parkland personnel. I wanted to find out more about the mother of Gordon Pryne's child. I scanned the website, searching under the last name "Pryne" for staff members, but came up empty. Most of the staff wouldn't be listed anyway. Just the physicians.

I gave up and went to the Texas Sex Offender Registry. Surely Gordon Pryne was a registered sex offender. Maybe it listed spouses' names or something. I typed in his name, and sure enough, there he was, along with a list of his sexual crimes. His last known address was in west Dallas. There was a map and everything. I wrote the address down.

I scanned the crimes. Pryne's mug shot bio had listed them only generically, but this list included more specific details. He had two sexual assaults on his record. He'd been convicted of sexual assault of a child at age nineteen and given probation. And he'd been convicted of raping a thirty-four-year-old woman at knifepoint, six years ago. I guess that was the aggravated sexual assault Jackson and McKnight mentioned earlier. The rape and attempted murder of the two Arlington girls wasn't listed. Maybe he was never formally charged with that crime.

I went to the website for the *Dallas Morning News* and searched the archives for the week of the knifepoint rape. There it was in Metro. A local doctor had been raped in her apartment. The article didn't list the victim's name, of course. Or Pryne's. The report had appeared the day after the assault, probably before there was a suspect. The victim was an OB at Parkland.

Back to the Parkland website. Of the ninety ob-gyns listed, fifteen were women. I clicked on each name, one by one. A brief bio and vita of each woman appeared, including photographs. I went back to the article for details. The victim had been thirty-four at the time of the assault. That would make her forty now.

I went back to the vitae and checked medical school gradua-
tion dates. Taking into account age, and whether or not the
physician was working at Parkland at the time, only one name
matched. I clicked on her name and saw a smiling photo of a
striking Hispanic woman. Her name was Maria Chavez.

Dr. Chavez was an assistant professor on the teaching faculty
of Parkland Hospital. She'd done her undergraduate work at the
University of Texas at El Paso, majoring in Spanish, graduating
with a B.A., then completed a second undergraduate degree in
pre-med at the University of Texas in Austin. B.S. in biology.
Ambitious girl. And smart. She'd gone to UT Southwestern
Medical School and done her residency at Parkland.

A knock on the door scared me almost out of my chair. A student intern stuck her head in the door.

"Sorry to bother you, Dr. Foster. Your eleven o'clock is waiting."

I checked my watch. It was ten after eleven. I was going to
have to improve my time management skills.

"Tell him I'll be right there."

I finished scribbling some notes and closed the computer files.

I floated through the rest of my day in a haze, anchoring for
fifty minutes at a time during sessions. Somehow I was able to
focus on my patients, which was probably the Holy Ghost inter-
vening on their parts, not mine.

I ate lunch at my desk and got caught up on paperwork and
phone calls. I called Randy's Right-Now Rodent Removal and
scheduled a visit for tomorrow morning. And then I spent some
time trying to track down Maria Chavez.

Getting in touch with a physician is even harder than trying
to reach a psychologist. They're always in surgery or at the clinic,
or in meetings, or with patients, and each time you call a different location, you have to leave a message with some nurse or
assistant who thinks you're a patient and starts the conversation

with "Date of Birth?" I knew this, of course. My dad is a surgeon. But still it frustrated me, and by the end of the hour, I'd finished about a third of my tuna sandwich and lost another third or so of my sanctification.

By the end of the day, I was shot out, bled dry, and globally pessimistic. I went for a long swim, in the indoor pool this time (I may be foolish but I'm not a complete moron), and tried unsuccessfully to clear my head.

By the time I got home, I was starving. And agitated.

I threw my keys and cell phone onto the kitchen table and checked my answering machine. McKnight and Jackson had both called to check on me. My father had called. He sounded angry and demanded an immediate call back. And my brother Guthrie had called. He'd just gotten the news about Dad and Kellee's pending progeny. Which explained the phone call from my dad. I was about to be assigned to settle Guthrie down, I suspected.

I ignored the messages and turned on the stereo. Axl Rose had gone out with the day's garbage. I popped in a Dave Brubeck CD and felt my spine decompress as he tapped his little black and white keys.

The mail had come, along with a brown package, sitting on my front step.

Given recent events, I found unexpected mail a little bone-chilling.

The package had no return address, just one of those UPS bar-code labels. It was in a plain brown box, neatly taped. I picked the package up and returned to the kitchen. I leaned in and listened for ticking.

Then I realized how paranoid I was being and took a pair of scissors to the tape and opened it.

Inside was another box, along with a note, written in purple crayon. "Happy Birthday, Dylan." Purple hearts were drawn on the margins of the note. I felt my spine tighten back up.

I went to the bathroom and got some tweezers, then picked up the note and set it aside. I was too curious and too anxious to wait for the police to come. I put on a new pair of Playtex rubber gloves ("sassy new color!" the package shouted), and with shaking hands, opened the second box.

Inside was a bright pink Barbie lunchbox.

I used a dishtowel to pick it up and examine it. Maybe there was something inside. I sniffed it. A body part? I shook it. It felt empty.

Pulling open the zipper, I peeked inside and saw another note, folded. I used my tweezers to pick up the note and spread it out on the table.

My fear quickly morphed into delight.

The package wasn't from Gordon Pryne at all. It was from my favorite five-year-old in the world, Christine Zocci, the niece of the student who had died last year. She had obviously picked out the gift herself. And drawn the card. Purple is her favorite color.

The note was from her mother, Liz. A chatty tome about their family, catching me up on everyone. Liz and Andy were doing great. Andy was running the family business now, and Liz was administering the family charities, which meant she was in charge of an enormous amount of money. Christine was in her second semester of kindergarten and had decided she wanted to be a queen when she grew up. When Liz explained that America doesn't have a queen, Christine had said, "Then I'll have to be queen somewhere else."

Her two younger brothers, "the little hoodlums" as the family referred to them, had recently gotten themselves kicked out of play group for biting the other children. Mikey, the older one, had decided to cut his own hair before school one day, and now sported a jagged bald spot where his bangs used to be.

I love this family.

The lunchbox had a picture of a red-haired Barbie, a thoughtful choice since my hair is auburn. She was wearing a sporty, striped sweater and pink pants. It had a shoulder strap and came with its own hot-pink Barbie sippy cup.

I picked up the phone and called the Zocci house in Chicago, knowing Andy wouldn't be home from work yet and that Liz would be wrangling kids and making grilled cheese sandwiches.

Christine answered the phone.

"Hi, Punkin, it's Miss Dylan," I said.

"Mommy!" Christine shouted. "It's Miss Dylan!" then said to me, "Did you get your present?"

We chatted about the various features of my new lunchbox and Christine told me about the boy at school she liked, and wondered if I still liked the same boy. I said yes, and thought about how little changes in the heart of a girl from age five to thirty-five. I guess we all want to be queen someday, at least in the eyes of the right boy.

Christine dropped the phone and Liz picked it up, shouting at the boys to get the goldfish out of the toilet. I wondered if it was a real goldfish or the Pepperidge Farm kind.

"Never have children," Liz said. "Save yourself while you still can."

Conversations with Liz always involve shouted instructions to the children, in mid-sentence, so that I have to concentrate on what she means when she says, "Andy and I went to a charity event right now Tommy get your brother off the kitchen table at the Four Seasons and saw Christine hand me the glass and I'll get you some milk."

But somehow their family life always grounds me. If I could, I'd live with them, just to know what it feels like to have that much chaos and unaffected goodwill swirling around me. I'm convinced I'd repair some of my fractured mental health in such an environment.

I felt better by the time I got off the phone—downright

loved, in fact, instead of my usual lost state of abject loneliness and vulnerability.

My cell phone rang then. I didn't recognize the number.

"Dylan Foster," I said.

"Dr. Foster, this is Maria Chavez. I had a message to call you."

"Dr. Chavez, thanks so much for calling me back."

"What can I do for you, Dr. Foster? Do we have a mutual patient?"

"Actually, no," I said, feeling suddenly awkward. "It's a personal matter." I took a breath. There was no good way to say it. "Involving Gordon Pryne."

She didn't respond. I thought maybe she'd hung up.

"Dr. Chavez?"

"Yes," she said.

"I'm sorry to intrude."

"How do you know Gordon Pryne?"

"I don't. Not personally."

"Dr. Foster, what is this about?"

"Gordon Pryne is a suspect in a murder."

"Drew Sturdivant," she said. "The police have already talked to me. Are you with the police department? Or was she a patient of yours?"

"Neither. I teach at SMU."

"I don't understand," she said.

"Drew Sturdivant was murdered with an ax. The ax that was used to kill her was left on my front porch the night she died."

"I see," she said slowly. "Do you know him?"

"No. And I don't know why he picked me."

"It's not the sort of question you always get an answer to," she said, her voice softening.

"Could we meet to talk?"

"I'm on my way home. The sitter leaves at seven. Why don't you just meet me there?"

"Are you sure?"

"I'd like to get this over with," she said. "No offense."

"None taken."

She gave me the address. We lived in the same neighborhood.

We agreed to meet at seven thirty, which was forty-five minutes from now.

I wasn't sure why I wanted so badly to talk to her. But something was tugging at me. I knew she was an important link.

I made myself a quick supper and got dressed to meet Maria Chavez.

13

~

Maria Chavez lived in a duplex in my funky little neighborhood, not four blocks from my house. Her yard was winter brown and her Christmas lights were still strung on her porch, a luminous little greeting committee. The flower beds on her half of the yard were neatly mulched and held climbing rosebushes, all trimmed and trussed for the winter. The beds on the other side were empty, tufts of Bermuda grass growing in the snaggle-toothed sneer of crooked liner rocks.

I stepped around a red tricycle and knocked on the door.

She answered quickly. She was a tiny woman, almost child size. And beautiful, even in her hospital scrubs, her brown hair pulled back in a ponytail, her face free of makeup, her eyes tired. She shook my hand and invited me in.

The house was pleasant, decorated in warm browns and reds. There was a stack of books by the couch and a magazine open on the dining room table beside an empty plate. Under the dining room table was a little array of toys. A dump truck, a rubber snake, and three plastic dinosaurs.

"Can I offer you anything?" she asked. "I was just about to have a glass of wine."

"No thanks," I said.

I took the opportunity to spy a little while she was in the kitchen. My initial glance around the room had suggested that Dr.

Chavez was a tidy woman and, like me, a tad bit obsessive. The room had a comfortable, lived-in feel without seeming cluttered or chaotic at all. I didn't know how old her kid was, but he was either old enough to corral his own toys or someone did a heroic job of wrangling the kid-gear so that it didn't take over the house.

I didn't see a television anywhere. She was atypical in that sense. I don't have one either, and know very few other abstainers. She did have a good stereo, though. I thought I recognized the piano music that was playing softly as Chopin, but I wasn't sure.

I've always thought you could learn a lot about people by studying their bookshelves, so I walked over to Maria Chavez's bookcase and indulged my nosiness. Stuck between *Gray's Anatomy* and a two-year-old *Physician's Desk Reference* was a copy of *Horton Hears a Who*. Other children's books, some in English, some in Spanish, were poking out from the cracks between the grown-up books.

She owned several Spanish textbooks, as well as a formidable collection of fiction written in both English and Spanish; some authors I recognized and some I didn't. She leaned toward weighty fiction. No suspense novels or anything like that. Many of the authors had Hispanic surnames. There was some poetry, several books on Cuba, and five or six books, in the top right-hand corner, on criminal psychology. I recognized several authors and titles. Most of the books were about the etiology of criminal behavior. Nature vs. nurture.

I made it back to my spot by the door before she returned. She gestured for me to sit on the couch. She sat in the chair opposite me, her feet together, her elbows on her knees, and her wine glass in both hands in front of her. She kept her head down for a minute, almost like she was praying. Or trying to gather herself. I waited until she looked up at me.

"Thanks for seeing me," I said. "And so quickly. I know this must be hard for you."

"What can I do for you, Dr. Foster?"

"Please call me Dylan."

She nodded and waited for me to answer her question.

"I'm not exactly sure," I admitted. "I'm trying to put a puzzle together, only I don't know what the picture is supposed to look like. And I don't know how the pieces are shaped. Or even where the edges are."

"And Gordon Pryne is one of the pieces," she said.

"I think so."

"And you think my story might fit in as well?"

"I do."

She didn't react at all. A cool customer, this woman. "What would you like to know?"

Of course, I had no idea what I would like to know. I just knew I was supposed to be sitting here talking to her, that she was somehow important. That I needed to hear what she had to say.

"I guess it might help if I explained what's happened so far," I began. "I was at home, getting ready for a date. I live just a few blocks from here, by the way."

"Really?" Her eyebrows went up. "Here in Oak Lawn? Which street?"

We talked for a minute about what a great neighborhood it is and how much we loved living there. A much-needed bonding moment and a distraction from the gravity of our other common ground, our connection to Gordon Pryne.

"So I'm at home," I continued. "This was last Saturday night. And I hear something at the door, and I go to answer it. And an ax falls into my doorway. Someone had leaned it up against the door. I didn't realize it until after I'd picked it up, but it was covered in blood. Drew Sturdivant's blood, it turns out. It was the ax that was used to kill her."

"And you just found it on your porch."

I nodded.

"Bizarre."

"Yeah. At least. I didn't find out her name until the next day, and by then I was in this weird situation where the police were suspicious of me, thinking I had something to do with the murder."

"Which you didn't."

It was a statement. Not a question or a guess. She knew, as I knew about her, that we were victims, not participants in Gordon Pryne's sick games.

"No," I said. "I didn't. And once they were over that, they told me the name of the suspect." I hesitated. "Gordon Pryne." I nodded toward her, hoping to show sensitivity and respect for what she'd been through.

"And how did you put his name together with mine?" she asked. "No one really knows…I mean, I don't talk about…"

I wanted to spare her the trouble of explaining herself. As if it were anyone's business.

"I'm a psychologist, Dr. Chavez."

"Maria," she said.

"Maria. Thank you. My point is, I realize I may have no more than an academic understanding of what you've been through. It's never happened to me. I feel awkward even bringing it up and I'm so grateful for your willingness to talk to me. I know this is the sort of thing you may not have talked about with anyone. Ever."

"Except the police."

"Right. The police."

"Did they give you my name?"

She didn't seem upset, though she would have been entitled. She had a right to take her secret to her grave, if she chose.

"They didn't tell me about you at all," I said. "I found out about your…about your connection to Pryne in a very round-about way. The police had told me that Pryne had a child whose mother worked at Parkland. So I went on a fishing expedition looking for her, thinking maybe there was a woman named Pryne on the staff. I guess I thought she could tell me something about him, maybe what he might do next or…something. I'm not sure.

"And that led nowhere. But in the course of trying to find her, I found out more about him and about his record, and I stumbled across his rape conviction, and found the *Morning News* story about the rape of a Parkland doctor. It was a rabbit trail, really, but it led me to you."

"So you never found the mother?"

"No. Only doctors' names are listed on the website. And she and Pryne may never have married. And if they did, she very well could've changed her name by now. I would have. From Pryne. Anything but that." I looked up. I hadn't thought to ask her until now. "You don't know her, do you?"

She took a sip of wine and sat back into her chair.

"It's a huge hospital system, Parkland," she said.

"I heard it has its own zip code. Anyway, I put you together with the incident six years ago through a process of elimination, really. Your name wasn't mentioned anywhere."

"You must be a good researcher," she said, smiling for the first time. "No one has ever… Not that I know of anyway."

"I think mainly I'm persistent." I smiled and made a little pinching gesture with my fingers. "And a teeny tiny bit obses- sive."

"Both qualities I suspect we share." She raised her glass.

I liked this woman immensely. She was careful without being suspicious, poised without being cold, and seemed wonderfully wise and intelligent.

"Gordon Pryne," she began, "broke into my apartment—this was when I was living closer to the hospital. Over off Harry Hines. I knew it wasn't a safe neighborhood, but I didn't have a car and the bus ride was short from there."

She said this without a trace of regret in her voice.

"My apartment was on the second floor, so I thought I was

safe from something like that, a break-in, but he climbed a wall at the end of the parking lot, and then jumped from one balcony to another until he got to my place. He broke the sliding glass door. Shattered it. In the middle of the day. It was a Saturday." She looked down and traced the rim of her glass as she spoke.

"I was in the kitchen making tortillas. My parents were coming in from El Paso and my father won't eat store-bought tortillas. So I was standing there and heard this enormous shattering of glass behind me."

"That must have been terrifying."

She nodded. "I turned around, and there he was with that knife. He looked...crazed. And angry. I remember that so vividly. My first thought wasn't 'why has this man broken into my house and what is he going to do to me?' It was 'why is he so angry?' Like it somehow had something to do with me. That anger. I couldn't think why he'd be so angry. At me. It seemed so personal."

She took a sip of wine and looked at me.

"Do you feel that way? That his leaving the ax on your porch was...personal?"

I thought about the note he'd sent me. It was personal. To him, anyway. But he was not a personal being. He was thoroughly impersonal. He had to be to do the things he did.

"It's hard not to. But I guess it isn't, is it?"

"No," she said. "It's anything but that. He's an angry man, and it's an anger that is...I don't know, comprehensive. Global. Universal."

"A general, all-purpose rage."

She smiled. "Something like that. Anyway, he just sort of ran from the spot where I first saw him and tackled me. He threw me against the wall in the kitchen, and knocked the wind out of me. Stunned me just enough to get me under control. I had a hot cast-iron skillet in my hand and I hit him with it. I hit him in the face. And I remember this—he didn't even flinch. He had this almost superhuman strength and that rage. He twisted the skillet out of my hand—he broke my wrist—and he dragged me by my hair into the living room, put a knife to my throat, and raped me. Right there on all those broken shards of glass. They took a hundred and fourteen stitches in my back." She looked down at her glass again. "I bet the whole thing lasted less than five minutes."

I didn't know what to say.

"And then he left. The same way he came in. He walked through the empty doorframe, hopped off my balcony to the next one, and jumped from one balcony to another. Then he scaled the wall and disappeared." She looked up at me. "Five minutes. And my life has never been the same."

"What did you do?"

"I called the police. The ambulance came. I was losing a lot of blood, but I asked them to take me to Baylor instead of Parkland. They did, which was kind of them. They didn't have to do that. They stitched me up, set my wrist, did the rape kit, photographed my wounds, the whole thing. I've done it a thousand times myself. Most crime victims are brought to Parkland, you know."

I imagined her performing these duties for rape victims, dragging this heavy secret around with her as she worked.

"I bet you take good care of them," I said.

"I do." She smiled again. "Do you like poetry, Dylan?"

"I'm more of a magazine girl."

"You don't know John Donne, then? English poet. Wrote a series of sonnets."

"Holy Sonnets," I said, the fog clearing from distant memories of high school English class. "Sixteenth century?"

"Seventeenth. 'Batter my heart, three-person'd God,'" she quoted. "'For You as yet but knock; breathe, shine, and seek to mend…Your force to break, blow, burn, and make me new…' Holy Sonnet 14. The image is of a metalworker, hammering and heating and hammering some more and polishing until he creates something beautiful, something that is his workmanship. And then at the end, there's this rape imagery. 'For I, Except you enthrall me, never shall be free, Nor ever chaste, except you ravish me.' I've read that poem every night. For six years."

"Mommy?" A child's voice called from the other room.

"Yes, Doodlebug, what is it?" she answered.

"Can I have a glass of water?"

"Sure, honey. Why don't you come in and give Mommy a kiss and I'll get it for you. There's a nice lady here that I want you to meet."

I waited until a little boy appeared, wearing Superman pajamas and dragging a worn baby blanket. He was maybe four or five years old.

He crawled into her lap and sucked his thumb. She kissed him tenderly on the forehead.

"Nicholas, this is Miss Dylan." Her eyes met mine. "Dylan, this is my son, Nicholas."

She was looking at me expectantly. I wasn't sure what she was waiting for.

And then I took a closer look at Nicholas, the sweet little boy in her lap.

His eyes were blue, his hair curly and wild. This little boy didn't look like his mother. He looked like his father.

He looked just like Gordon Pryne.

14
~

H e's beautiful," was all I could think of to say. He was, too.
I studied his face. He had Gordon Pryne's wild features—crazy
curly hair, bright blue eyes, and a sort of animal energy, which
seemed to be in hibernation at the moment, all sweet and small
and slumbery. But he looked like the kind of kid who could be
hell on wheels after a good dose of sugar and no nap.

She smiled at him and kissed him again on the forehead. "Yes,
he is." Then to him, "Let's get you a drink of water, and then
straight back to bed. Okay? Doodlebugs need lots of sleep."

She left with him in her arms, his blanket trailing behind
them. He sucked his thumb and watched me over her shoulder
as she carried him away. I heard her in the kitchen, and then she
walked back through the den to his bedroom and tucked him
back in bed.

"You sure you don't want a glass of wine?" she said. "You look
like you could use one."

"No, I'm good."

She sat down and waited.

"You kept the baby," I said, almost to make myself believe it.
"You got pregnant, and then you kept the baby."

"I did."

"When did you…? I mean, how did you…?"

"Which question do you want me to answer?" she said.

I shrugged. "Pick one."

"I didn't realize I was pregnant until I was four and a half months along."

"Surely there must have been symptoms. And aren't you a…?"

Pretty soon I was going to regain my ability to finish a sentence. I could feel it coming back to me.

"Ob-gyn. Yeah, it's not like I wouldn't know what to look for. But I'm a small woman. I didn't gain any weight. I was nauseous all the time. But I was on pain medication and experiencing symptoms of posttraumatic stress. Nausea, vomiting, insomnia, anxiety, moodiness, fatigue. I'm sure you see it all the time. And my cycle is crazy anyway. Very irregular. So I really didn't put it all together. Not until I was in my second trimester."

"And by then…" So much for my ambition to finish sentences.

"I couldn't do it. I just couldn't do it." She looked up at me, suddenly animated. "I mean, no one would have blamed me. I realize that. Everyone, or almost everyone, I guess—the pope springs to mind as an obvious exception—makes an allowance for rape."

"Did you think of adoption?" I asked, and instantly regretted it. Of course she had.

"I obsessed about it. I don't know how many nights I spent pacing the rooms of this house, like a caged cat. Back and forth. And that's how I felt. Caged. Angry. So, so angry."

"Why did you keep him?"

"You know why?" She smiled at me. "Because I was afraid. Afraid of how this poor little innocent child would turn out. The adoptive parents would have to know how he was conceived— and by that time, by the way, I knew I was carrying a boy. I'd already named him Nicholas in my mind. Nicholas is the patron saint of children. Did you know that?"

"I didn't."

"If I'd placed him for adoption, would his new parents look

at him differently? Would they look at him and see a rapist?"

"Don't you?"

"Oh, yes. I absolutely do. But that's the point."

"I'm not following you."

"Don't you see? I know his father. I know how angry he is. How cruel. I know he has no capacity for empathy or for kindness or for anything that makes us…human. I know he has no conscience. But I don't know *why* he's like that. Is it because he had a terrible life? Or is there something in him, in his genes, that makes him…?" She looked up at me.

"Evil?" I said.

She nodded. "Evil. Is that a genetic trait? Or is it something that happens to you?"

"Maybe it's spiritual."

"Maybe it is spiritual. But the point is, we don't know. I don't know. And I wanted to protect this little boy from evil. I wanted to do everything I could to love it out of him. I knew that the second I saw the sonogram and heard his heartbeat. He needed someone who knew his story. He needed *me*." She looked up at me. "I'm his mother."

"Surely you knew you'd be stuck with Gordon Pryne for the rest of your life. The minute he found out he had a son—"

"He never found out. I've never told a soul. Not even my parents. No one knows who his father is. No one in the world. Other than me. And now you."

"But the police are the ones who told me he had a child. They obviously know."

"Jackson and McKnight," she said. "I met them. The day after Pryne came by with the teddy bear. I called the police when I got home that night and he was here. But I never told them how Nicholas was conceived. Or even that he was Pryne's child. I think they arrived at that conclusion on their own. He does look like his father."

"But they know about the rape."

She shook her head. "My name never appeared anywhere in the record. Except in the case file, which I'm sure they haven't checked. They weren't involved in my case. I agreed to a plea to settle the case without a trial. I never had to testify." She leveled her eyes at me. "They don't know I'm the woman he raped. You're the only one that knows that."

"If Pryne doesn't know about Nicholas, why did he show up with a teddy bear?"

"And how does he know where I live? I was hoping you'd know the answer to both questions," she said.

"Me? How would I know? I've never even met him."

She rose and went to the kitchen. She came back with the wine bottle and a glass for me. I'm not wild about red wine, but I had the feeling I was about to need it. She poured us both a glass, set the bottle on the table and sat down.

"I pulled a double shift today," she began. "Three-to-eleven, eleven-to-seven."

I looked at my watch. She'd been up since about two in the morning. It was after eight p.m. now.

"Three-to-elevens are always crazy. You know how Parkland is. Anything can happen. It's where they take all the indigents and criminals for treatment."

"The unwashed and the unclean."

"Exactly. So around four this morning this homeless woman is brought in. Cervical tumor. She was in pain and had lost a lot of blood. Alcoholics do that. Their liver functions are way off. Their blood can't coagulate. Sometimes you can't save them. They bleed out fast."

"How did you know she was an alcoholic?"

"The smell. You know that smell when it's coming out of their pores?"

"Happily, no," I said.

She chuckled. "Good for you. I wish I didn't. Anyway, she was conscious when she came in, but not lucid. Hysterical. Babbling. We hung a couple of units of blood and tried to get her stable for surgery. I was the attending OB. That's why they called me in. I'd never met her, you understand."

Stories like this one make me appreciate my job.

"But she seemed to know me. Kept grabbing for my hand and calling me Maria. Shouting at me to listen to her. Maria is a pretty common name for a Hispanic woman. I didn't think anything about it. I thought she was hallucinating. We gave her a shot of morphine and she settled down, and I went to check on a couple of patients who were in labor.

"When I got back she'd crashed. Her heart had stopped. Too much blood loss, probably. And no nutritional base to start with. She'd probably been living on bourbon for years. You're that mal-nourished, you really have no shot. But they were working on her. You know, with the paddles."

"My dad's a heart surgeon," I said.

"Oh. Then you know. De-fibbing her. So I watched them work on her, but she was still flat-lined. And then all of a sudden, she came to. Just opened her eyes and looked right at me."

"Was she conscious? Or was it a reflex?"

"She was conscious. And alert. You know what she said?"

I shook my head.

"She said, 'Maria, I've spoken to the authorities about you.'"

"The authorities? Did she mean the police?"

Maria smiled. "I think she meant a higher authority than that. She said, 'Maria, I've spoken to the authorities about you. Your help will arrive tonight.'"

"What did you do?" I asked.

"I didn't know what to do. Everyone was staring at me. I just wanted to settle her down, so I answered her. I said, 'But I don't need any help.'"

I leaned in. "What did she say?"

She said, 'The authorities have spoken. Your help will arrive tonight.' And then she died. Just like that." She paused and said quietly, "Her name was Willie." She looked up at me. "And then you called. Just a few hours after that."

"You don't think I'm the help?"

"Yes. I do."

"I can't imagine any sort of help I could provide."

"Do you know much about nightmares, Dylan?"

I felt my skin prickle. "Why? Have you been having night-mares?"

"No, Nicholas has. He wakes up in the middle of the night screaming. Always at the same time."

"What time?" I knew what the answer would be.

"Three thirty."

"Has he told you anything about the dreams?"

"No. But he's been drawing them, I think."

She got up and let herself quietly into his bedroom, return-ing a moment later with a coloring book. She handed it to me and sat back down.

I flipped through the pages. The book was published by the Audubon Society—*Birds of the Americas*. Simple outline drawings of cardinals and ducks and hummingbirds. In the margins of some of them, he had written his name in crude capital letters. The askew script of a five-year-old.

Nicholas had colored the images in broad strokes of wacky, kid-chosen colors. The cardinal was lemon yellow, the Mallard duck Day-Glo orange and mint green. As I flipped through the book, the colors got darker, the strokes more unruly and wild.

When I got to the picture of a dove, I froze. Nicholas had left the picture white, but x'ed out its wings with black crayon. He'd drawn a red slash between the bird's wings on its back.

I looked up. "Did he tell you anything about this?"

"It's the white man. That's what he said. The white man from his dreams."

I flipped through more pages. The wings were crossed out in each image now, the red slash drawn violently across each bird's back, the image left white, colorless.

"He sang a song the other day while he was coloring," she said. "To the tune of 'Jesus Loves Me.'"

"What were the words?"

"Peter wants me this I know. For the Bible tells me so. Little ones to him belong. They are weak but he is strong. Yes, Peter wants me. Yes, Peter wants me. Yes, Peter wants me. The Bible tells me so."

I felt sick.

"Who is Peter?" she said.

"The man with the slash in his back. His name is Peter Terry."

"Who is he? Is he connected with Gordon Pryne? Some criminal friend of his? A pedophile or something? How do you know him?"

"He's not a person. He's a…spirit, I think. A demon."

I watched her eyes. She didn't flinch.

"What does he want with my son?"

"The same thing he wants with all of us. Peter Terry is a hunter," I said. "He's hunting souls."

15

~

I left Maria's duplex thoroughly spooked by our conversation and once again enraged at Peter Terry. The sky started to spit out little icy pellets, which were drumming onto the windshield of my pickup and already sticking to the roads.

Once or twice a year maybe, during what Texans call a "hard freeze," which means anything below twenty-five degrees, we get freezing rain or snow or some mixture of the two. Every exposed surface ends up coated with a glassy sheet of ice.

Since Dallas has no winter storm equipment—snowplows, sanding trucks, and road salt are not urgent budget items in a city south of the Red River—roads are essentially impassable until the ice melts. The city simply shuts down to wait it out.

This sort of event in Dallas excites a uniformly childish sense of glee. Meteorologists, suddenly thrust blinking into the spotlight and flushed with self-importance, chart the impending storm with morbid enthusiasm. A gossipy string of warnings is passed along by everyone you met the day before. And after the ice storm has arrived, everyone pops out of bed at 5:00 a.m. and flips on TVs and radios to see if schools and businesses have been shut down for a longed-for snow day. If our luck is good, we get to go back to bed, sleep late, and then start a pot of chili sometime that afternoon.

Somehow, I'd managed to miss the buzz completely.

I needed supplies.

My favorite hardware store is called Elliott's. I love Elliott's Hardware because it is a real hardware store, not like those huge national chains that sell very little hardware and are in fact the place to go when you want track lighting or vinyl flooring or maybe a spiffy outdoor grill.

Elliott's is the sort of place where you can describe some obscure plumbing part from a faucet that was discontinued forty years ago, using words like *thingy* and *doodad* and *doohickey*. And the face of the sixtyish hardware expert you're talking to will light up and he'll say, "Follow me," and he'll walk you over to aisle twenty-seven and open a drawer of a hundred similar doohickeys and pull one out of a slot and hand it to you. And the part will cost twenty-five cents. And as an added bonus, they're open until nine on Tuesdays.

I steered my way over there, parked my truck in the lot, which had already been sanded and salted, and scooted in the sliding glass doors at ten minutes to nine.

"Welcome to Elliott's," the man said cheerfully. "How can we help you tonight?"

"Mice," I said.

"You have mice?"

"Or rats. I'm not sure which."

"How big is the hole?"

I made an okay sign with my fingers.

"Rats," he said.

"Rats, then. My exterminator is supposed to come tomorrow, but with the weather, he might not be able to get there for a couple of more days. What do you think? Rat poison, maybe?"

"Don't recommend it," he said.

"Why?"

"You want rodents dying behind your walls and smelling up your living room?"

"Nope."

"Follow me," he said, and walked me over to aisle twelve.

"You have your standard rattrap," he was saying, picking up a sample to show me. "Bait it with peanut butter and clock 'em on the back of the head. Snapping sound can be a problem. Scare you out of your wits in the middle of the night. And then there's the problem of carcass disposal. Plus you'd need a dozen or so of these little babies to do the job. Wouldn't be my first choice. Next you have your glue traps, which are essentially trays of industrial glue. Little critters get stuck and either starve to death or rip themselves open trying to get out."

I winced. "Doesn't sound too humane."

His eyes lit up. "Follow me."

He walked to the end of the aisle and gestured toward the shelf, like Carol Merrill on *Let's Make a Deal*. Door number three.

"Repeater Clear Top Multiple Rat Trap. We have two brands. Woodstream or Rover. Either one will do you just fine. Catch you some rats with this little beauty and then drive on over to your enemy's house and let 'em go."

"I'll take it."

"Excellent choice. How are you for salt? Ice storm tonight. Blue norther rolling in."

"Definitely need salt."

"Scraper for your windshield?"

"Yep, need one of those."

"Flashlights or lanterns in case the power lines snap?"

"I think I'll use candles."

"Matches?"

"Sure."

"What kind of car do you drive?"

"A '72 Ford pickup."

"You'll need sandbags."

"Roger that."

He got me fixed up, loaded the sandbags into the bed of my truck himself, refused a tip, and reminded me to fasten my seat belt and drive slow.

Elliott's renews my faith in mankind. I should spend more time there.

My next stop was the grocery store. I loaded up on chili fixings, of course—it never hurts to hope—along with other sundries I'd need, including peanut butter to bait my new humane Rover brand Repeater Clear Top Multiple Rat Trap. And then I headed home. The roads were already slick, but since everyone else had gotten the word about the storm, I was the only one dumb enough to be out. I had the streets to myself.

My house was near arctic temperature when I arrived. I unloaded groceries and ran around the house kicking on space heaters and lighting the gas fire in the bathroom. I even turned on the gas stove and opened the door—which I know you're not supposed to do (methane gas or something), but I needed all the heat I could get. I walked over to the water heater closet and leaned in to listen, breathing a quick thank-you to my good friend Jesus. It was knocking just like it was supposed to.

It was late and I'd had a long day, but I wasn't tired. I was wired. I turned on the stereo, changed into jammies and scooted into my slippers, made myself some hot chocolate (with marshmallows to reward myself for finding Maria Chavez), and sat down to think.

What was Peter Terry up to? I'd articulated it for the first time to myself when I said the words to Maria. Peter Terry was hunting souls. But why Nicholas Chavez? And what did that have to do with Drew Sturdivant? There was no doubt in my mind now that Peter Terry was connected to Drew's murder. Somehow. The link to Maria Chavez and her son was too strange to be coincidental. With or without Willie the homeless person's weird prophecy about Maria's help arriving tonight.

And what was I supposed to help her with, anyway? Protecting her son? How exactly did one go about protecting a five-year-old from a spooky demonic white dude with a slash on his back who enjoyed twisted practical jokes like breaking water heaters while wearing a lumberjack outfit and inserting his name into "Jesus Loves Me"?

"What a sicko," I said out loud.

My phone rang. I checked the clock. It was almost ten thirty. Who would be calling at this hour?

"Hello?"

"Did you see this coming?"

"Hey, Guthrie."

"Why is it that the worst specimens are the ones who insist on replicating themselves?" he said. "Have you noticed that? Ever been to a truck stop? Or, like, the state fair?"

"How did you find out?"

"They sent me a T-shirt."

"World's Greatest Uncle?"

"It should say brother, for starters. Kellee and her room temperature IQ."

"It's about forty-five degrees in my house right now."

"My point exactly."

"There's nothing to do but make peace with it, Guthrie."

"Why does this bother me so much? I'm an adult."

"That's a matter of opinion."

"Happy birthday, by the way. I forgot. As usual."

"So did I, almost."

"What is this? Thirty-six?"

"Thirty-five."

"We're old."

"Speak for yourself. How's Cleo?"

"She left."

"Left? What do you mean, she left?"

"I mean she put her clothes in the new red Volvo I bought her and drove away."

"She left you?"

"Is there another kind? Leaving is leaving."

"Cleo left you."

"Only after I asked her to."

"What happened?"

"What didn't happen? We never should have gotten married in the first place."

I tried not to act relieved. One negative, critical person in the family is enough, and since I'd had no success in changing my personality, Cleo had to go.

"I'm sorry, Guthrie. Really. I am."

"Liar. Besides, don't be. I can't stand pity."

"There's a difference between pity and empathy," I said.

"Okay. Feel my pain. Someone needs to."

I heard him rattle ice in a glass. Guthrie was a gin man.

"Where are you?"

"At the club. She's at the house picking up the last of her stuff."

"Don't drive home, okay? Not if you've been drinking."

"What makes you think I've been drinking?"

"Guthrie."

"Okay. I'll get a ride."

"Promise me."

"Scout's honor."

"You got kicked out of scouts."

"So did you."

"Not the point."

"Okay. I swear on my golf clubs."

"Better. Did she take the cats?"

"Are you kidding? The woman's not an idiot. We've had those cats for half a decade and they still can't find the litter box."

I laughed. "Well, at least you won't be by yourself. Is this just a separation? Or what?"

I heard him order another gin and tonic. "Or what, probably."

I didn't know what to say. "Tough week," was all I could muster.

"A little. What about you? Anything happening down there?"

"Not much."

"I heard you guys got snow and ice coming."

"It's already started."

"Sticking?"

"Yep."

"You got chili stuff?"

"Absolutely. Picked it up on the way home tonight."

"You make good chili."

I smiled. "We could play poker and listen to old records if you were here."

"And think up baby names."

"You going to be okay?"

"I'm always okay."

"Call me tomorrow and check in."

"You're not therapizing me, are you?"

"No. Sistering. You're my brother. I love you."

"I don't think you've ever said that to me before."

"I'm trying to improve my personality and become a nicer person."

He laughed. "Don't. I can't handle too much change at one time."

We said our good-byes and hung up.

Sometimes at the end of my day, I take inventory. Add up the good, the bad, and the ugly. Most days are at least a little more good than bad. And ugly doesn't happen too often.

Today had been an ugly day.

On ugly days, I sometimes go see a sad movie and have a good cry later in the bathtub. I skipped the movie this time. I filled the tub, grateful at least for the hot water, squirted in some eucalyptus bath oil for the sinus headache I knew would follow my tears, and sank into the sadness. I cried into my bath water until I couldn't cry anymore. For myself, for Drew Sturdivant, for Maria Chavez, for Nicholas, and now for my brother. Whose crummy marriage was coming apart around him and leaving him with a houseful of cats he didn't like.

And then I blew my nose, took some decongestant and some aspirin, and tucked myself in, hoping Scarlett O'Hara was right. Tomorrow had to be a better day.

16

~

It might have been, too, if my telephone hadn't rung in the middle of the night. At 3:42 a.m.

It was Maria Chavez.

"He's here," she said, whispering.

"Who? Who's there?" I strained to hear her answer. "I can't hear you, Maria. Who's there?"

"Gordon Pryne," she whispered.

"What are you calling me for? Hang up this minute and call 911!"

"I'm looking at him right now," she said.

I flipped on my nightstand light and sat up.

"He's not inside the house, is he? Is he standing right there or something? Does he have a knife?"

"He's outside. In the driveway."

"What's he doing in your driveway?"

"Skating," she said.

"With skates?"

"No. Just sliding around on the ice. Playing."

"You're kidding."

"I wish."

"Can he see you?"

"If he can, he's not showing it. He's just…skating."

"How did you know he was out there?"

"Nicholas told me. He woke me up and said Daddy wanted to know if he could come outside and play."

"Geez."

"I called the police."

"Jackson and McKnight?"

"911. They're sending a squad car. But with the ice…"

"Do you have a gun?"

"Of course not."

I made a mental note to buy myself a gun tomorrow.

"I'm going to call Jackson and McKnight. I'll call you right back."

"No! Don't hang up! Don't leave me. Please."

"Okay. Okay. Hang on."

This would probably have been a good time to know how to use the handy-dandy, three-way calling feature on my expensive local telephone service. But instead, Maria had to wait while I got my cell phone and dialed Jackson. I held a phone to each ear.

"Detective," he said in a groggy voice.

"It's Dylan Foster."

"What's wrong?" He was alert now.

"Gordon Pryne is at Maria Chavez's house. I'm on the phone with her right now."

"How do you know Maria Chavez?"

"Did you hear what I just said? Gordon Pryne is at her house. In her driveway."

"Did she call it in?"

"Yes, but I think it's taking them a while to get there. I have her on the other line. What should she do?"

"Ask her if her doors are locked."

"Maria," I said, "are your doors locked?"

"Of course. But that didn't stop him before. He could break a window."

I repeated her answer to Jackson.

"Does she have a gun?" he asked.

"No," I said.

I heard him knocking around for something. "Address?" he said finally.

"Maria, what's your address?"

I repeated her answer to Jackson.

"What's her number? I'll call her directly."

I repeated the question to Maria.

"No! Don't hang up."

"He can just beep in, Maria."

"I don't have call waiting. Please don't hang up," she said. "Please. I don't want to be here by myself."

I repeated what she said.

"I'll call you back," Jackson said, and hung up.

"What's he doing now?" I asked Maria.

"Still skating."

"Where's Nicholas?"

"He's right here. He fell asleep in my bed. I don't think he ever woke up completely."

"Are you okay?" I asked.

"No."

"What's Pryne doing now?"

"He just fell down. He's trying to get up, but it's very slick out there. He just fell again."

"That could be helpful."

"Here they come," she said. "I can see the squad car at the end of the street."

"Lights on or off?"

"Off."

"Does he see it?"

"He just did." She paused. "He's crawling toward the edge of the driveway. To the grass."

"Do they see him? Are they there yet?"

"He made it to the grass. He's standing up. He's trying to run."

"Which way?"

"To the back of the house."

"Is your yard fenced? Is your gate locked?"

"No. There's no fence." She started to cry.

"Maria, listen to me. You have to stay calm. Where are the police now?"

"Still coming down the street. They're going so slow."

"Can you see him?"

"No. He got his footing on the grass. He's going to the back of the house."

"Is your bedroom door shut?"

"Yes."

"Locked?"

"It doesn't have a lock."

My cell phone rang. "Hang on, Maria."

"Detective?"

"Are they there yet?" Jackson asked.

I heard Maria scream. "He just broke a window," she said. "I heard a window break."

I told Jackson what was happening.

I heard the crackle of static as Jackson repeated my description into a radio.

"Maria, is there a dresser or something?" I said. "Something you can push in front of the door?"

"I can't move," she said.

"Maria, push something in front of the door. Now."

I heard her struggling with something while I told Jackson about the window.

"They just pulled up in front of the house," she said. "They're getting out of the car. Something's coming in on their walkie-talkies. They're talking to someone. Is that Jackson?"

"I think so."

"Where is he now?" Jackson asked.

"Maria, do you know where he is?"

"No. I can't see him."

"Do you hear anything in the house?" I asked.

"No."

I repeated her answers to Jackson.

"Tell her I'm on my way. Tell her do not, I repeat, do not leave the bedroom until I get there. Which window is her bedroom window?" Jackson said.

I asked Maria and then relayed the information to Jackson.

"Tell her to stay in the bedroom," he said, "away from the windows, down low. I've got more cars on the way."

I repeated his instructions. "Is Nicholas sleeping near the window?"

"No," she said. "I don't want to wake him up. I don't want him to get scared."

"Okay. That's good. Just stay calm."

"They're there," he said. "Two more cars. Three more on the way."

"Maria, some more cops just got to the house. Just stay put, okay? You're going to be fine."

"Okay."

"Did you move something in front of the door?"

"A chair."

"What kind of chair? Not a little one?"

"A wing back. I can't move the dresser. It's too heavy."

A wing back. Not heavy enough.

She started to cry again. "Someone's pounding on the front door."

"Who? Is it the police?" I asked.

"I can't tell."

I asked Jackson if the police were at the door.

"Maria, it's the police. Jackson just told them you weren't going to answer. Did it stop?"

"Yes. Where are they? Did they go around back?"

"Detective, did the police go to the back of the house?"

"They're surrounding the place. He's gone."

"Are you sure?"

He spoke into his radio again.

"They've got someone on every side of the house," he said.

"Are you sure he's not in the house? What about the broken window?" I asked.

He spoke into the radio again. Then back to me, "Looks like he threw a rock through the kitchen window. Hole's not big enough for a man to fit through."

"Are you positive?" I asked.

He spoke into the radio again.

"Affirmative. Footprints confirm it. He walked right past the window. Didn't even stop."

I repeated this to Maria.

"Where are you?" I asked Jackson.

"Two miles away," he said. "McKnight's on his way to your place."

My place. Pryne was headed my way. I hadn't even thought of that.

"Is he the only one?" I asked, suddenly envious of all the squad car activity at Maria's house.

"No," he said. "Do not answer the door until you hear a confirm from me. To anyone."

"Okay," I said. Then into my other phone, "Maria, are you still there?"

"Still here," she said.

"Jackson's almost there. Hang on, okay?"

"Okay." She paused. "I'm glad you answered the phone."

"Me too."

"Willie was right. I do need help."

"You and me both."

Jackson showed up at her house a few minutes later, and McKnight eventually got to mine, along with a half dozen young buff Dallas Police Department officers who called me ma'am and stood solemnly at intervals outside my house, drinking my hot chocolate and leaving little puffs of steam in the cold night air as they spoke to one another.

Gordon Pryne's footprints went straight through Maria's back yard, into the alley, and down toward Lemmon Avenue, a major thoroughfare that cuts east–west through the city for miles. They lost his tracks there.

The police took Maria and Nicholas to a friend's house and put a car on her street.

Since Gordon Pryne never showed up at my place that night, and since I had nowhere to go, they put a squad car in front of my house and left me alone.

I paced around for a while, unable to settle myself down. At 5:00 a.m. I checked the weather report. Freezing rain and snow all day. Temperatures in the twenties.

I went back to bed and miraculously got some sleep. I woke up at noon, checked to see if the DPD had abandoned me during the cold, dark night. They were out there, in plain view, right in front of my house. A little gossip fodder for my neighbors. I gave the cops a wave and went into the kitchen to start a pot of tea.

My eye caught the rattrap I'd baited before I'd gone to bed last night. I peered inside to see if I'd caught anything.

The trap was empty. The peanut butter was gone.

Sneaky little beasts.

17

~

Eating chili alone is an unsatisfying experience. In fact, in Texas it just isn't done. It's practically a sin.

So while I fried up the bacon to produce the grease to brown the onions in, I racked my brain for someone to call.

I tried David, of course. Snow days are excellent boyfriend days, if you have one who is good company, which I do. But he was iced in way out in Hillsboro, which would do me exactly no good at all. He did express appropriate sympathy at my plight and anguish that he could not hop in his car and race all the way to Dallas to dine with me. Thin consolation.

I put some bread in my new pink Barbie toaster—my Christmas gift from Christine Zocci—and got my address book, flipping all the way up to *L* before I found someone I thought I could stand to spend the afternoon with. Helene Levine. She'd moved in from the suburbs last year and now lived about two miles away, in a high rise down on Turtle Creek. In this weather, that was less than an hour's drive.

I called her but got no answer. Where could she be with the roads like they were? She was sixty-eight years old, had arthritic knees, and drove a Mercedes sedan. Plus she's from New Jersey and hates the cold. No way was she out on the ice today.

My toast popped up, a little silhouette of Barbie browned into the bread. I spread some mayonnaise over Barbie's face, sliced some tomatoes, made myself a bacon, lettuce, and tomato sandwich, and kept flipping through my address book.

M was populated solely by John Mulvaney. No thanks.

As I flipped past empty pages, I was reminded once again that I had essentially no friends. This horrifying thought had flitted through my mind a few days before when I'd been trying to think of someone to stay with. The day the note came from Gordon Pryne. But I hadn't had time to let it bother me. Now it settled on me like a bad smell.

What was wrong with me? I'm a likeable person. Okay, I'm a little tense. And I tend to diagnose people whether they ask me to or not. And I have a teeny case of obsessive-compulsive inclination. And I can be pretty negative and a tiny bit hostile. And I'm a little controlling.

I scrolled back through my mind and tried to remember the last time I'd let David pick the movie. That could have been months ago.

Oh, and my thighs were liquefying even as I sat here eating thick-slab maple-sugar bacon between two slices of Barbie-toasted Wonder bread smeared with Hellmann's Real Mayonnaise. I can't help it if I hate fat-free. At least I work out.

I finished my sandwich and started chopping an onion, taking my frustration out on it by hacking it into tiny, satisfying little bits. I threw them into the pan and smiled at the sizzle. I stirred them around, wondering if the aroma was making the rats hungry. It could be just them and me for snow-day chili.

The phone rang.

"Dr. Foster, this is Detective Jackson with the Dallas Police Department." As though I knew lots of other Detective Jacksons. "Bad news and worse news. Which one do you want?"

"You pick."

"Okay. Starting with worse. Gordon Pryne is still at large."

"That's not exactly news. What else?"

"We found a print on the note."

"And?"

"It's not his."

"Whose is it?"

"The print remains unidentified."

I translated. "You mean, you don't know whose it is."

"That is correct."

"Why is that bad news?"

"It means he's working with someone."

"Oh." That *was* bad news. "But you're still running the prints, or whatever, to find a match."

"Ran it through AFIS this morning."

"What's that?"

"Automated Fingerprint Identification System. Should have come up with a match by now, unless his prints have changed."

"How would someone change their fingerprints? I thought that was impossible."

"Meth addicts get burns on their fingers. Burn heals, the print changes. Manual labor can wear the prints down. Brick laying, things like that. Guy like Pryne doesn't know anyone respectable. He's running with someone, they got a record. They got a record, they got a print."

It started to rain again. Not exactly rain, though. More like one of those Slurpees from 7-Eleven.

"You still there?"

"Yeah, I'm here," I said.

"Cruiser still outside?"

I checked. "Yep."

"Would you like the officers to escort you to a hotel?"

"Not really. I'm making chili."

"Good day for chili."

"Want to come over?"

I'd just invited humorless Detective Jackson over for chili.

That's how sad my life had become.

"I'm on duty."

"Have you talked to Maria today? Is she okay?"

"I believe she's decided to stay with a friend for a few days."

"Do you have a number for her?"

I wrote down the number he gave me and thanked him for calling.

I threw a little bit of crushed habañero pepper into the pan, just for grins. Might as well make the chili hot, since I didn't have anyone to breathe on. Besides, I'd read somewhere that really hot chilies cause the body to release endorphins, producing an opiate-like effect. I could definitely use an opiate-like effect.

I threw some ground beef into the pan, watching the grease splatter onto my stovetop as the meat started to brown. I began contemplating my clean-up strategy even as I made the mess. I'd take the whole stovetop apart later and scour it down with Antibacterial Soft Scrub with Bleach. It would give me something to do with my brain. The stove needed a good scrub anyway.

I dug in my rodent-defiled pantry for cans of crushed tomatoes and green chilies and for chili powder and cumin. I disinfected the containers with Clorox and opened them up.

I finished browning the meat, helped myself to a spoonful, added more salt and pepper, then stirred in everything else, put the lid on the skillet, and left the chili to simmer.

At my desk, I fired up my computer and started searching for information on Drew Sturdivant. Maybe Pryne's buddy was someone she knew. It didn't take long to scare up her phone number and address. She had lived pretty close to SMU, in a huge village of apartments populated almost entirely by college students. I wondered if any of her neighbors were aware of how she made her living. I wrote down the address.

Next I looked up El Centro College. I perused the website and was surprised to discover I knew a couple of faculty members. El

Centro is a community college, not a four-year school. Professionals in the community sometimes teach at this level because it allows them the stimulation of teaching college-level courses without the mind-numbing hoop-jumping involved in a full-time academic career.

Community college professors are doing it for fun, in other words, and make real, actual money at their day jobs. They drive better cars than we do, are genuinely interested in their courses and their students, and are hardly dull at all, unlike most of my colleagues.

My accountant was teaching as an adjunct in the business department. And one of the psychology instructors had been a graduate student of mine a couple of years ago. He was a crummy student, had a pretty dynamic personality, and had figured out quickly that he wasn't cut out for academic life. I'd heard he was doing well in private practice. He'd asked me out a couple of times. I'd always dodged the issue by hiding behind the professor/student thing.

I'm sort of afraid of my accountant. He's always demanding receipts I don't have, and I never get my tax stuff in on time. So I decided to try my ex-student first. The school was closed today, of course, but I shot him an e-mail anyway.

Since he was in private practice, I thought it was possible he might be seeing patients today. No play, no pay, as the saying goes. I looked up his office number in the business pages.

A woman's voice answered.

"May I speak with Mitch Dearing, please?"

"He's with a patient."

Bingo. I checked the clock. It was twenty minutes before two. He'd be out in ten minutes if he worked on the hour.

"May I take a message?"

"Would you have him call Dylan Foster when he gets a minute?" I gave her my number.

"Are you calling for an appointment?" the woman asked. "I can help you with that."

"No."

"May I ask what this is regarding?"

Nope. "It's a personal call."

"Of course. I'll give him the message."

I hung up the phone and decided to do a perimeter check of my house. I checked the locks on all the windows and doors, peeked into the backyard to make sure there were no murderers or demons lurking in the bushes. I checked the garage door to make sure it was down. And double-locked the door between my bedroom and the garage, since I knew Peter Terry preferred this exit route. I even looked in the closets and under the bed, just to satisfy my burgeoning paranoia.

I knew it was a stupid decision to stay in my house. Any idiot would opt for the safer choice and leave. But I'm not just any idiot. I'm a stubborn idiot.

Honestly, I just didn't want to make the concession. It's my house. I'd fought to regain this ground the last time Peter Terry came sniffing around. I didn't want to cede the territory. To Gordon Pryne or to anyone else. Especially if Peter Terry was the one stirring this brew in the first place.

I was betting all my chips on something a friend once said to me: *As children of the King, we're entitled to protection.* I would have felt more confident in the veracity of this little ditty, of course, if I'd bought myself a gun before the ice storm hit, like Detective McKnight suggested. Just in case the Lord Almighty Himself needed a little help keeping me protected.

The phone rang as I stepped back into the kitchen to check the chili. I looked at the clock. Ten till two. Right on time.

"Dr. Foster, Mitch Dearing," he said.

"Thanks for calling me back, Mitch. How are you?"

"I'm well, thanks. Enjoying private practice. You?"

"Not bad," I said. "I'm calling to ask about an El Centro student. Drew Sturdivant."

"The murdered girl."

"Did you know her?"

"No, but a colleague of mine had her in class this semester."

"Is she a psych major? Was she, I mean?"

"Design, I think. Had she applied to SMU or something?"

"Not exactly."

"She wasn't a patient of yours, was she?"

"No. My interest in her is more...indirect." I wasn't about to elaborate. "Do you think your friend would talk to me? I'd like to find out more about Drew if I could."

I heard him clicking his electronic data thingy.

"Got a pencil?"

"Yep."

I wrote down the name and phone number of Drew's psychology instructor, thanked Mitch, lied about what a great student he'd been, and got sucked into an invitation to lunch. All in about thirty seconds. My boundaries needed a little work.

I phoned the instructor on her cell phone.

"Catherine Keene," she answered.

I made my introductions, explaining that our mutual, close personal friend, Mitch Dearing, had given me her number and got right to the point.

"I'm calling about Drew Sturdivant. I understand she was a student of yours."

"She was in my Intro to Psych last semester."

"How was she? As a student, I mean?"

"Extremely bright. Very conscientious."

Not what I was expecting.

"I understand she was a design major."

"That's right."

"Interior or fashion?"

"Fashion. Very talented," she said. "She'd landed a summer internship in L.A. Prada or something. No, that's in Italy. Someplace. I can't remember. It doesn't matter. She was due to graduate from El Centro this spring. Early."

"You're kidding."

"No. She had a very bright future. Which makes her death even more tragic, I think. It's rare that a student makes such a positive impression. At least in the community college system. Most of our students are there because they don't know what else to do. Or because they're cleaning up some mess they've gotten themselves into." She paused. "Juicy something. Juicy Fruit."

"Juicy Couture?"

"That's it," she said.

"Speaking of messes, did you know how she was supporting herself?"

"You mean the stripping?"

"Yes."

"No idea whatsoever. I read about it in the paper like everyone else. But she was an odd bird. Quirky. Ran with a strange crowd."

"Can you elaborate?"

"What's your interest, Dr. Foster? Do you mind my asking?"

I did, of course, but needed to offer up something or this woman was going to stop talking to me.

"A friend of mine knows the suspect."

"The police have a suspect? Who is it?"

"His name is Gordon Pryne," I said, hoping I wasn't breaking any sort of police investigation rule or anything. "Does the name sound familiar?"

"No. Was he a student at El Centro?"

"I don't know anything about his academic interests, but I think it's pretty safe to say he never attended El Centro."

"How did she know him?"

"The police think maybe through her work."

"The strip joint?"

"Right."

"Which one was it?"

"Caligula. Down on Harry Hines Boulevard."

"So seedy. I can't imagine how she ended up there."

"Hard to imagine how anyone ends up there."

"You know who you should talk to, Dr. Foster? Her room-mate. Her name is...what is her name? Carla, I think. No, Charlotte."

"Charlotte what? Do you know a last name?"

"No, wait. Sharlotta. With an *S-H*." She spelled it out for me. "She might be able to help you out. I don't know her last name. Sorry."

"That's okay. Thanks."

"I hope they catch the guy," Keene said. "Drew was a special young woman. Sad and a little lost. But really quite extraordinary."

"Any idea what the sadness was about?"

"I wouldn't know."

"Thanks for your time, Catherine. You've been a big help."

"Good luck."

I hung up and dialed Helene again. This time she answered.

"Where were you?" I asked. "I called you an hour ago and you didn't answer."

"I went to the grocery store."

"You took your Mercedes out on the ice?"

"I took a cab."

Southerners never think to call a cab. We're not into public transportation.

"Cabs are running?" I asked.

"Of course they are."

"How?"

"Ever hear of snow tires?"

I invited her over, but she didn't want to get out again.

"Cold weather hurts my knees," she said. "And your house isn't really very warm."

"Oh, for crying out loud. It's not that bad."

"You really should get some friends," she said. "And central heat and air."

Like it was that simple.

She thanked me for the invite and hung up.

I dialed Drew Sturdivant's home number and had a quick conversation with Sharlotta. She agreed to see me. I hung up the phone feeling victorious, put the chili in the oven on warm, and called myself a cab.

18

~

The cab ride from my house to Drew's apartment, which in good weather would have been about a ten-minute excursion in my trusty Ford, was more like a white-knuckle crossing over the River Styx on a greased rope bridge. Backwards. And maybe blindfolded.

The cab reeked of hashish. My cabbie's dreads were so heavy in the knit cap on his head that he looked like he was carrying a watermelon in there. And the dude was clearly from the Caribbean, from the lilt in his patois. Which would be irrelevant if it weren't for the ice. This guy no more knew how to drive on ice than he knew how to fly.

Well, come to think of it, he clearly knew how to fly. He was flying right at that very moment. Soaring, as a matter of fact. Right there in the front seat. Miles high in the Dallas sky.

Daylight was fading, leaving the city twinkly with ice and streetlights and the occasional leftover Christmas display. I tried to enjoy the view, thinking it might be the last thing I ever saw. If the streets hadn't been deserted, I'm sure it might have been.

But after sliding through at least half a dozen red lights, skidding against several curbs, and shattering one expensive ceramic planter filled with frozen pansies, we made it. I tipped the guy because I'm weak and guilt-motivated in such situations, and because he knew where I lived. I called another cab as he drove away, figuring it would take at least half an hour for it to arrive, then slid my way to Drew Sturdivant's apartment and rang the bell.

No answer. I checked the address and rang again. Still nothing. I leaned in and laid my ear against the door. It sounded like she had an entire orchestra in there. Playing something serene and swannish.

I slid down the walk and peered at the lit rooms from a distance. I definitely saw movement. Someone was home. I knocked this time. Hard.

At last the door swung open and I was looking at a young woman of maybe twenty-two, with gorgeous chocolate skin, a head bursting with wiry braids, and a blistering white smile. She wore ballet gear, all limp and soggy with sweat: lavender leotard, pink tights, and striped leg warmers, with a little black chiffon skirt. There wasn't an ounce of fat on her. She was stout for a ballerina, but one solid muscle. I fought off a thigh-shame relapse.

I gave her a little wave. "Hi. Dylan Foster," I shouted over the music.

Sharlotta stepped back and let me into the apartment, holding up a finger for me to wait while she snapped the music off.

"Tchaikovsky?" I asked.

"You know it," she said. She held out her hand. "Sharlotta Dumaine."

"Dylan Foster," I said again. "Thanks for seeing me."

"No problem. I was about to juice some vegetables. Want something?"

"No, thanks."

I followed her into the kitchen, seating myself at the dinette as she shoved carrots and celery into a juicer, just like those people on the infomercials. She flipped the switch and the machine started shrieking. Orange sherbet-colored liquid dribbled out of the spout and into a glass. She picked up the glass, swirled the juice around, and tasted it.

She looked at me. "Sure you don't want some?" she shouted.

"Pass," I said.

She shoved more carrots into the machine until she got the juice the way she liked it and flipped off the switch. The abrupt silence was almost numbing. She sat across the table from me with a bowl of grapes and an apple.

"Do you always eat this healthy?" I asked.

"I'm a raw foodist."

"Foodist? Is that like nudist?"

"A live, raw foodist, actually. I only eat raw foods. Live, if at all possible."

I tried to get a visual. "So, do you just cut a hunk out of the cow while it's walking by? Or what?"

"No animal products of any kind. No meat, no dairy, no eggs. One hundred percent organic."

"Are vegetables dead or alive?"

"Depends. Sprouts and wheat grass and like that? They're alive. Tomatoes and such, they're dead." She took another swig of juice and looked at me like she was making perfect sense.

"Nuts?" I asked, going for the double entendre.

"Nuts are dead. But like, almonds? You can soak them in water for 24 hours and sprout them. Then they're alive."

"Don't they resent your eating them after you bring them back to life?"

"They've never said one thing about it," she said, without missing a beat. She grinned at me with big white teeth.

I thought about my chili in the oven and my BLT on toasted bread. Definitely dead, cooked food. Did that make me a dead cooked foodist?

"How long have you been eating like that?"

"Forever. I grew up on a communal farm."

"Where?"

"East Texas," she said. "Life of Christ Community?"

"Life of Christ? You grew up in a Jesus commune? I never heard of such a thing."

She shrugged. "Check your Bible. Those early Christians, honey, those folks shared everything."

"Yes, but didn't they eat little baby lambs? And a wide variety of goat products?"

"Well, I didn't say they were perfect, now, did I?" Her smile faded and she said, "Drew and I grew up together."

"You're kidding. Drew Sturdivant grew up in a Jesus commune?"

"Yep." She took another swig of juice and studied me. "How about you?"

"My parents were in the Peace Corps for a couple of years." Why was I trying to compete over weird hippie childhoods? Mine had been traumatic enough without making a contest out of it.

"No, I mean how did you know Drew?"

"I didn't." I took a breath. "Her psychology professor gave me your name."

She waited for me to explain.

"I'm looking into her murder."

"You said you were a shrink, I thought. Not a cop."

I nodded.

She raised one eyebrow at me. She had a compelling, vibrant way about her. Maybe it was all that live raw food. I don't like lying to nice people. I decided to shoot straight.

"The ax that was used to kill her was left on my front porch after the murder."

She nodded, perfectly unruffled. "You're the one."

"You knew?" I hadn't seen anything about it in the news reports of Drew's death.

"That detective told me. Jackson."

"Pardon me for asking, but were you and Drew close? I mean, you don't seem too broken up."

"Hard to break me up." She got up to rinse out her glass. "We used to be close. But she'd gone off in some direction. Something nasty I didn't know about. She was a real private girl. Real private."

"What do you mean by that—some nasty direction?"

"Stopped calling her friends. Started getting things pierced and tattooed. I got no problem with that sort of thing, you know. But there are things that shouldn't be pierced and tattooed, is what I'm saying. And then going on down to Caligula. That strip place. That wasn't like her. Wasn't like her at all." She shook her head. "She wasn't herself. No, she wasn't."

"When did this start?"

"A little after she moved in. She seemed better lately. Since she started dating Finn."

"Finn? What kind of name is that?"

"Beats me. Maybe he's Irish."

"Finn is the boyfriend?"

"If you can call him that," she said. "Definitely a boy. Not a man. And a friend, but not much of a boyfriend."

"Why?"

"Just immature. Doesn't have much backbone. He's kinda wimpy. She liked wimpy guys, though. That was Drew."

"When did she start seeing him?"

"Last summer, I think. Sometime after school started."

"She meet him at El Centro?"

"At a party. He's not in school. I'll give you his number if you want to go see him. He's out in Arlington."

"I'd appreciate that," I said. "Can I see her room?"

"Sure." She motioned for me to follow her.

The living room was small and sort of dumpy. Decorated in the celebrated and much-copied "early college" style. Unmatched chairs, lumpy couch, simulated wood veneer coffee table. In the corner was a large wire cage with wood shavings in the bottom, the size of a couple of big aquariums. I couldn't tell if there was an animal inside.

The bedrooms branched off a small hallway. We passed Sharlotta's room. A twin bed was shoved against one wall, along with a tiny, rickety dresser bursting with bright, multihued clothing. Otherwise, the room was empty of furniture, its walls stark, smudgy white, the overhead lighting dim, yellowy, incandescent. I didn't even see a bedside lamp. A ballet barre dominated the middle of the room, set on a flat of wood flooring in front of the mirrored closet doors. The doorjambs of both bedroom doors were stuffed with ballet shoes, their pink ribbons dangling down in a little curtain of satin.

"What's with the ballet shoes?"

"Breaking them in."

She shoved Drew's door open, though it wouldn't open all the way because of the toe shoes, and we stepped into the room.

Drew had painted her room a deep pink. Somewhere between Pepto-Bismol and dead roses. She'd done the woodwork in a dark gunmetal gray. Black chiffon curtains hung across the window, moving a little with the air as we walked into the room. Her furniture was industrial. The dresser and night table were stainless steel, brushed to a rough finish with steel wool or something. Her bedside lamp was made out of a combat boot. The headboard on the double bed was made of plywood, spray-painted with graffiti. It was cool, in an angry, nihilistic sort of way.

On the headboard, slapped on the plywood at an angle, was a small poster that read "Anael Watches," like an ad you'd see at a construction site or something. Around it were spray-painted crosses and silhouettes of angels. And in the center of the headboard, in black, an ankh.

I walked over to the bed and studied the graffiti, then turned around and looked at Sharlotta, who was watching me closely.

"Know what it means?" she asked.

I shook my head. "You?"

"No clue."

"These aren't Jesus commune phrases?"

"I don't even know what language that is."

"It's Hebrew," I said.

She shrugged.

"What about the watch ad? Did she wear that brand or something?" I asked.

"She didn't wear a watch."

I dug in my bag for a notepad and a pen, squinting at the wood to make out the Hebrew characters. I recognized the letters, but my Hebrew was so rusty I had no idea what they meant. I saw several characters for God. And something that started with the Hebrew letter *nun*, the equivalent of the English *N*. Possibly. Hebrew *N*s look just like *B*s and *G*s to me. That was the best I could do. After two years of busting rocks in graduate-level Hebrew while I was in seminary, I had plenty of self-mutilation stories to tell. Trouble is, I could tell them only in English. None of the Hebrew stuck.

I finished copying down the characters and moved on to Drew's desk. She'd made the desk as well, it seemed, out of a door and some file cabinets. She'd laid plywood over the door, but this wood was clean of graffiti.

The desk was littered with pencils (lead and colored), erasers, and sheets of paper with design sketches on them. I picked one up and studied it. The dress was a combination of combat gear and ballet gear. A floaty little skirt not unlike the one Sharlotta was wearing, with a long-sleeved scoop-neck top, black, and a military style green khaki jacket.

"I like this," I said.

"She was good."

"That's what I hear."

"I saw it coming," Sharlotta said.

"Saw what?"

"I knew she was going to die."

"You mean because of who she'd been hanging out with? How she was living?"

"I mean I knew. I know things sometimes. Before they happen. I have, like, a radar."

I put the drawing down. "Did you know it was going to be murder?"

"I knew it would be violent."

She didn't seem like a nutcase or anything. And I have that kind of radar sometimes. That's how I'd always thought of it. I could always seem to see a little farther down the road. Or around corners. It seems to come and go, at least for me.

"Any feeling about who did it?" I asked.

As she shook her head no, a little furry face poked out from under the bed. I watched its nose wiggle and sniff the air for a second before I realized it was a rabbit. After a few seconds, the bunny hopped over to me and sniffed my foot.

"She hasn't been out from under that bed since Drew died," Sharlotta said. "Not even to eat."

"Can I pet her?"

"Sure. She's sweet. She won't bite you."

I picked her up and held her to my chest. She was warm and soft, her ears lopping over to either side of her face. She sniffed my face and then snuggled in, seemingly content to settle in my arms. I was charmed. And ridiculously flattered.

"What's her name?"

"Melissa," she said. "Named after Melissa Auf Der Mauer."

I tried not to look stupid, since of course I didn't know who that was.

"Bass player for Courtney Love's band. Hole?"

One of those bands I was too uncool to know anything about.

"Melissa was Drew's birthday present from Finn. She's still a baby. Four months old. Or five."

"I've never seen a red rabbit before. Her hair's the same color as mine."

"They're kinda rare, I think. Drew said, anyway. Do you want her? She likes you."

"I wouldn't know how to take care of a rabbit."

"She's litter-box trained."

"You're kidding."

"Nope. She uses a litter box just like a cat. She just hops around the apartment most of the time. She's real sweet. She likes to play outside when it's warm. But she never runs off."

I rubbed Melissa's ear against my face. It was velvet. I could see why all those studies say blood pressure goes down when you hold a pet.

"Her parents haven't cleaned out her room?" I asked.

"I haven't heard from them," she said.

"You're kidding."

"They shunned her."

"Shunned. What is that? That sounds like commune talk."

"Shunned. Disowned. After the divorce."

"She was divorced? She was only nineteen."

"They marry 'em off young at the Jesus commune."

"You're not married."

"I left before my time," she said flatly.

"When did she get married?"

"Seventeen. He was forty, maybe forty-five. She hated him. She moved in with me right after she left him. That was two years ago."

"Do the police know about this? I mean, maybe he should be considered a suspect."

"He died in a car wreck a couple of months after their divorce."

"Oh. That's a pretty good alibi."

She nodded. "Hard to kill someone when you're dead already."

I held Melissa in one hand while I poked around in Drew's

closet, self-conscious at the voyeuristic intimacy of touching someone else's stuff. I felt myself descend into melancholy as I fingered the sleeves of her T-shirts.

Drew Sturdivant had been a talented, interesting young woman. But broken, it seemed, into little pieces. Pieces shaped like sadness. And anger.

I suspected she'd had some secrets. More than just the ones I knew about. Most people do, of course, and the darker secrets are usually the ones that hurt the most and leave the ugliest scars—the very ones we should never, ever leave ourselves alone with.

I wondered what had happened to her at the Jesus commune and what had happened to her in that marriage. And why she went to work at a filthy strip joint when she had so much else to offer.

I'd seen enough. I followed Sharlotta out of the bedroom and back into the kitchen. Reluctantly, I handed Melissa over to Sharlotta, who put her into her hutch and gave her a carrot. I'd gotten attached to the little rabbit in the few minutes I held her, but I really didn't need a pet right now. And then there was the little detail that it seemed wrong somehow to adopt a helpless bunny into a demon-possessed home. Peter Terry would take one look at Melissa and stick her in a pot on the stove. Like Glenn Close did in *Fatal Attraction*. That would be just like him.

Sharlotta bagged me up some apples ("Dead, raw, organic," she said as she handed them to me), and wrote down Finn's phone number and address. I thanked her for her hospitality and left her my number as well, then stepped out into the cold air just as my cab arrived.

My sorry luck held. It was the same cabbie. I slid into the backseat, thanked the Almighty Lord of all creation for saddling me with this yahoo again, cranked the window down to let out the fresh pot smoke, and fastened my seat belt for the ride back to my house.

19

~

I got home to a message from Detective McKnight. Gordon Pryne had been arrested.

I called the number he'd left on my machine.

"Detective. This is Dylan Foster."

"We bagged him."

"Where was he?"

"Caligula. Owner called us."

"Why would he go back there, knowing you guys were looking for him?"

"He was stoned. Crystal meth."

"Not a lifestyle that lends itself to intelligent, goal-directed decisions," I said.

"No, ma'am."

"Where is he now?"

"Interrogation. Detective Jackson is in with him. I stepped out to take your call."

"How's the questioning going?"

"Interrogation. You interrogate suspects. You question witnesses. He's a suspect."

"Okay. How's the interrogation going?"

"We're just getting started."

"Is he coming off the meth?"

"I think he's down already. He seems okay."

"Has he started crying yet?"

"He hadn't before I stepped out. You think he will?"

"Depends on how much he used. And when. I'd bet on it with him. He's so volatile. They tend to be criers."

"You have experience with meth?"

"Some. I did a rotation on a drug rehab unit during my internship." I checked my watch. It was eight thirty. "Detective, is there any way I could come down and watch the interrogation? I mean, is that allowed?"

"Not really."

"Maybe I could offer some insight," I said. "I'd like to see what he has to say."

He paused for a long, excruciating minute. "I'll send a squad car over. You at home?"

"Yep."

"Fifteen minutes?"

"I'll be ready."

This journey wasn't nearly as precarious as my cab ride had been. Chalk that up to a sober driver, I guess.

The officer who drove me had Detective McKnight paged as we drove into an underground garage. I thought we were near police headquarters, but had lost my bearings in the canyons of downtown Dallas. We got out of the car, slammed the doors to the cruiser, and waited by a steel door marked "Restricted. Identification required." McKnight arrived a few minutes later, swiped a card into a slot, and led me into the secure area.

Dallas County Central Intake is a compendium of wretched depravity. Within its blue and yellow walls are specimens of every imaginable malignant mutation of the human soul. Prostitutes, pimps, drug addicts and their dealers, murderers, rapists, child molesters, thieves, burglars, small-time crooks, petty criminals, drunks—every suspect in every arrestable crime in Dallas County passes through these doors, in various stages on the continuum of repentance. From defiant to pathetic. DCCI has them all.

A half dozen dejected men were seated just inside these doors, in neat rows of metal folding chairs, like school children. They each wore white coveralls and bright orange Keds—the kind without laces.

I raised my eyebrows at McKnight with the silent question.

"Trustees," he said.

"Doing what?"

"Waiting for vomit to clean up. Whatever."

I pointed to the lines of men and women taking off their shoes as they waited behind a white line for processing.

"And the shoes?"

"Shoe laces are weapons in here," McKnight said.

I thought back to my brief but unfortunate incarceration in Chicago's Cook County Jail. They'd let me keep my shoes. Thank God for simple dignities.

I followed McKnight through a series of card-swipes and locked doors, down hallways shiny with putty-colored linoleum, until we arrived at Interrogation Room Three. He opened the door and we were in a bare little room furnished with a single table with a monitor on it.

We stood and watched the monitor as Jackson talked to Gordon Pryne. A uniformed cop stood between them both and the exit.

I leaned in and peered at the small screen.

Pryne was cuffed at the wrists, with a chain that tied his cuffs into a D-ring in the floor. He was agitated, twitching with anger, each word from his accuser landing on him like a stone. He squirmed and fidgeted, bending to accommodate the cuffs and running his shaking fingers through that wild snatch of hair.

"What do you think?" McKnight said.

"He's not off the meth yet. I'd say he's about to blow. One way or another. See his hands, how they're shaking? And look how pale he's gotten, just since we've been standing here. He's starting to get clammy, to go kind of gray. You can see the sweat stains starting here," I pointed at the screen, "around his collar. And under his arms."

Pryne's chains rattled as he began shuffling his feet rhythmically.

"When we step inside," McKnight said, "we'll be behind a one-way mirror in a room next to the interrogation unit. Then I'll step into the room, leaving you behind the mirror. He can't see or hear you. He won't even know you're there. The room is pretty soundproof. But I'd advise you to turn off your cell phone or pager and to be as quiet as you can. Don't scoot your chair or anything if you can help it."

I nodded and turned my cell phone off.

"Ready?" he asked.

I nodded again and followed McKnight into the room. Three other men were watching the interrogation. McKnight nodded to them and pointed me to a chair. Then he swiped his card again and stepped inside, closing the door behind him. It locked with a crisp click.

Pryne looked up and tensed. He sniffed the air. He dropped his voice, narrowing his eyes to slits.

"Get her out of here," he said.

I felt my chest tighten.

"No one in here but us, Gordon," Jackson said. "Just you and us and your guilty conscience."

Pryne pulled against cuffs and screamed at McKnight, "Get her out of here!"

I saw a quick glance pass between Jackson and McKnight. I could feel the other men behind the mirror looking at me.

"Who are you talking about, Gordon?" McKnight asked.

Pryne fought against his chains again, drawing blood on his wrist, and threw his head back convulsively. Jackson and McKnight both leapt backward. Pryne shoved the table, which tipped over and crashed onto the linoleum.

A sound filled the room. Something feral and desolate and primeval. We all stood, riveted, as we realized collectively what it was. Gordon Pryne was howling.

Profane screams were punctuated by the cracked syllables of words in a language I didn't recognize. He threw his head back again, knocking himself to the floor as his chair flew backwards. He struggled to his feet and leapt at the end of his chain, a mad, rabid yard dog. He lunged toward the mirror and looked me straight in the eye.

I flinched and took a step backward.

He screamed and lunged again at the mirror, slamming himself against his chain. Deep red stains began to spread at his wrists.

The man next to me touched my elbow and escorted me out.

He was a cop, I think, judging from his empty holster and the respectful brown suit he wore. He didn't introduce himself, just said, "Wait here," and went back in.

I found myself alone in the outer room, the fluorescent lighting buzzing in my ears. My legs were trembling and I was cold and dizzy. My heartbeat was loud and fast in my ears, my face hot, and I couldn't stop shivering. There were no chairs in the room— only the table with the lone monitor—so I crossed my arms and sank to the floor, my back to the wall, and put my head down on my knees.

I huddled there for a minute or so, my head down, breathing. In and out, I told myself. In and out.

I could hear Pryne's shrieks, tinny now through the monitor. He seemed far away, though in fact I'd only increased the cushion between us by a few feet and one locked door. The distance didn't seem nearly enough.

I closed my eyes instinctively to pray, my head still down, breathing, though the words wouldn't come.

The screaming stopped abruptly.

I looked up at the monitor.

Pryne had collapsed and lay motionless on the floor. Jackson and McKnight were leaning over him.

I stood and walked to the monitor.

"He's conscious," McKnight said. Then shouting to Pryne, "Can you hear me? Gordon?"

Pryne balled himself up and began to weep, his body heaving with each tormented sob. He began babbling, this time in English. I leaned in, straining to hear the words.

"Why can't they leave me alone?" he said. "No, no, no. Leave me alone."

The man in the brown suit entered the room and said something to Jackson and McKnight. They left the interrogation room and came to find me.

"Parkland's coming," Jackson said to me, without a hello. "Need to bring a stretcher through here."

"Should I...?"

"If you could wait," McKnight said. "We'll have someone drop you back at headquarters. Couple of blocks from here. We'll be about fifteen minutes or so."

He opened the door to the hallway and stopped a uniformed cop walking by.

"Take Dr. Foster back to HQ and put her in the conference room on 5. And get her a cup of coffee or something, will ya?"

I rode with the cop, parked myself in the conference room, and declined the coffee, which infused the entire area with a burnt, acrid smell—like it had been sitting there cooking on that credenza for days. I waited alone at the large oval conference table, until McKnight and Jackson appeared.

They helped themselves to coffee and sat down at the table.

"What do you make of that?" Jackson said. "He got the DTs or something?"

I shrugged. "You mean delirium tremens. Maybe. He's not

a drinker, though, is he? You know anything about his alcohol habits?"

"Uses everything else on the street," McKnight said. "Assume he drinks. Would that explain it?"

"I guess if he'd stopped drinking a few days ago, just cold turkey, maybe. But that wouldn't explain the…personal nature of his behavior. He seemed to be responding to me. Literally to me. It happened the minute I stepped behind the mirror. I don't know how else to interpret 'Get her out of here.' And the fact that he looked me straight in the eye and lunged at the mirror."

Jackson was shaking his head emphatically. "Gordon Pryne had no way of knowing you were in that room. No way. I didn't even know you were back there. I just knew McKnight stepped out a couple of times and came back in. That's it. Pryne had no access to that information. Zero."

"Not through the regular channels, anyway," I said.

"What's that supposed to mean?" McKnight asked.

"Look, just…throw away all your logic for a minute. Everything you know to be true about the normal rules and regulations of the planet."

They looked at one another and then at me.

"What's your gut feeling? What did you see in that room? You were standing right there." I waited. "Didn't you feel it?"

They were silent for a minute. The air in the room began to smell of sweat and tension.

"Evil," McKnight said at last.

"Yeah," Jackson said reluctantly. "That's it. Evil."

"Okay. So you guys, between you, have done how many interviews over your years on the force?"

"Hundreds," Jackson said.

"At least," McKnight said.

"Have you ever felt that before?" I asked.

They both considered the question, looking down at their

stained coffee cups.

"No," Jackson said at last. It felt almost like an admission, he was so reluctant to say it.

McKnight nodded in agreement. He put his cup down and crossed his arms.

"I seen some very bad things," Jackson was saying. "Some very bad things. Heard some terrible stories. What people can do to one another. You have no idea. But that…that evil thing. I never seen that before. Never felt that."

"I think we're dealing with something here that's…beyond Gordon Pryne," I said. "Something outside the bounds of…I don't know…what you might consider normal reality. The ugly things people do to each other, as you say, that's people doing it, right? Ugly, sick people, but people. But this thing, this thing that Gordon Pryne just showed us…that's something else, I think. Something else entirely."

"What?" McKnight asked. "What is it exactly?"

"I'm not sure it's quantifiable in any exact sense. I think it might be—"

"You mean, like paranormal. Supernatural," McKnight said.

"Something like that. Otherworldly, maybe. That might be a way to think about it."

"How do you know that?" McKnight asked. "I mean, how could that possibly be true?"

"I don't know. And if I hadn't seen it myself, I would never have considered it as a possibility. I mean, the guy is just a serial offender, right? Just another in the long line of violent, angry people who shuffle through here, one after another. But didn't you feel like you were watching something—"

"Like that *Exorcist* movie," Jackson said. "It was like that."

"Is it possible he's just crazy?" McKnight asked. "Just crazy and loony and out of his mind from all the drugs and whatever other garbage he puts into himself?"

"Maybe," I said. "Do you really think that's what it is?"

McKnight shook his head, kicked the conference table and shoved his chair back.

"Anyone recognize the language he was talking?" Jackson asked. "Dr. Foster?"

"No. I've never heard anything like it before."

McKnight got up and filled his coffee cup again, then put the cup down without drinking anything and paced the room.

Finally, he looked up at me. "What do we do now? I mean, what would you recommend?"

I shrugged. "Are they sedating him or something?"

"Probably," Jackson said. "They should call us here in a minute and let us know."

"They're restraining him, I hope," I said.

"Absolutely," Jackson said.

"Do you guys have a chaplain?" I asked.

They looked at one another and shrugged. "Martinez," Jackson said at last. "I think his name is Martinez."

"You think I could talk to him?" I asked.

"We'll try to find him," Jackson said. He nodded and McKnight left the room. Jackson excused himself after an awkward moment, leaving me sitting there alone again.

I got up and turned the coffee pot off, then picked up the carafe in one hand and the rest of the machine in the other and walked down the hall, looking for a kitchen. I found one a few doors down and emptied the coffee into the sink. I peeled the wet filter away from the grimy plastic and threw it away, then searched the cabinets for something to scrub with. I found some crummy, industrial paper towels and a bottle of store-brand dish soap. Not my preferred weapons of choice, but sometimes you have to make do in a pinch.

I turned on the hot water, holding my fingers under the stream until I was satisfied with the temperature, and started scrubbing.

20

~

I spent the next hour or so dissecting the video with officers Jackson, McKnight, and Martinez. As the tape began to roll, we stared at the dusty screen in silence, the grim, grainy images gripping us just as they had in real time.

Pryne started the interview like any other offender. Innocent. Wide-eyed shrugs, a studied look of bewilderment, and emphatic, unequivocal denials.

He didn't know anyone named Drew Sturdivant. He'd never been to Caligula. Okay, maybe once or twice, but everyone goes to strip joints, you guys know how it is, and that don't make you guilty of murder. That Arlington rap was a frame. He never broke into no apartment and he never raped no one. Some other dude must look just like him.

"The evidence," McKnight reminded him, "all points to you, Gordon. We got fibers. We got footprints at the scene in your shoe size. You wear a size ten shoe? 'Cause unless I'm missing something, you got a size ten foot. I can see 'em right there." McKnight pointed at Pryne's orange jail shoes. "Am I right? Want me to take a look at the size for ya?"

Pryne scooted his feet farther under his chair.

"You wear lug-sole boots, Gordon? 'Cause we got people tearing up your place right now looking for 'em," Jackson said.

"We got a witness that puts you with Drew Sturdivant right

before she was killed." McKnight put his hands on the table and stared into Pryne's eyes. "You were the last person seen with her before she died, Gordon."

"That's probably just a coincidence, huh?" Jackson said.

A frame. Somebody was always trying to frame him. He'd never done anything like that in his whole life. Not in his whole life.

"You were convicted of rape six years ago," Jackson reminded him.

A frame. He was never there. That woman made that whole thing up. Women are always trying to trap you. You have to watch out for women. All they want is to trap you. Everyone knows that.

He didn't own an ax. He wasn't on Harry Hines that night. He hardly ever went down to Harry Hines. And he never killed no one.

Denials, lined up and ready to go. Prefab, packaged up, and portable.

The buzz of the coffee maker and the pall of the greenish flat lighting squeezed in on me as I watched the tape. I'd never seen a criminal interrogation before. It was more mundane than on television, of course, but also more depressing because it was real. I pressed my fingers into my temples to keep the headache out of my brain and tried to fight back the urge to give up entirely on any remnant of hope I held for humanity.

It was Martinez who pointed out the first sign of change in Pryne. He paused the tape about fifteen minutes into the interview.

"Anyone notice that?" he asked.

"I did," I said.

"What did you see, Dr. Foster?" Jackson asked.

"He's getting agitated." I turned to McKnight. "What was the last question again?"

He rewound.

"Watch his hands," I said.

Jackson's voice came through the speaker. "You're an innocent man, then? That's what you're telling us. What do you think of that, Detective McKnight? We got us the wrong guy, we're so dumb."

We watched as Pryne began to twist his hands, the chains beginning to clink. His face contorted and he shuddered briefly but violently.

"Right. That's it," he said, nodding quietly. "The wrong guy. It's not me. Not me."

McKnight stopped the tape.

"So what?" Jackson said to us.

"He looked like he thought someone was behind him," Martinez said.

We watched it again.

Sure enough, as his hands began to move, Pryne glanced back over his shoulder, just for an instant, and then turned back around and shuddered. He made a quick movement with his hands as if he was shooing away a pest.

"Keep going," I said, feeling the now-familiar sense of dread.

As the tape rolled and the questions continued, Pryne began to deteriorate. I recognized symptoms of crystal meth detoxification. Twitchy agitation. Ridiculous grandiosity followed, rapid-fire, by quaking paranoia.

"You know what's interesting to me?" I said to McKnight and Jackson. "As Pryne decompensates, you guys are picking up the tension in the room. Like it's contagious."

It was true. As Pryne became more agitated, McKnight, Jackson, and the cop guarding the door all started to shift uncomfortably. McKnight was the first to loosen his tie. Jackson began to pace, moving closer to the exit. The uniformed cop moved his hand to his gun and kept it there.

Martinez stopped the tape. "Normally you'd get calmer, right? As he got more upset? To settle him down?"

"Normally, yeah," McKnight said.

I looked at McKnight and Jackson. They looked at one another, then back at me.

McKnight started the tape again. We all watched as Pryne's distress intensified and the officers' behavior mirrored right along.

Pryne's attention seemed focused on the back corner of the room. The cops started moving away from that same corner. An inch or two at a time.

"What's going on?" I asked at last. "Am I missing something?"

McKnight paused the tape. He and Jackson looked at one another again. Martinez crossed his arms.

"It seemed like it started getting cold in there," McKnight said at last.

Jackson nodded.

"Cold?" I asked. "What do you mean, like temperature cold?"

"Cold. And…I don't know…empty. Like the air was almost leaving the room," Jackson said.

"Stuffy? Like someone turned the air off?" I asked. "Maybe the heat went off."

"No. Not stuffy," McKnight said. "Dead."

"Dead," I repeated. "I don't understand what that means."

"It seemed like I got kinda nervous," McKnight said.

Jackson nodded. "Yeah. Like that."

"Keep talking," Martinez said.

"It was almost like a panic-type of a feeling. Like something you'd feel if—"

"If maybe you heard someone break into your house," Jackson said, "and maybe the noise woke you up in the middle of the night. Like something bad was about to happen. Something very, very bad."

"Or maybe someone stuck a gun in your ribs," McKnight said. "That happened to me once. Like that."

"Could it have been a reaction to Pryne's change in demeanor?"

Martinez asked me. "Could they have noticed it and been responding to it subconsciously?"

"Possibly, but that doesn't seem sufficient to explain panic," I answered. "You both felt it, right?"

They looked at each other and nodded.

"Did it feel like something came into the room with you? Is that why you're scooting away from that corner?" Martinez asked.

"Nothing came into that room," Jackson said loudly. "The door was locked and guarded. We were in there alone. Look at the tape. For the love of Pete. Do you see anyone else in there?"

"Why do you ask?" I said to Martinez.

"My grandmother was from Mexico. Deep Mexico. Where you still have to kill the pig yourself before you eat it. She was a very superstitious woman. They're like that in that part of the country. Real Catholic, but almost tribal about rituals and superstitions. Always running down to the *curandero* to ward off one spirit or another."

"What's that?" I asked. "*Curandero*?"

"It's basically a magic shop. It's got charms, incense, dolls, crosses—all like that—for getting rid of bad spirits or calling on one saint or another for protection, or maybe for putting a curse on someone. It's from the Spanish, *curar*, which means to heal or cure. You see them in the barrios here in the states.

"Some woman will be running the place and she looks like she's four hundred years old, sitting there smoking a pipe and looking at you all suspicious-like. And when you pay for your stuff, she'll say something really eerie like 'Your girlfriend has had a change of heart,' and you don't know what she's talking about. You were on an errand for your grandmother to get a St. Jude candle or something. And then two weeks later, the girl that just broke up with you will call you and want you back." He grinned. "At least, that's what happened to me one time."

"You don't believe in that stuff, do you?" McKnight asked.

"I'm just saying I saw some funny things when I visited my grandmother's house in the summertime."

"What's your point?" Jackson asked.

"Yaya used to say that you can always tell when a spirit comes into the room. The air gets cold and dead. Those were her words. Cold and dead. Or, technically, *frio y muerto*. She didn't speak English."

I raised my eyebrows at him. "Yaya?"

Martinez blushed. "*Mi abuelita*. My grandmother. My brothers and I called her Yaya."

"That's very touching," Jackson said impatiently. "Can we move on?"

"Hey, do you guys really have a witness that saw him with Drew?" I asked.

"Six thirty the night of the murder. On Harry Hines," Jackson said.

"Who is it?" I asked.

"Name's Skinny," McKnight said.

"Drug addict," I said.

McKnight nodded and started the tape again.

Twice during the interrogation, McKnight's cell phone buzzed and he stepped out. The first time to take my phone call. The second, to escort me into the station after I arrived.

We watched him return the second time, leaving me behind the mirror.

Pryne tensed immediately on his return.

And then we watched the scene again. Pryne sniffing the air. Pulling at his chains. Screaming "Get her out of here," at increasing volume. And the howl. That macabre, almost lupine howl.

We watched the whole thing without saying a word.

The tape continued to run, replaying Pryne's collapse, his begging. Balled up there, on the bloodstained floor, crying and chained and snared like an animal, he looked small to me. Helpless. A wretched, pathetic little shell of a human being.

McKnight and Jackson turned away from the screen and started talking with Martinez. I watched the video as the stretcher was rolled in and the paramedics worked to get Pryne stable, then chained him to the gurney and rolled him out of the room.

Broken was the word that kept ringing in my head. The man looked broken.

I joined the conversation at that point. No one bothered to turn off the tape. It ran as background noise, muffled voices mumbling in the distance as the camera stared at an empty room.

We talked vaguely about Pryne, about evidence and forthcoming legal procedures, about the unlikelihood that he would confess. We discussed the particulars of methamphetamine withdrawal, but everyone knew we'd witnessed something far more ominous than that—something so grisly and disturbing that no one was up to talking about it at that moment. It had been a long, unpleasant day.

McKnight and Jackson, both shaken and irritable, excused themselves to write up their reports.

Martinez turned to me. "What's your background, Doctor? Are you an M.D.?"

"Psychologist," I said. "I teach at SMU. How about you?"

"Fifteen years with the DPD. Became chaplain a couple of years ago."

"How do you get to be a chaplain with the Dallas Police Department?" I asked.

"You end up being the one people call. The one they don't mind confiding in. You know how that is. Probably happens to you all the time. Eventually, the department just makes it official. Throws you a couple of hundred bucks a month to add it to your résumé. And I took some theology in college. That helps."

"Really? Where did you go to school?"

"Trinity University in San Antonio. I grew up down there."
He shrugged. "Yaya wanted me to be a priest."

"How does she like you being a cop?"

"I waited until she passed before I joined the force. She's
probably still bugging St. Jude about it, trying to get him to talk
me into changing my mind. Poor guy."

I smiled. "Maybe the chaplain thing is a good compromise."

"It'll have to do for now," he said. "And your spiritual background, Dr. Foster? Do you mind if I ask?"

"Just a regular, white-bread American type of Christian person. We don't know about *curanderos*. Or Yayas." I decided to
confess. "I studied theology, too."

"How'd you end up in psychology?"

"I'm not well-behaved enough to be a professional Christian.
I thought I'd go for civilian life instead. Besides, like you, I suspect, I like working with people. I'm more interested in their
stories than their sins."

"So what's his story?" he said.

"You mean Pryne?"

He nodded.

"Don't know. I think there's more to it than meets the eye. Do
you know anything about him? His background? Where he grew
up or anything?"

"We've got it all in a file somewhere, I'd bet. Want to take a
look at it? I can probably get that cleared."

"Sure."

"I'll give you a call tomorrow. We'll find a time to meet."

I wrote down my number for him.

"You look tired," he said, reaching for the card.

"Headache. I think my brain's trying to escape my skull
through my eye sockets."

"I have some aspirin in my office."

"I'd be grateful," I said.

He nodded and left. I massaged my temples, my eyes closed against the light.

The tape was still running. I heard something on the monitor as someone came back into the empty interrogation room. I looked over and saw a janitor wheel in a mop and bucket. He pushed the table and chairs back against the wall and then walked toward the camera, his image becoming huge and finally dissolving into a dark swatch of shirt as he reached for the tripod to move it.

The image cleared as he scooted the camera out of his way. It was pointed at the mirror now—Pryne's view during the interview.

I squinted at the monitor and froze the image. I could see the whole room now, including that corner that made everyone so nervous. I pushed play and watched for a few minutes until I saw it.

There. In the mirror. A quick, fleeting image and he was gone.

Peter Terry was there. Standing in the corner. Laughing.

21
~

Free-range anxiety is a lot like a free-range rooster. It can move about at will, and if provoked, it just might peck you to death. My anxiety, already pushing hard against the fence, broke loose at this point and jumped the chicken wire, clucking madly and scattering feathers everywhere.

Out of sheer gut will, I got myself home in one piece so I could fall apart in private, thank you very much, with only the demon inhabiting my home as a witness. And the rats. I'd almost forgotten about the rats. They could enjoy the show, too, for all I cared.

Before I left, I asked Martinez for a copy of the interrogation tape, which he promised he would get for me, along with the copy of Pryne's file. The cop who drove me home seemed to sense my distress. He walked, or rather slid alongside me to my door, checked the place for bogeymen, and salted my sidewalk for me before he left.

My house was cozy with the smell of chili, which I'd completely forgotten about. After I checked every lock in the house three or four times and turned on my space heaters, I pulled the chili out of the oven and spooned myself out a big helping, loading it up with cheddar cheese and sliced jalapenos for zip. I ripped open a bag of Fritos—since Fritos are made out of corn, I was counting that as a vegetable—and sat myself down to supper.

I ate like a plow horse after a long day of sod-busting. I tried to block out visions of fat cells exploding in my thighs as I crunched my way through the first handful of Fritos. I thought about the rats as I ate, wondering if they were watching me, their little beady eyes mapping out grids on my kitchen floor in preparation for a late night reconnaissance mission for Frito crumbs. The smell of chili warming in the oven all afternoon must have driven them crazy, the nasty little vermin.

Speaking of nasty little vermin, Peter Terry knew Gordon Pryne, it turned out. And Gordon Pryne clearly knew Peter Terry. I felt my stomach flip as I let this thought enter my conscious mind.

Could Peter Terry be Gordon Pryne's accomplice? But no, it was the fingerprints that had pointed Jackson toward a second offender. I didn't know enough about demons to know if they had fingerprints, but it seemed unlikely.

I couldn't think clearly. The day had been too long. It would be an exercise in foolishness to let myself speculate about fingerprints and demons and stalker notes and ax murderers. I could feel my brain winding up for it, the clucking and pecking getting louder by the second, urging me to run blindly around in circles, only to get nowhere and scratch myself all to pieces on the way.

I got up from the table and paced a circuit around the kitchen instead, pausing to open the water heater cabinet. My water heater stared back at me, opaline white, a glowing, sanctimonious reminder of my obsessions run amok. I knew better than to check underneath it for rat poo. Instead, I reached out my hand, felt the heat, then shut the cabinet and cleared the table.

I cleaned the kitchen, allowing myself the small comfort of a Comet-scoured sink and a humming dishwasher, and got ready for bed, besotted with gratitude that my water heater still worked.

Sometimes Jesus just throws me a little bone.

I tossed up a quick prayer of thanks, tucked myself in, and

proceeded to toss and turn for the rest of that long night.

With morning came a break in the weather, along with the general collapse of my mania. I simply could not keep it up any longer. I'd finally worn myself out.

I fixed a cup of tea and looked out my kitchen window.

The lumpy rain had stopped, and the sun was making a welcome but meager showing through the clouds. I pried the newspaper off the front porch and checked the weather. The temperature was supposed to ease all the way up to thirty-four, starting the melt that would liberate the city by late afternoon. If it froze again that night, we'd be in for another slick day tomorrow.

I sat, wrapped in one of my mother's quilts (I still had no bathrobe), drinking tea at my kitchen table and listening as my eaves began to drip onto the hard, crunchy snow. I scribbled on notepads all morning, trying to bring some order to my thoughts and generate a to-do list.

Randy of Randy's Right-Now Rodent Removal made an appearance just after noon. I listened grimly as he assessed my situation.

"With your rats," he said, nodding gravely at me, "you've got your entry problem and your exit problem."

"My entry problem and my exit problem?"

"Let's start with your entry problem. By that I mean, where are they coming in? What is their point of entry?"

"They're coming in behind the water heater." I pointed dumbly at the hole. Was the man blind?

"Yes, but your original point of entry is what I'm asking, Miss Foster."

"I don't follow you, Randy."

He took a scrap of paper and a ball-point pen from his pocket protector, clicked the pen like he was cocking a gun, and began to draw.

"Your walls of your typical house in this neighborhood are

framed like this, sitting on a foundation you call a pier and beam. What you have with a pier and beam is a crawl space, some sixteen to eighteen inches in clearance, between your subflooring and your ground. We do it like this in Dallas because the ground in North Texas likes to move around a little bit here and there. A slab foundation, like you might have up in the panhandle or somewhere, would crack quick as a wink."

I nodded, already overwhelmed with unfamiliar and, to my mind, unnecessary information.

"Now you have a concrete base on this pier and beam construction, and if you're lucky, a high performance vapor barrier above the soil in your crawl space. If that barrier is damaged in any way," he punched the pen at his drawing to emphasize what I hoped would be the climax of his little speech, "you can get yourself rodents, mold, all manner of problems."

"So you're saying my vapor barrier is damaged, you think?"

"House this age probably never had one, Miss Foster. I hate to tell you that, but it's the awful truth."

"So how can I find out?"

"What I'm going to do is, I'm going to slip on my coveralls and go down there and take a peek. I'll be right back."

He left for a moment and came back from his truck wearing a pair of filthy white coveralls with a red-and-white patch on the back in the shape of a mouse, with *Randy's Right-Now Rodent Removal* stitched into it, and the motto below: "Because you needed us yesterday."

"Where's your trap door?" he asked me.

"My trap door?"

"House like this, you have a trap door that goes down to the crawl space. Usually in your bedroom closet. Mind if I take a look?"

I shook my head no and trundled along behind him into my bedroom. I tried not to feel violated as he opened my closet door and parted my clothes with his thick, hairy arms. He removed handfuls of blouses and tossed them on the bed. I grabbed them up and placed them neatly in stacks, holding my hand out for him to hand me the next batch.

Randy let out a mighty grunt as he eased himself down on one knee and began taking my shoes out of the closet, shoving them off to the side. I placed them in tidy rows on the hardwood floor, arranged by type and heel height.

Going through my closet tickled an inkling to return to Drew's room. I made a mental note to go back over there and take another look.

Randy located the trap door, pried it open with the largest screwdriver I'd ever seen, and squished himself through the gap. He completed this maneuver, miraculously, without the aid of the slab of butter I'd deemed essential to get a man that size into a hole roughly the width of a couple of shoeboxes.

Frigid stale air snuck into my already-chilly house as I waited by the open trap door, peering through at the dirt below. I could see Randy's flashlight bobbing in the darkness, illuminating cobwebs and dead bugs I was better off not knowing about. I backed away from the hole and sat on the floor by my bed.

He was back in a minute, smashing his elbows into his ribcage and puffing back up into the room in a cloud of dust.

"Miss Foster, I'm sorry to inform you that you have no vapor barrier."

"That is unfortunate news."

"Additionally, your foundation is cracked directly underneath your water heater. A recent crack, it looks like to me. Have you had any unusual settling in your house lately? Heard any loud creaks?"

"Something like that, yes." My hatred for Peter Terry bloomed into a red-hot, billowing mushroom cloud in my head.

"I'm afraid I can't help you until you address your foundation problem, Miss Foster."

"You mean I'm stuck with the mice?"

"Rats."

"Whatever. Can't you just run them off or something? I thought that was what you did."

"Well, this is getting right into your exit problem, Miss Foster. See here, right now they have both. Entry and exit. You can do whatever you want, but they will continue to enjoy full access to your property. What you have to do is seal off that crack and then address your rodent infestation."

"Infestation? Is that an official word? What exactly is that?"

"That's a significant rodent problem, Miss Foster, which is what you have here." He took out his pen again. "Now what I can do," he said, drawing me yet another diagram, "is fix a steel plate over the hole behind the water heater. And I can seal up the crack in your foundation, but it will only be a temporary fix. You'll have to call for foundation repair for a more permanent solution."

"That's expensive, isn't it?"

"I can recommend someone who's reliable and very reasonably priced."

"You don't have a brother named Fred, do you? Fred's Forever Foundation Repair?"

Randy didn't laugh.

"In the meantime, I can leave you some glue traps," he said sternly.

"I bought a humane trap a few days ago."

"Caught anything?"

"Nope."

"I'll leave you some glue traps."

"Why can't you just poison them?"

"Back to your exit problem. Seal off your exit and you're stuck with dying rodents between your walls. I wouldn't wish that on my worst enemy."

I would.

He went to his truck again and spent the next hour drilling and hammering and applying various fixatives to my water heater closet and to the crack in my foundation, then handed me an astronomical bill, a stack of glue traps that smelled like new tires, and a business card for Metroplex Foundation Repair. I thanked him, wrote a check that almost cleaned out my teensy checking account, and sent him on his way.

I loaded my clothes back into my closet, re-sorting them by type, fabric, and color, of course, which gave my brain something to do besides worry. I found a pair of flowery jeans I'd forgotten about and a neato Bob Dylan T-shirt someone had given me last year for my birthday. I have a thing for him since I'm named after him. I showered, slipped the T-shirt on underneath a roomy sweater, and started making phone calls.

Sharlotta was first. She said I could come back tonight to take another look at Drew's closet. I tried to reach David on his cell phone, but had to leave a message. Then I called Helene to see how her knees were, and Maria Chavez to see if she'd moved back into her house since Gordon Pryne had been arrested. I left messages for both of them. I checked my messages at the office. Nothing that couldn't wait. I'd return the calls tomorrow when everyone was back in action. No way we'd get away with another snow day, no matter how slick the streets were. We'd already had two days off—unheard-of wealth in a Texas winter.

By the time I'd finished making phone calls and fussing around the house with chores, the sun was almost down again, the thin January daylight dimming and the freeze bringing the dripping water to a dead stop.

My doorbell rang then, and despite my recent bad luck answering my door, I ran to open it, glad for the company.

It was David, carrying a bouquet of grocery-store roses, a fluffy new pink bathrobe with matching slippers, and some news.

"Linda Fortenberry called me today."

"Who's that?" I asked, as I started filling a vase for the roses.

"She's the medical examiner for Dallas County."

I looked up.

"You met her at the Christmas party," he said. "I had lunch with her Tuesday."

"What did she want?"

"She owes me a favor. I asked her to call me about Drew's autopsy."

I turned off the faucet. "What? What did she say?"

"Drew Sturdivant was pregnant when she died."

22

~

She was only four weeks along. She may not have even known she was pregnant. The ME's office was running DNA tests to begin the process of identifying the father.

I was back at Drew's apartment within an hour, poking through her closet and digging through her drawers, with Sharlotta's toe shoes thumping against the floor in the next room and Melissa the redheaded bunny rabbit hopping around my feet.

Once again, I wasn't sure what I was looking for. I made myself hold back and observe without jumping to any conclusions about anything I saw. It's an old therapy trick. Curiosity is the key to learning anything about anybody. If you allow yourself to indulge in a little unfettered curiosity, even the most stubborn, predetermined conclusions tend to evaporate pretty quickly, opening up any number of possibilities you may have otherwise overlooked.

Drew had the wardrobe of an anarchist. An anarchist with talent and a quirky sense of style. Almost everything she had was black or camouflage fabric, with whimsical dashes of Drew-like originality thrown in. A bright yellow fake fur collar was sewn on to a ripped denim jacket with poetry written on the back in black Sharpie. Lace spilled from the pockets of a pair of camouflage painter's pants. Delicate pink ribbony trim was sewn on to a black leather micro-miniskirt.

She owned only five pairs of shoes—admirable parsimony in the birthplace of Neiman-Marcus. (We take shoes seriously here in Dallas.) There was a pair of black stack-heel Mary Janes, two pairs of combat boots—one red leather, one black and scuffed—a pair of black sneakers, and a pair of black ballet flats.

Necklaces and scarves hung on plastic racks just inside the closet door. I ran my hand along the scarves. A faded black leather newsboy cap hung on a peg.

The top shelf of her closet was stuffed with cardboard liquor boxes. I climbed onto her desk chair and pulled them down, one by one.

The boxes, stained and weakened by time and use, held Drew's childhood. Stuffed animals and dolls were packed in one. Another held her school papers and report cards from the Jesus commune. The report cards bothered me. In addition to the usual marks in writing, math, and history, there were courses with names like "Biblical Behavior," "Spirit-filled Living," and "Submission to Authority"—as though such things could be mandated and quantified. Drew's grades were abysmal, as mine would have been in such a militaristic, follow-the-dictator environment.

The report cards stopped coming after her sophomore year. I guessed that was about the time she got married.

The next box held what looked to me like early sewing projects. One smock-like number, the original design surely intended to serve as a sweet little outfit for a young girl, was stained with red ink blotches and scrawled with the words "Daddy's little girl." The shoulder buttons were little metal skulls.

I looked up as Sharlotta entered the room with two mugs of hot tea and a carrot for Melissa.

"Valerian," she said, handing me a mug. "Good for the nerves."

"Thanks. I guess it's okay to cook tea, then?"

She smiled with those fabulous teeth. "Technically this is an herbal brew rather than tea. With herbs, you really shouldn't boil the water all the way. It bruises the leaves."

I took a sip. It tasted sort of weedy.

She pointed at the jumper I was holding. "What do you think?"

"I think Drew had some unresolved anger issues."

She laughed. "You got that right. That's from seventh grade home economics. She got kicked out of class for that."

"What happens to you when you get kicked out of class at the Jesus commune? Do you have to go to hell without passing 'go' or something?"

"Close. You get K.D."

"What's that?"

"Kitchen duty. Up at 4:30 a.m. to grind the wheat and make bread for 150 people."

"You guys ground wheat and made your own bread?"

"I had my first slice of store-bought bread when I was seventeen years old. The year I left."

"What did you think of it?" I asked.

"Not nearly as good as homemade. But sweeter."

"All that processed flour, I guess."

"No. Because no one got punished to make it."

"I saw her report cards. Who decides what biblical behavior is?"

"Not us, that's for sure." She climbed on the chair and pulled down the last box. "This is the one you should be looking at."

She sat down on the floor, cross-legged, pulled the flaps of the box open, and handed me a stack of photographs.

I sat down next to her and studied the first one. It was the face from the newspaper photo, but much younger, with wispy black hair and sad, lonely eyes.

"Third grade," Sharlotta said. "The year her dad died. That's the year her mom brought her to the commune."

"How did he die?"

"Car wreck."

"Same as her husband."

"Almost exactly. They both fell asleep driving."

"You're kidding."

"Same road too. Out in East Texas. Off I-20."

"Autopsies?" I asked.

"No idea."

"Will you write their names down for me? And the approximate dates they died?"

She got some paper off Drew's desk and wrote down the information for me. I tucked it in my purse.

She went through the photographs with me, chronicling Drew's demise from sweet, sad little eight-year-old girl into fuming, lost teenager. The last picture, at the bottom of the box, was Drew's wedding picture. She wore a dress that was clearly of her own design—ripped pink chiffon with gray satin trim—combat boots, and, as a final accessory, a look of unconflicted rage. Her husband was dressed in a brown suit with a wrinkled blue shirt, a terrible tie, and a comb-over hairdo that made him look like a Nixon-era insurance salesman.

"Not quite her type," I said.

"You got that right."

"Who's this?" I held up a photo of a woman with brown, Reagan-era hair and a crooked smile.

"Drew's mother. Brigid."

"Odd name."

"It's some goddess name. She picked it out herself."

"Is that a Jesus commune thing?"

"She's not a Jesus commune person."

"I thought you said she took Drew there when she was in third grade?"

"To drop her off. Drew was raised by her aunt and uncle. Bob and Alison Sturdivant. They're still at the Jesus commune."

"What happened to Brigid?"

"She never saw her again." She got up and pulled something out of a book on the desk. "Drew tracked her down a couple of years ago."

It was a letter, postmarked Shreveport.

"It's the only one she got."

I opened the envelope. The handwriting was erratic and barely legible.

> *My darling daughter,*
> *Your letter caught me by surprise. I'll need*
> *some time to think it over. Remember, your*
> *mother is where you find her. The earth will care*
> *for you, darling girl.*
> *Brigid.*

"What a nut-ball," I said.

Sharlotta hooted. "You got that right."

"Is it just me or did Drew Sturdivant have an unusually crummy life?" I asked.

The mirth drained quickly from her face. "It's not just you."

"There's no last name on the envelope."

"I don't think she uses one. She uses this instead." She pointed at a symbol drawn at the bottom of the page.

"An ankh. Same thing that's on the headboard. Know anything about it?"

"Just that she liked them. She wore one on a necklace. Never took it off. After I saw the letter from her mother, I figured that was why."

I looked through the pictures again. Drew wore the ankh in every photo, including that third-grade picture. A tiny gold one on a delicate chain. Like most little girls wore hearts or crosses. Where else had I seen an ankh recently? Somewhere. It had made a vague impression, but I couldn't conjure up the memory. It was the ankh that had driven me back to this room, though. I realized that now. It was significant in some way. I could feel it all the way into my bones.

"Can I see the bathroom?" I asked.

Sharlotta led me to Drew's tiny windowless bathroom. I opened the medicine cabinet and found the usual items. Aspirin, mouthwash, Band-Aids with cartoon figures on them, razor blades. A toothpaste tube squeezed from the middle with a glob of white toothpaste oozing out from under the cap. And a box of tampons. I opened it. Only a few were missing. I didn't see any forms of birth control. I shut the medicine cabinet and went back into the bedroom.

Melissa was still working on her carrot. She left it and hopped over to me. I picked her up and snuggled her to my cheek. I couldn't believe how soft she was.

"You sure you don't want her?" Sharlotta asked. "She loves you."

"I don't need a pet."

"No one needs a pet," she said. "That's not what pets are for. They're extra."

I stood there, hugging Melissa.

"Come on," Sharlotta said. "She loves you."

I could feel myself weakening. "I wish she weren't so cute."

"Her hair's the same color as yours."

I sighed. "I can't believe I'm doing this."

"Great. I'll tell you everything you need to know."

We parked Melissa in the bathtub while we loaded her gear into my truck, and Sharlotta briefed me on the basics of bunny care. It didn't seem too complicated. Put the litter box where she can find it and change the litter daily, keep hay in her hutch, fresh veggies and water out for her all the time, don't leave the front door open, stuff like that.

"You have to check her teeth regularly," Sharlotta said.

"For what? Cavities?"

"Rodent teeth never stop growing. You have to clip them if they get too long."

"How am I supposed to know if they're too long?" I was already starting to regret my impulsive, uncharacteristically optimistic decision to embark on pet ownership. With a rodent, no less. The irony was a little annoying.

"Hers probably won't. She has nice straight teeth. They grind down by themselves."

"Oh. Well, good for her, I guess. Anything else I should know?"

Sharlotta grinned. "She's a raw foodist."

"I figured that."

"And she only likes root vegetables and lettuces and parsley. And firm fruits like apples. No broccoli or asparagus or anything like that. Nothing at all from the cabbage family. She won't touch it."

"Picky."

"Discriminating," Sharlotta said.

She went back inside and came out a few moments later with Melissa and an enormous paper bag full of carrots and radishes. "Raw, dead, organic," she said, handing me the bag. "Live, cute, and yours," she said, handing me my new bunny. "She likes the vegetables at Whole Foods. The purple carrots are her favorite."

"Thanks."

I drove away with Melissa on my lap, a little stunned at what I'd just done.

I set up her kennel in my bedroom, since it was the warmest room in the house. I said a prayer over that corner for good measure, hoping to keep Peter Terry as far away from my new roommate as possible.

Melissa explored the house for an hour or so and then settled in at my feet, her head resting on one of my new fluffy pink slippers as I sat at my kitchen table in my bathrobe and examined my notes again. I had a stack of them by now.

Sharlotta had let me take the third grade photo of Drew, along with the letter from Brigid, Drew's mother, and a few other photographs.

Drew's photo was now on my fridge. I spread the letter out on the table in front of me.

"The earth will care for you." Who says a nutty thing like that to a daughter they abandoned ten years before? I dug her picture out of the pile and stared at it. What a loon.

I looked up the address on the Internet and with a few other quick searches had a phone number for a psychic in Shreveport listed only as Brigid. I dialed the number. No answer. I left a message. I found no listing for Bob and Alison Sturdivant anywhere in East Texas, but I did write down a number for the Jesus commune. I'd have to work up to that one. I called David instead and asked him to make some calls to the county medical examiners along the I-20 corridor where Drew's father and husband had died.

I did a Google search for Anael watches and found nothing. I'd start calling jewelry stores in the morning.

And then I called my old friend, Eli Beckman. He agreed to meet me tomorrow for coffee.

I put glue traps around the house before I went to bed, with apologies to Melissa since technically, rats were her distant cousins. And then I tucked Melissa into her hutch for the night, flipped off the light, and hoped for the best.

23

~

Eli Beckman is one of those coffee people. Coffee with him is a religious experience. He orders his beans from a wholesaler in California and stores them in the sort of expensive, tiny refrigerator with the glass door most people use for wine. He grinds his own beans, of course, in a Rube Goldberg contraption on his spotless granite countertop in his massive commercial kitchen, then lovingly concocts his brew in another machine that cost, I'm positive, at least twice as much as my pickup.

Since he is such a coffee snob, he won't drink the coffee at commercial coffee houses. He insists it's not oily enough. As though oiliness in a beverage is somehow a desirable feature. In fact, there is only one place in the entire city of Dallas where Eli Beckman will drink the coffee. So I parked my truck in front of the good rabbi's house in North Dallas, knowing there was no tea in my future. I'd been invited for coffee. Coffee was what I would get.

Rwanda A, Gikongoro Bufcafe was on the menu that day.

Eli handed me the empty bag and pointed at the label as I settled in on a barstool.

"This is one of the finest coffees in the world," he said reverently. "It's grown by Rwandan farmers at an elevation of between fifty-five hundred and sixty-two hundred feet, give or take. Small farms, small harvest. Gikongoro is the name of the wet mill where the coffee fruit is removed from the bean. It has a low-acid taste, compared with, say, a Kenyan AA, which is a high-acid bean. High acid is a compliment in coffee, but I think this Rwandan is lovely. Just lovely."

"And Bufcafe?" I asked, studying the label. "What does that mean? It's, like, buff? Does it work out? Lift weights? What?"

"The exporter, Dylan. That's the name of the exporter." He tsked. "What you know about coffee—"

"I drink tea."

"—could pass through the eye of a needle."

He poured me a cup and placed it in front of me as though he were offering me his firstborn.

"Cream and sugar?" I asked.

He glared at me. I smiled sweetly at him until he scooted the sugar bowl in my general direction and then opened up his Sub-Zero and handed me a carton of 2 percent.

I doctored my coffee, sniffed it and tasted it, rolling it around in my mouth like I'd learned in a wine-tasting class once. I waited a moment before I pronounced my verdict.

"It tastes like coffee."

Eli shook his head again and began to gesture wildly with his hands.

"What's the matter with you? Can't you taste the fruit tones?" He closed his eyes as if in worship and took a delicate sip of his nonsugared, noncreamed coffee. "I'm getting banana, chocolate, honey, flowers…a hint of raisin. The mouthfeel is supple, smooth. The finish, resonant but gentle."

"You're mentally diseased," I said. "It tastes like coffee."

"And you have the palate of a chimpanzee."

"Rwandan or Kenyan?"

He threw back his head and laughed. "And what can I do for you, my friend? Since your palate cannot be salvaged? You have some sort of Hebrew emergency, you said?"

"That's exactly it. A Hebrew emergency."

"Who knew such a thing was possible?" he said, clearly delighted. "All my years in Hebrew school, for just such an occasion!"

I spread out my notes from Drew's room.

"What do you want to know about Lot and his daughters?" he asked, glancing at my papers.

"Is that what it says?" I peered at the figures I'd copied from Drew's headboard.

"Your Hebrew—" he began.

"Is like my palate. I know. Don't make fun of me."

"Two years of Hebrew and she doesn't know the word for daughter."

"Tell me what it says, Eli."

He ran his finger along the words.

"It says 'daughter of Lot, lost and little.'" He looked up at me. "A pun. In English, not in Hebrew."

"I don't get it."

"A little versus a lot."

"Clever. What else does it say?"

"'The Nephilim return.'"

"What's that? Nephilim?"

"Genesis 6. Half-breed humans."

"Come again?"

"I thought you went to seminary."

"Shut up and tell me what it means."

He held up a finger, signaling me to be patient—not my best thing—and left the room, returning a moment later with a small stack of books. He set them down and flipped one open, running his finger right to left, lovingly following the lines of Hebrew characters, searching.

"Ah!" he said. He read it first in Hebrew, which of course did me absolutely no good. And then quoted, "'The Nephilim were on the earth in those days, and also afterward, when the sons of God came in to the daughters of men, and they bore children to them. Those were the mighty men of old, men of renown.'"

He looked up.

"You're looking at me as though you've answered my question," I said.

"Weren't you listening?"

"I-don't-know-what-it-means." I drew it out slowly, punching each word.

"I thought you went to seminary," he said again.

I glared at him and picked up my spoon to put more sugar into my coffee.

He waved his hands at me. "Okay, okay. Stop that."

I put the spoon down.

"The Nephilim," he began, "were a mysterious race of beings, pre-flood. The passage, as you can see, seems to indicate that they were some sort of half-blood race."

"Half what and half what?"

"Sons of God—the Hebrew word there is *ben eloheem*—which in the Greek Septuagint—I hope you at least remember that—is translated *angelos*."

"Angels."

"Yes. Angels. But fallen ones, judging from the passage."

"Why do you say that?"

"The phrase 'went in to the daughters of men,' this is a phrase of some…force, you might say. The indication in Hebrew is that this was not a consensual act. In fact," he pointed to the page and I leaned in to look at the word, "the very word Nephilim is from the verb *naphal*, meaning to fall—often associated with violence, or translated 'to overthrow or fall upon.'"

"You mean rape?"

"Yes. Exactly."

"Demons, then? That's what it means? That demons raped

human women and the resulting race was this...Nephilim bunch?"

"That's the scuttlebutt."

"That's so bizarre. How come I don't remember this? I mean, this is the sort of event that makes an impression—something a person should point out if you were studying Genesis 6."

"Either you weren't paying attention or your professor skipped right over it. That's the traditional method for teaching this passage."

"What? Skipping it?"

He nodded. "This is one we like to keep in our pockets."

"Why?"

"Because nobody really knows what it means. It's one verse. An obscure reference. And the implications...shall we say, my friend Dylan, they're rather far-reaching, don't you think? If it's true?"

"Are these people still walking around?" I asked, thinking of course of Peter Terry.

"Don't you remember what happens in Genesis 7?"

"What?"

He threw up his hands again. "Dylan Foster, you're breaking my Jewish heart."

"The flood!" I pointed at him.

"Precisely."

"So they were wiped out with everyone else."

"Sort of."

"You're making me crazy, Eli."

He flipped pages until he found what he wanted. "Numbers, chapter 13." He looked up at me. "Post-flood, of course. Moses has sent out a reconnaissance team to scout Canaan. 'So they gave the sons of Israel a bad report of the land which they had spied out, saying 'The land through which we have gone...' blah blah blah...hm... Ah, okay...'and all the people whom we saw in it are men of great size. There also we saw the Nephilim (for the sons of Anak are part of the Nephilim) and we became like grasshoppers in our own sight, and so we were in their sight.'"

"What? What does that mean? They were giants?"

"Precisely."

"Like Goliath."

"Goliath was Anakim."

"What's that?"

"Sons of Anak. The phrase 'part of the Nephilim'—this is translated in a number of ways. It's not very clear."

"No kidding." I took a sip of coffee. "What happened to the Anakim?"

"Apparently wiped out by Caleb and his crew." He shrugged.

"And the Nephilim?"

"No other mention of them exists in the Hebrew Bible."

"What about in the Christian Bible?"

"That," he said, closing his Hebrew scripture, "would be your department."

I nodded.

"What about the Lot reference? What do you think that means?"

"Lot's daughters—their story is a very sad one."

"Do you have the Old Testament in English anywhere?"

He shoved a book across the countertop at me. I flipped through the pages of Genesis, scanning as I read. I found what I wanted in chapter 19 and looked up at Eli.

"I'd forgotten about the angels."

"Keep reading."

I read to the end of the chapter.

"Oh. I forgot about that part too. They *were* lost, weren't they?"

"Most definitely. And little, one could argue, in the sense that they were overmatched by the evil around them."

"'Daughter of Lot, lost and little.'" I said.

"Makes sense, no? Now tell me. What is all this about?"

I told him about Drew Sturdivant. About her sad life and her even sadder demise.

"And what is her fascination with Anael?"

"I don't know. I'm going to start calling jewelry stores after this."

"Jewelry stores? What ever for?"

"Anael watches. I thought it was a brand of…" And then, of course, I realized. "'Watches' is a verb. Anael *watches*. Who is Anael?"

"That, my dear friend, is a very good question."

"What about the ankh?" I pointed again at the page. "Do you know anything about ankhs?"

"That would be a question for an Egyptian scholar, not a Hebrew scholar."

"The Hebrews were enslaved in Egypt for centuries," I argued.

"Yes," he said, pouring me more coffee. "But unfortunately for you, we didn't take notes."

24

~

The sun was bright, piercing, as I left Eli's house, the cold snap officially broken. Water dripped everywhere, and the chilly air was ripe with the wet, loamy smell of thawing earth. Pansies, their petals emerging unscathed from their ice shrouds, perked up in their beds, bright little patches of optimism and resilience.

It was almost noon. I was hungry and had work to do. I swiped my card in the touchpad and pulled my truck into the lot at SMU, grateful once again to be teaching on such a lovely campus with that rarest of commodities in university life—ample and convenient faculty parking.

I dumped my stuff in my office and went to the kitchen to fix myself a cup of decaf herbal tea, careful not to boil the water, and stuck my Tupperware bowl of leftover chili in the microwave to heat it up. Then I settled in at my desk and ate lunch, my head spinning from my visit with Eli, my hands jittery from caffeine. Two cups of coffee was my normal quota for a year, not for one morning.

I was just starting my research on Anael when I heard a knock at my door. I held my breath and waited quietly for the intruder to leave, hoping the tapping of computer keys hadn't betrayed my presence.

"I know you're in there."

It was Helene.

"Oh, all right," I said.

The door swung open. "You never fool me with that routine." She settled her considerable bottom into a chair, looked at me over her glasses, and pointed at the floor beside my desk. "What is that?"

I looked down. "What does it look like? It's a lunchbox."

"You're thirty-five years old and you carry a pink Barbie lunchbox?"

"It was a gift from a friend."

She rolled her eyes.

"Is that the purpose of this visit? To insult my taste in lunch-boxes? I'm working."

"That's what I wanted to talk to you about. Your work."

"What? Is there some problem?"

"Your review is coming up."

I grimaced. "I hate reviews."

"That's because you have a reflexive dislike for authority."

"Aversion. A reflexive aversion to authority."

"See what I mean?"

"What?"

She rolled her eyes again.

"I have all your teaching reviews. I need your publication record to date. And you need to submit whatever you're working on and a report on how it's going. And your anticipated date of completion."

"I guess I'd better start working on something, then."

"I thought you said you were working. When I came in."

"I am working. I'm just not working on work."

"What, then?"

"Know anything about Genesis 6? The Nephilim?"

"No."

"I thought you went to Hebrew school."

"Only until I was thirteen. I stopped going the day after my bat mitzvah."

"Stayed in just long enough to get the loot, huh?"

"That's one way to look at it."

"What's the other way?"

"It was important to my father. He was dying of cancer."

"Oh. Sorry."

She waved off my apology. "This will be peer review. You know that, don't you?"

"Who's on the committee?"

"The tenured faculty. Harold."

"Francine?"

"Yep. Crazy Francine. She'll go easy on you." She named a few more. "And John."

"Mulvaney?"

"He's the only John we have."

"You're kidding, right?"

"Do I look like I'm kidding?"

Lord help me, she didn't.

"How did John Mulvaney end up on my committee? The man knows rats and mice. That's it."

"He's tenured, Dylan."

"That's absurd. I don't want John Mulvaney anywhere near my review."

"That's not up to you."

"Who is it up to?"

"The committee. You'll have to petition to get him removed."

"I have to petition the committee John Mulvaney sits on? That committee?"

"Yep."

I sighed. "Helene, in addition to the fact that he knows nothing about my work and is therefore not qualified to evaluate it, the man has strange, delusional fantasies about me. I don't want him on my committee."

"Then you'd better start practicing the fine art of kissing up."

"Tell me who to kiss up to and I'll do it."

"I'd start with Harold, if I were you. He likes you. Save John for last. Maybe the others will help you with him. None of us can stand him either."

"Done."

She eased herself out of her chair.

"How are your knees?" I asked.

"This is Texas, not New York. It's supposed to be warm."

"You should have picked San Antonio. Winter lasts, like, two weeks down there." I handed her a bottle of aspirin. She shook a couple into her hand.

"You need to suck it up and get the knee replacement," I said. "Your doctor told you that two years ago."

"I don't need your advice, Dylan."

"Coward."

"And I don't want to be laid up for a month to recover."

"Oh, it's not a month, you big baby. Do it this summer. I'll bring you casseroles."

"I can make my own casseroles. And my own medical decisions." She turned to leave. "Go see Harold. He's in this afternoon."

An Internet search on Anael turned up a strange underworld of angel worship I knew nothing about. I looked at dozens of websites, most of them ominously black, with drawings of gaunt, sneering beings. They all hailed the power of angels, making little if any distinction between angels in service to God or to Satan. To the angel worship crowd, it seemed, the difference was inconsequential.

I scrolled past references to angels with names I'd never heard of—all ending in "el." Elaborate organizations of angels were described, a detailed pecking order. Many of the sites referenced spells and incantations. One actually referred to night feeding. As in vampire-like night feeding.

I pulled my concordance off my shelf and looked up *angelos* and its Hebrew equivalent, *malak*, then spent most of the afternoon looking up every reference to angels in both testaments, scribbling pages of notes.

I found two strange New Testament passages I'd never noticed before. In 2 Peter, angels that sinned were "committed to the pits of darkness," which sounded pretty unpleasant to me. Since other demons are free to roam the earth, according to most of what I'd just read, I took this to mean that a particularly wretched batch of losers had, at some point, gotten themselves chained up in some sort of fiery hoosegow. The book of Jude seemed to back this up, referencing angels "who did not keep their own domain, but abandoned their proper abode," and had gotten themselves incarcerated for their trouble.

All four commentaries I checked suggested that these passages pointed to the demons in Genesis 6, who had forced themselves on unfortunate human women and spawned the weird race of half-breed giants.

I wondered if Peter Terry could be one of the demons in the Nephilim scheme. Seems like he'd be locked up with the rest of his foul cronies. Unless he'd broken loose somehow. Surely God had posted some sort of celestial guard duty down there. Still, what of their reappearance in Numbers 13?

My phone rang, jolting me out of the ether and back into my decidedly earthly office.

"Dylan Foster."

"I got some dirt for you."

It was Eli.

"What?"

"I called my friend Menachem Levy."

"Let me take a wild guess based on the name. He's Jewish, right?"

"Better than that. He's a rabbi. A real one with credentials. Not like me. And an expert in Jewish mysticism. He teaches at Ben Ilon in Tel Aviv."

"That's a university?"

"*The* university. At least on this topic."

"Jewish mysticism. What is that exactly?"

"Apocryphal literature. Angelic lore. Kabbalah. Like that."

"I don't know anything about that. Except Madonna and Demi Moore and that ugly red bracelet. Seems a little hootie-hoo to me."

"Oh, that all comes from some nut factory in California. The real Kabbalah is an ancient tradition of rabbinic teaching. You're not even allowed to study it until you're forty years old. It's considered to be too powerful, to require too much maturity for a simpler mind to handle."

"I'm out on both counts. What did he say?"

"I asked him about the Nephilim and the Anakim. I got a whole slew of stuff for you."

I grabbed a pen and a clean notepad. "Shoot."

"According to Levy, Anakim are traditionally thought to be from a race that includes Rephaim, Nephilim, Emim—there's a whole bunch of them. Emim, I think, is referenced in Deuteronomy 2 and 3. I haven't looked that up yet."

"Slow down and spell them all for me."

I wrote them all down and underlined the common suffix. "Cherubim and Seraphim end the same way. Do you think they could all be angelic tribes or orders or something?"

"I guess it's possible."

"Most of the tribes you see in the Old Testament end in 'ite.' Canaanite, Hittite, Jebusite."

"Good point. I never noticed the distinction."

"Okay. What else?"

"Hang on a second. I'm taking notes."

I sipped tea while I waited for him to catch up. It was tepid by now.

"Okay. I got it," Eli said. "There are lots of strange stories that describe the Anakim. Do you know about the books of Enoch?"

"Book? Or books?"

"Either. But technically there are five parts—written in...some language. Transcribed eventually into Latin and Greek." I listened while he scanned his notes.

"Is it part of the Apocrypha? The Catholic Bible?" I asked.

"It's apocryphal, but Jewish, not Catholic." He flipped through pages. "I can't summarize all this for you. I'll fax you the references. It's pretty freaky stuff. Levy said that Enoch references the rape from Genesis 6. And that the demons taught the women spells and sorcery and stuff like that."

"Did he mention Anael at all? Anything about angel worship?"

"Anael is associated with Anakim. That's all he said. But he did mention the Watchers."

I felt the room get cold. Cold and dead.

"Who are the Watchers?"

"It's the word for demons in the book of Enoch."

"Watchers? Am I hearing you right?" I asked, scribbling furiously.

"Yes. Watchers."

I wrote the phrase "Anael watches" in the margin and underlined it.

"I found a few things," I said. "But this was all on Internet sites, so who knows if it means anything?"

"About Anael?"

"Listen to this." I scanned my pages. "Anael is supposedly the angel of the second heaven, whatever that is."

"That's from Enoch. He went through all seven of them."

"Is that where 'seventh heaven' comes from?"

"Search me."

"Anael is apparently the guardian of Friday. And the angel of love."

"Please don't tell me the moon is in the seventh house."

"Sadly, yes. And Jupiter aligned with Mars." I laughed.

"Is this the dawning of the Age of Aquarius?"

I groaned. "I hope not. I barely lived through it the first time."

"Make love, not war, baby," Eli said.

"Speaking of war…Anael is also apparently one of seven archangels. I think there are only two mentioned in the Bible. Michael and Gabriel."

"Write down Uriel," Eli said, spelling it for me.

"Uriel? Never heard of him."

"He's the one that led Enoch around in heaven. His tour guide. According to the book of Enoch, anyway. And he's supposedly the one that delivered the message to Noah about the coming flood."

I wrote it all down, took another sip of tea, grimaced, and pushed the cup away. "Enoch sounds important."

"I'd spend some time on him if I were you."

"I'll go down to Perkins this afternoon."

"Oh. One more thing about the Anakim." I heard him flipping papers.

"What?"

"They were known by some phrase…" he kept flipping.

I tapped my pen against the desk, impatient as usual. "And the phrase would be?"

"Wait for it… I'm looking, I'm looking… Ah! Here it is." He cleared his throat. "Wearers of necklaces. The Anakim were known as the wearers of necklaces."

25

~

The thing about ghosts and haunts in the movies is that they're easily satisfied. Basically, they're interested in geography. You've built your house on a graveyard, or some kid was murdered in the bathtub upstairs in your Victorian-era dream home. Or maybe one twin got whacked and keeps wandering around your living room in a permanent bad mood, playing *Blue Skies* in the middle of the night on your aunt Betty's upright piano. Something like that. The point is, their primary goal is for you to leave them alone so they can haunt their little square of land in peace.

They're parasitic, not predatory.

Demons, it seems, have far grander ambitions. They're not content to scare you half out of your mind. Or out of your house, for that matter. They do seem interested in forcing you to forego your concern for your property values and give them their space. But they rarely have the courtesy to announce the rest of their agenda. And, perhaps worst of all, unlike ghosts and other less formidable spooks, demons are portable. Like my sanity, it turns out, they can come and go at will.

And that, among other things, is what makes the little devils so dangerous.

I stared out my window at the sun, which was giving up the fight and slipping behind the trees for the day, and thought about Peter Terry, picturing the sky full of creeps like him.

It was five thirty. My normally tidy desk was littered with open reference books and pages of hastily scribbled notes. I sighed and slumped back into my chair. I had arrived at information overload. I couldn't crack one more book tonight. Bridwell Library, down at the other end of campus at Perkins School of Theology, opens at ten on Saturdays. I promised myself I'd be first in line in the morning.

I needed to call it a day and go home to my new pet. Melissa was probably sick of her hutch by now and craving organic carrots. I cleaned off my desk, organized my notes and stuck them in my bag, and locked my office for the night.

I considered calling Jackson and McKnight on my way home but decided quickly against it. What was I going to say? I think a demon killed Drew Sturdivant? Quite possibly she was being watched by an angel named Anael? This is the dawning of the Age of Aquarius?

That's the thing about this stuff. If you talk about it out loud, you sound like a screwball.

Martinez might find my theories semi-credible, because of the chaplain thing and the *curandero* bit. I still needed to get a copy of the video anyway. I put in a call to the DPD switchboard and left a message for him as I walked to my truck in the dimming light.

I decided to make one quick Drew-related detour on the way to my house.

Harry Hines Boulevard in Dallas is home to many perfectly reputable businesses. Warehouses, discount shopping centers, wholesale fabric outlets, automobile repair shops. Anything that doesn't require easy accessibility or attractive walk-up appeal might be found on Harry Hines.

Unfortunately, Harry Hines is also home to a wide and fairly disgusting variety of "adult" businesses (as though real, emotionally mature adults would actually go to such places). Any deviant sexual activity one desires is within easy reach. On demand and on a budget.

I drove my truck past prostitutes dressed for August rather than January, slouching on street corners in sequined halter tops and teeny skirts, all big hair and platform shoes. They looked cold and sad to me. I wanted to stop and take them to Denny's for pancakes and find out how they'd gotten here. I couldn't imagine any amount of money that would possibly be worth selling yourself off like that.

I drove past Caligula, thinking I should probably go in and check it out, maybe talk to the owner, see if anyone knew anything about Drew I hadn't already learned on my own. But I couldn't bring myself to do it. The thought of walking into a place that was crawling with men who were crawling with desire to see a woman crawling naked along a stage floor was too much for me. For once in my life, I backed away. I just wasn't up to it.

Instead I drove around on Harry Hines until I spotted Critter Cars. I pulled into the lot at ten after six.

The lot was small, by car lot standards. Maybe a half acre or so sandwiched between a pawnshop and a discount denim outlet. It was surrounded by a chain-link fence topped with razor wire. The gate was shut and padlocked. I walked up and peered through the fence.

"Can't give you much of a trade-in on that truck," a voice said.

I turned around. An attractive woman of maybe fifty was standing with one foot in a red Lexus convertible parked in the driveway next door, the car door open, lights on, engine running. She was dressed for a cocktail party, her long fur coat swinging open to reveal a tiny black minidress.

"Oh, I'm not looking to trade it in."

She shut the door and walked over to me, her hand extended. "Kay Basieri," she said.

"Dylan Foster. Do you work here?"

"I own the place. Just locked up. I'd be glad to show you something if you know what you want. Browsing, I don't do after closing. You'd have to come back tomorrow."

"Thanks. I just wanted to take a look around."

She studied me. "You don't look like our typical customer."

"Who's your typical customer?"

"People with bad credit."

"What's the interest rate? Just out of curiosity."

"Fifteen percent add-on."

"What does that mean?"

"Prime plus fifteen percent."

"That makes it about…"

"Twenty-three percent, give or take. Cash only." She reached into her bag and lit a cigarette with a thin, gold lighter. "The property's not for sale."

"I'm not here to check out the property."

She took a drag and looked at me, waiting for me to state my business.

"I'm looking into a murder. I understand a girl's body was found around here?"

"Cops have already been here."

"I'm not a cop."

"Reporter?"

"No, just a friend."

I shivered. Once again, I'd left the house that morning without a coat.

She must have taken pity on me, because she said, "I've got a few minutes. No sense standing out here in the weather."

She stubbed out her cigarette, locked her car, and opened the padlock on the gate. She swung the gate open, its wheels protesting with loud creaks. It was a big job for one person, much less a 100-pound woman in a cocktail dress and three-inch heels. Kay

Basieri manhandled that thing without breaking a sweat, closing it behind us and locking us in. She didn't even snag her stockings.

We stepped inside the office, a single-wide trailer complete with space heaters, window unit air, a water cooler, and a waiting area with tramped-down shag carpet. A tall counter with a window in the center dominated the room. She unlocked the inside door, motioned me to follow her behind the counter, and locked the door behind us. She offered me a seat at the desk, switching on the space heater behind her with her foot.

The credenza behind the desk held a picture of a longhaired guy in a tropical print shirt laughing at the camera. He held a beer in one hand and made a peace sign with the other. I could see a beach and blue water behind him.

"He looks like he's having fun." I pointed at the photo.

She grinned. "That's Critter."

"I take it Critter is a nickname."

"Party Animal was too cliché. My late husband."

"I'm sorry."

"Me, too. The only happily married couple we knew and the son of a gun up and died on me."

"Heart attack?"

"Cancer. Went just like that." She snapped her fingers. "Still haven't forgiven him for it." She took out a pack of Virginia Slims, lit a new cigarette, and crossed her legs. "I threw the coffee out or I'd offer you some."

"No thanks. But I appreciate your staying. You look like you're on your way somewhere."

"New Year's Eve party."

"It's almost February."

"We like to wait until the crowds have cleared."

I smiled. "I hate crowds."

"You and me both, honey."

I renewed my commitment to myself to get some friends. I

hadn't even gone to a New Year's Eve party on New Year's Eve. What a loser.

"Were you here when they found the body?" I asked.

She shook her head. "One a.m., give or take. The dog handler found it. He does random checks throughout the night."

I looked around. "Where's the dog?"

"She comes in at seven."

"A.M?"

"P.M. A handler brings her and then picks her up twelve hours later."

"So it's not your dog?"

She shook her head and tapped her ashes into a waiting seashell.

"A rental."

"I've never heard of renting a dog before."

"A guard dog," she corrected me. "She's an employee, not a pet. She works the night shift." She opened her top drawer and handed me a business card. *Junk Yard Dogs—guard dogs for sale or rent. Results guaranteed. Expert handling.*"

"Does she have a name?"

"The dog? Elaine."

"You're kidding me."

She exhaled a blue stream of smoke. "Nope."

"So the handler has a key to the lot?"

She nodded. "I lock up at six. The dog handler comes at seven, opens our padlock and puts Elaine inside the fence, gets her set up with water and everything. She has a heated bowl for cold weather. Then he locks the gate behind him and adds his own chain and padlock."

"Do you have the key to that lock?"

"Nobody but the dog guy has that key."

"Any way a person could have gotten past Elaine to put Drew's body in the trunk of one of your cars?"

"Only if they broke the lock and then shot Elaine first. That dog would tear my arm off if I tried to get in. And I own the place." She blew another stream of smoke. "She found the body."

"Elaine did?"

"She scratched up the trunk of the car trying to get to it. Dug a hole right into the pavement by the trunk, she was so agitated." She checked her watch. "The dog handler comes in half an hour if you want to talk to him. Or meet Elaine."

"What kind of dog is she?"

"Rottweiler, I think. She's real sweet until the gate closes. Then she knows she's at work and she does her job."

"Which is?"

"Keep everyone out of the lot. No exceptions."

"Even employees?"

"Even me."

"So there's a window of time between six and seven when no one's on the lot and Elaine isn't here yet."

She nodded. "Depending on what time we make it out of here."

"I think the police said Drew was last seen at six thirty p.m.," I said.

"Gate's locked at six. How'd he get the body in?"

"Over the fence?"

"Razor wire around the entire perimeter. Sometimes people throw a mattress over the wire and crawl over."

"Seems like it'd be hard to do dragging a body."

"And where's the mattress? I don't think they found anything."

"Would blankets work?"

"If you had enough of them. There's a lot of fibers on that wire. Cops took samples."

"Can I take a look?"

She put her coat back on and handed me a man's jacket that

had been hanging on a peg behind the desk. It smelled like smoke. I put it on and followed her out the back door of the trailer.

The back gate wasn't ten feet from the trailer. It was chained and padlocked. A dumpster sat beside the gate.

"Here's where people get in," she said. "They climb onto the dumpster, throw something over the razor wire, and climb in."

"Why haven't you had the city move the dumpster?"

She looked at me sideways. "You haven't lived in Dallas long, have you?"

"A few years."

"Might as well ask the city to give me a pedicure and wax my legs for me while they're at it. The cars are all locked and insured. Sometimes someone will bust a window and take a stereo or something."

"Where do you keep the car keys?"

"In a safe inside the office. Building's all locked up and alarmed. That glass in the customer window is bulletproof. We never keep cash on hand after hours. And then there's Elaine. We really only have that one hour of vulnerability. We've been here fifteen years. Very few problems, knock on wood."

She walked around the building and stopped in the back corner of the lot. I bent down to see where she was pointing.

"Elaine tore up the pavement here. Dug right into the asphalt. Car's trunk was scratched to pieces. Her paws were bleeding."

"How'd the body get in the trunk if the keys are locked in a safe?"

"It was a Honda," she said.

"Come again?"

"You don't need a key to get into the trunk of most foreign cars. Hondas have a latch. Pops it right open."

I pointed at the back gate.

"Any chance that gate was left open that night?"

She shook her head. "Only time we ever unlock it is to take

the trash out. I didn't close that night. My receptionist and our mechanic did. He took the trash out, then went back into the office for a few minutes. The gate was open maybe ten minutes at the most. Yolanda locked it before she left. She clocked out at 6:57. A little later than usual. She does that sometimes. Four kids. She needs the money."

"But it's possible. If someone saw her leave it open, they could rush in, stick the body in the trunk, and get out before she got back."

We both stared at the layout for a minute, thinking. Finally, I held out my hand. "Thanks very much. You've been extremely helpful."

"I hope they catch the guy."

"They have someone locked up."

"Who is it?"

"His name is Gordon Pryne."

"Doesn't ring a bell." She threw her cigarette on the ground and screwed it delicately into the asphalt with the toe of her dress shoe. "Doesn't matter who it is as long as they got him. I don't like the idea of a killer wandering around in my alley."

We said our goodnights and she let me out, locking the gate behind us both and driving off into the night. The wind was starting to whip. Could be another storm coming.

I walked around the lot and stepped into the alley.

A six-foot wooden fence ran most of the length of the alley, with open gateways every twenty yards or so. That takes care of your entry problem and your exit problem, as Randy the rodent man would say. Anyone would have free access to the alley. The one chain-link was the fence around Critter Cars, making it the only property fully visible from the alley.

I wondered why Pryne hadn't just put the body in the dumpster. On such a cold evening, no one would be poking through trash bins in the middle of the night. It would have made a decent hiding place and it was much more accessible.

Gordon Pryne was impulsive. Sloppy, really. Not a plan-ahead type of guy. He'd left a wide, messy trail of damning evidence behind him in each of his other crimes. He was just the type to dump her body in a trashcan. Or even leave it out in the open. Either option was convenient and conveyed an impersonal, contemptuous attitude toward the victim.

Why the sudden finesse with Drew's murder?

And Drew Sturdivant had been killed within the first couple of blows. For a violent act, it was as humane as possible. Pryne liked to make his victims suffer. That seemed to be the point, actually. Drew's killer had used multiple blows, the paper had said, but most of them had been inflicted in a frenzy after she'd died. Which sounded to me like she knew her killer in some loaded, personal way.

Did Pryne have that sort of relationship with Drew? I doubted he had that sort of relationship with anyone.

And why did he leave the ax on my porch? I still had no answer to that nagging little question—the one that had gotten me into this whole mess in the first place.

I was creeping myself out standing at the scene of the crime in the dark. And I definitely didn't want to stick around and meet Elaine. I got in my truck and drove to my house, surprised at the pleasant sense of anticipation I felt knowing that sweet, fluffy Melissa would be there to greet me.

26

~

The moon had gone by then, ducking behind the gathering night-clouds and leaving the street to swallow up the slim reflection of my headlights on the ice as I drove home. My house was dark when I got there, all shut-down and shuttered. I felt depressed and alone just looking at it.

I'd apparently forgotten to turn my porch light on when I left this morning. It's a tough call, that porch light situation. Leave it on all day and announce to local ax murderers that you're not home? Or leave it off and come home to a pitch black house? It's one of life's stubborn dilemmas.

I pushed the button on my garage door opener, expecting the familiar, reluctant groan and the gape of yellow light as the door yawned open. But the door stayed firmly clamped shut. I let out a string of cuss words, followed by an all-purpose prayer for forgiveness, and parked my truck in the driveway. I'd forgotten to give Kay Basieri her smelly coat back before I left the car lot, so I peeled it off now and left it on the front porch to air out overnight.

I unlocked the front door and threw my stuff down. The air was stony cold and smelled flat and dank, like the underside of a rock. I locked the door behind me, flipped the switch in the foyer, and found myself standing in dead darkness. No electricity meant no space heaters, no lights, no working refrigerator. Just a water heater (thank you, Jesus), a gas oven, and the dinky gas wall heater in the bathroom. If it was something other than a breaker switch, it was going to be a long night. I felt my way to the bedroom and reached under the bed for a flashlight I keep there. It's about the size and weight of a baseball bat, which renders it a multi-purpose instrument. Should the need arise.

I pushed the button on the flashlight and walked behind the beam to Melissa's hutch. The cedar shavings were all piled up in one corner, the rest of the hutch floor almost bare. Her bowls had both been knocked over. The big plastic milk bottle I'd cut open at one end and turned on its side (for a handy hide-out, in case Peter Terry came calling) was empty.

"Melissa," I cooed. "It's your Aunt Dylan."

It didn't seem right to refer to myself as her mom. Drew was her mom, of course. I was just the crazy woman Melissa got stuck with after she was orphaned. Besides, I needed to get used to thinking of myself as an aunt—since I'd already been crowned World's Greatest Aunt by my father and his idiot wife Kellee.

I expected the rust-colored mound of shavings to shift and for Melissa (who always seemed to emerge from hiding when I entered a room) to poke her nose out of the pile and hop on over to me, happy to see me after her first day by herself in her new home. But nothing happened.

"Melissa, sweetie, I'm home."

I dug carefully into the shavings, pulling them away from the center until I got to the bottom of the pile. The hutch was empty.

I heard a piercing squeal come from the kitchen. Like the sharp screech of metal against metal. Did rabbits scream? I had no idea.

I rushed to the kitchen and flipped on the light, forgetting momentarily that I had no electricity. I pointed the beam in the general direction of the screech. Melissa was there, on the kitchen floor, running around in quick, tight circles, pawing at the cabinet door under the kitchen sink. She'd peed on the floor, leaving a tiny pool of urine in the middle of the kitchen. I walked over and pointed my light at the mess. Dirty paw prints recorded a frenetic, circular dance on my linoleum.

"Melissa!"

She ignored me and kept scratching the door.

I heard the screech again and flinched, my whole body cringing, a rush of naked fear surging right up from the floor to my hair.

The screech came from her general direction, but I could tell now that it did not come from Melissa. It came from behind that cabinet door.

"Melissa," I said again, more gently this time. "Hey, Melissa. Settle down, honey."

I walked over to her, put the flashlight down on the countertop, and picked her up. She fought me and freed herself from my grip, thudding to the floor awkwardly and scrambling again to the cabinet door. The bottom edge of the wood was raw from her scratches. I pulled her away again and held her firmly against the floor with one hand.

I would rather have jumped into a pool of battery acid than open that door. Some poltergeist was back there. But of course, I stood up, clutching Melissa tight, picked up my flashlight, and opened the door slowly with my foot, swinging both sides open. There, in a reassuring assembly of order, were the soldiers in my war against germs, all lined up at attention, labels pointed forward. From Ajax All-Purpose Cleanser to Zep Orange Industrial Degreaser.

As I leaned down to shine my light into the cabinet, Melissa wriggled free again and hit the floor running. I expected her to head once again for the open cabinet, but she high-tailed it to the other end of the kitchen and turned to stare at me, her back to the wall, her eyes bright, reflecting the light back at me as I pointed it in her direction.

She twitched her nose calmly. She'd cornered the monster. Slaying it was apparently my job.

I knelt on the floor and pointed my light again into the cabinet. At first I didn't notice anything out of place. And then I saw a bottle of Tilex lying on its side in the back. I began to remove bottles from the cabinet, one by one, setting them on the kitchen floor. When I reached for the Tilex, the screech returned and the Tilex bottle began to jerk wildly. I yanked my hand away and pointed my flashlight.

Glaring back at me were two tiny eyes, red in the light. I pulled back again and let out a little scream. I heard Melissa take off for the bedroom.

I stood up and rummaged through a drawer, producing a pair of kitchen tongs. I used them to reach once again for the Tilex, pulling it away gingerly, shining my light directly at the red eyes, which glared, unblinking, back at me.

It was a rat. Caught in one of Randy's glue traps.

As I leaned in to get a closer look, the rat let out another screech. I flinched and pulled away, sitting back on my heels.

Now let me just say here that I've read the research on animals and emotion. Animals supposedly do not experience complex feelings like we do—only the simple, primal ones necessary for survival. Like fear. But anyone who has spent any time at all with animals will tell you with great conviction that their pets feel love, shame, joy—the whole rock and roll. Of course, the academics all choose to ignore them in favor of their own rat-maze-with-a-mild-electric-shock experiments. As though anyone subjected to electric shock would give you an honest answer.

This rat, I swear to you, was enraged. And what it flung at me with those eyes was hatred. I can't find another word for it. Simple, pure, unflinching hatred.

The rat was dark brown with a long, black tail. It was maybe eight or nine inches long, nose to tip. Its belly was stuck to the glue trap, stem to stern, and in its struggle, it had disemboweled itself. The rat was dying. A slow, hopeless, miserable death.

He screeched at me again. We both knew, at that moment I believe, that his doom was inevitable. And we both knew I could not and would not save him.

A strange mixture of remorse and revulsion washed over me. The scene was grotesque, to be sure, but it was the look of revilement, of sheer contempt on this rat's face that slapped me backward and bowed my head. I'd never been directly responsible for another creature's suffering before.

"I'm sorry," I said out loud.

He screeched at me and kicked his back legs, ripping his wound some more and spilling another centimeter of his life onto the brown, smelly glue.

I wanted to put him out of his misery, but I couldn't think what to do. So I sat back on my heels and started to cry. Strange, gulping sobs. I heard a soft scuffling behind me. Melissa had scuttled back into the kitchen and stood by the door, taking in the scene.

My cell phone rang. I jumped up to answer it, grateful, for once, for the intrusion.

"Dylan, this is Enrique Martinez."

"Oh. Hello." I sniffed and wiped my eyes. "How are you?"

"Am I catching you at a bad time?"

"It's perfect timing, actually. I needed to hear a friendly voice."

"Is anything wrong?"

"No," I lied. "Everything's fine." I pulled a paper towel off the roll and wiped my nose.

"I was wondering if you were going to be home later. I'm coming off overtime. I could drop the video by for you. I couldn't get clearance for the file."

"What time?"

"I could be there in ten minutes."

"That would be great."

I hung up and returned to the kitchen cabinet, compelled back to the morbid scene. It seemed somehow fitting that I should witness the death I'd caused, though I'm sure the rat would rather have died alone. He screeched at me again, baring his sharp, yellow teeth.

It occurred to me that Gordon Pryne, and other bilious souls like him, had witnessed many such scenes. Pryne's victims, of course, were human. People with lives and minds and souls. People who, with the burden or advantage of language, depending on your point of view, could articulate their suffering—plead for mercy, shout for help, and if they were so inclined, curse their executioner.

What sort of person can inflict torment without succumbing to empathy? What could such profound absence of tenderness feel like? Apathy? Or perhaps emptiness. Maybe a person must be emptied of his very self in order to muster a true capacity for cruelty. I could not imagine, no matter how deeply I looked into my sometimes dark and conflicted heart, how anyone could blithely, intentionally impose pain on another being.

I heard a knock at my front door. Ten minutes had passed quickly. I took my flashlight and answered the knock.

David was standing there, dressed up for a date, all snazzy in scuffed cowboy boots, Levi's, and a wool blazer.

"You forgot, didn't you?" he said.

And of course I had. "We had supper plans, didn't we?"

"You were supposed to meet me an hour ago."

I looked at my watch.

He stepped inside and brushed past me. "I'll go flip the breaker. The rest of the block's not out. It must be you."

I shut the door and called after him. "You want the flashlight?"

"No," he said, without turning around. I heard him walk

through the kitchen and into the garage. By the time I made it back to the kitchen, the lights were on. The refrigerator shuddered to life with a jolt.

David walked into the kitchen and pointed at the bottles of cleaning products lined up on the floor. "What's going on?"

"A rat. Caught in a glue trap."

"Since when do you have rats?"

"Since...I don't know. I found out on Sunday."

He leaned down, still without looking at me, and peered into the cabinet. "Thanks for mentioning it. And since when do you have a pet?"

"Since last night."

"What is it? A gerbil or something?"

"Rabbit."

"Thanks for mentioning it." He studied the rat. "Does it have a name?"

"The rat?"

"The rabbit."

I moved in front of him and shut the cabinet doors. "David, look at me. I apologize. I feel terrible about this. I do."

"This isn't really about how you feel, Dylan."

"What's that supposed to mean?"

"It means I'd like to have a girlfriend that pays attention."

"What's that supposed to mean?"

The hurt in his eyes shifted to anger. "Don't make me explain it to you. You're not an idiot."

I took a step backward as the first tears began to sting my eyes. "Explain it anyway."

"It means I don't like sitting at a restaurant for an hour by myself waiting for you without even the simple courtesy of a phone call."

"I apologized, David. What else do you want me to do?"

"You say that like it matters. 'I apologize.' What does that mean, exactly? That it won't happen again? Because it will, Dylan. Next week or next month or on my birthday or someday when we're due at my mom's for Christmas. It's just a matter of when."

I took a step back and crossed my arms defensively. "That's not true. I've never stood you up before."

"No, you usually just cancel at the last minute. Or you have some big catastrophic *über*-disaster in your life that demands all your time and attention. Flies or demons or suicidal patients or a bloody ax on your porch or who knows what? I'm…just…"

"What? You're just what?"

"Sick of it, Dylan. I'm sick of it." He jammed his fists in his pockets and shifted his weight to one foot. He looked down at the floor and took a breath. "I'm a patient man, Dylan. I really am. But there's just too much…I don't even know what to call it… Chaos, I guess. I don't like it, standing in the middle of all that wind."

The doorbell rang. David flashed me an I-told-you-so look.

I threw up my hands. "I need to answer the door, David. Can you just…hang on a second? Please? I'll be right back. We're going to finish talking about this. And I'm going to grovel. And you're going to forgive me. I feel certain of it."

He sat down on a barstool and threw his keys onto the kitchen table.

Officer Martinez was standing on my porch, tape in hand.

"Oh, hey. Thanks for coming by," I said.

"I saw your lights come on. Everything okay?"

"My electricity was out. I guess it was the breaker or something. I'm fine."

"Want me to check the house?"

"No, that's okay. I just—"

"I checked it already." David's voice came from the doorway behind me. "She's all safe and sound." He walked over to us and extended his hand to Martinez. "David Shykovsky."

Martinez smiled and shook his hand. "Enrique Martinez."

David looked at me. I couldn't tell if he wanted to cry or hit something. Maybe both. "You could have told me, Dylan."

"Told you what?"

He kissed me on the cheek. "I'm leaving. I'll call you later. Nice to meet you," he said to Martinez. "Good luck."

He walked out the door, glancing down at the Virginia Slims jacket as he strode by. Then he got in his car and drove off. Just like that.

"I guess I came at a bad time," Martinez said.

I shook my head. "It's just a misunderstanding. I'm sorry. It's not you."

As I shut the door, the rat screeched again in the kitchen.

"What's that?" Martinez asked.

"A rat. It's caught in a glue trap under my kitchen sink."

He walked past me and into the kitchen, squatting down to peer under the sink. "Want me to get rid of it for you?"

"Would you?"

"Sure. Where's your dumpster?"

I pointed. "Behind the fence to the left."

"Garbage bags?"

"Pantry."

He opened the pantry and pulled out a big black Hefty Handle-Tie garbage bag, the kind you put leaves and grass in.

"Are you going to kill it?" I asked. "Or just throw it away?"

"Which do you want me to do?"

"I'd like for you to put it out of its misery."

"You might want to wait in the other room."

I walked around the house turning on heaters, then went into the bedroom and found Melissa, who was hiding under my bed. I held her for a minute before I put her back in her hutch, more for my comfort than for hers. She was shaking, her big rodent teeth chattering, her brown eyes darting around. I wondered if she knew, somehow, that it had been a relative of hers, however distant, suffering behind that cabinet door. Had she been trying to save it?

I heard a scuffle in the kitchen, a few Spanish words I didn't know, and then the slam of the back door. Several minutes passed before the door opened again. By the time I met Martinez back in the kitchen, he was standing at the sink washing his hands.

"Well?"

"Rats are hard to kill," he said.

"You look a little green." I smiled sheepishly. "I owe you one. I didn't know what to do."

"I had to throw your…" He made a pinching motion with his fingers.

"Tongs?"

"I threw your tongs away. I didn't think you'd want them back."

"Good call. Can I offer you something? Dr Pepper? Cash? My firstborn? Or I think I have some Shiner left from the last time I made Shiner Bock stew."

"I'll take the *cerveza*. Gracias."

I opened the fridge, reached in for a Shiner Bock and motioned him to the kitchen table. He dried his hands on a dish-towel and pulled out a chair.

"Have you eaten?" I asked. It was past nine.

He shook his head, no.

"I could warm up some chili."

He brightened. "Snow-day chili?"

I opened up a fresh bag of Fritos and dumped them into a bowl for him, then warmed up the chili, dished it into a couple of bowls, and served it with some cheddar cheese on top. I sat down across from him and we dug in.

"I spoke to Gordon Pryne today," he said.

"You saw him?"

"Paid the man a visit. In my official capacity as DPD chaplain."

"How was he?"

"Jittery. He needs the meth. It's not going well."

"That's no surprise. Where is he? Parkland?"

He shook his head. "Cell. Lying on his cot like an old dog."

I winced. "Did he say anything?"

"He did."

"He didn't confess, did he?" I grinned. "Maybe he thought you were a real priest. You've got the whole Catholic vibe."

He took a long pull on his beer and looked at me. "He asked for someone."

"Who?"

"You."

"Why would he ask for me? I've never met the man."

"Not by name," he said. "He asked to see the girl behind the mirror."

"He saw me, then."

Martinez shook his head. "Nope."

"Then how?"

"He told me he had a dream. About a lake and a rope. And a necklace and a girl. And the girl in the dream was the girl behind the mirror. He told me he needed to talk to the girl behind the mirror. He said you're the one that can help him."

27

~

How I'd gotten myself elected to help anyone was a big pile of stinking mystery to me. Not only was I not qualified for the job, I had no memory of applying for it and was positive I did not want it. But apparently, at least according to a dying, hallucinating homeless person in the Parkland ER, and a serial murderer and rapist coming down off a crystal meth intoxication, I'd been summoned. Twice now. By powers way up there in the corner office. The references were weak, though. So I figured I might still have a chance to get out of it.

Martinez asked what I thought it meant, that I could help Gordon Pryne, and I told him that I didn't know. Which I didn't, though I had my suspicions.

I thought about popping the interrogation tape in and pointing out Peter Terry, the source of all things vile and villainous in my life, but I didn't know Martinez well enough to risk it. What if I was the only one that could see him? What if he wasn't there this time? This whole thing could quickly deteriorate into something like those old *Bewitched* episodes, with Darren/Dylan the buffoon/crackpot always talking to the walls and seeing things nobody else saw. I needed that like a tomato in the face. Besides, since I don't have a TV, the question was moot anyway.

Martinez stayed longer than he should have. I was shaken by the rat thing—as was he, I think—and we both seemed to need the company. He didn't leave until long after his second bottle of Shiner was empty and the label peeled off entirely, bit by tiny bit.

"A nervous habit," he'd said.

He didn't say what he was nervous about.

Enrique Martinez is a handsome man. Very male, if you get my meaning. All dark and inward, with a pleasing sense of trouble about him. He seemed to me like a guy who had gotten into enough hot water in high school either to straighten himself out for good or to land in a permanent state of delinquency. I had a feeling he rarely told his stories.

He talked a little, listened a lot. You could feel his brain tumbling things around.

He asked about David.

"Over a year," I'd said. "Maybe a year and a half."

"Nice guy?"

"Very."

He'd nodded and peeled the dot off the i.

What bugged me about the whole thing was that I felt like I was cheating. Like I should call up David and confess or something.

I owed David an apology, for sure. More than one, it sounded like to me. Probably entire volumes could be drafted and bound to accommodate the necessary supplications. But Enrique Martinez wasn't the reason I'd flaked out on David tonight. I was the reason I'd flaked out on David tonight. And that was a much tougher problem, in my opinion. Here I was, thirty-five years old, and still waiting for my better self to arrive. She had yet to show up, the irresponsible little brat.

But I must admit, as I sat there listening to myself talk to Martinez and liking the way he considered me as I prattled on, I found myself in a little bit of a flutter. Just a tiny one.

Don't get me wrong. David Shykovsky is quite nearly the most perfect man I've ever met. Funeral home or no. Even that strike couldn't contaminate his otherwise perfect boyfriend record. But I'd been wondering lately if we really had the mojo.

We're very different, for one thing. David is all sweetness and light. Grade-A, #1, Sugar Pie material. There is absolutely no guile in the man. Not one drop. And he has the longest fuse of anyone I've ever met—an endless supply of forbearance. He'd forgive me until he turned blue. Me, I'm always the one standing there red in the face.

Another thing is, he's optimistic. The glass is always half full with him. Not only is my glass half empty, I'm the sort that will sit there and calculate the time before it dries up entirely.

David has been talking about commitments lately. And truthfully, he'd be great at it. The man is a block of concrete when it comes to reliability. He's got family man written all over him. I'm always the one running away from things. I can't commit to finishing a sandwich.

So when Enrique Martinez, with his slight tilt of an accent and his quiet way, sat at my kitchen table until two a.m. and listened and laughed and peeled the label off his Shiner, I felt something I hadn't felt in a long time. I'm not sure what to name it. *Settled* might be the word. And I couldn't possibly have been more surprised.

I didn't even bother to clean up the mess in the kitchen until after he left. That's how comfortable an evening it was. I actually sat there for three hours with dirty chili bowls on the table and all my cleaning products sitting out on my kitchen floor.

After he left and after I'd hosed down the kitchen, I walked around and picked up all the glue traps and threw them away. I pulled out my humane traps again, loading them up this time with the rest of the chili. Maybe all those days of anticipation would lure the little monsters in.

Morning brought a modicum of renewed energy. Nothing untoward happened during the night, which was enough of a relief to revitalize me a bit. That and a decent night's rest, with heat in the house and a pair of warm socks.

My traps were empty when I woke up. The chili was gone, of course.

I'd been ignoring phone messages for a while now, so I made myself sit down and make a slew of calls, cleaning up all the loose ends I'd left flapping the last few days. It was fortuitous timing, actually. Saturday mornings are a great time to return calls. Almost no one ever answers the phone.

I left a message for my dad and Kellee—sure, I'd love to come to a baby shower...no, wait. I forgot I have a seminar to give that weekend (writing myself a note to schedule a seminar somewhere the first weekend in June, as far from Houston as possible). I returned a call from Guthrie, who was on the golf course when I talked to him, so he didn't sound too bad. And one from Maria Chavez, who was back in her house and wondered if I'd like to get together sometime. I said sure and wondered if I was actually making a friend.

I called David, who did not pick up, though I left lengthy, appropriately contrite messages at his house, on his cell phone, and on his office line at the funeral home. I figured he'd call me back when he was good and ready.

I left messages for both Jackson and McKnight. We seemed to have gone into separate corners, working from different points of view and with different agendas.

I knew where they were coming from and what they wanted. They were cops and they wanted Gordon Pryne convicted and off the streets. My point of view was cloudy and my agenda wasn't even as clear as that. I was on one of my compulsive, maniacal searches for some speck of truth out there in the darkness somewhere. Flying around the yard in circles, headless, wings flapping.

I once read about a rooster that survived six months without a head. Its owners fed it corn kernels through its gullet until it finally gave up the fight and died. I'm serious. That would be just my luck. Six months on life support and then die in the dirt anyway, without ever knowing what hit me.

I placed another call to Brigid, Drew's birth mother, who apparently never answers her phone. And then summoned my courage to call Drew's adoptive parents at the Jesus commune in East Texas. I'd found only one phone number for Life of Christ Community. I called it and reached someone named Esther who said she would give the Sturdivants the message to call me. No, they certainly did not have a phone, she said. I could tell she wasn't even writing down my number.

My last calls were to the three most amicable members of my review committee. I needed to start greasing the system to get John Mulvaney kicked off the panel. Otherwise, I was in for a fight, no matter how solid my work was. He'd jump me through hoops just for the sheer entertainment of it. He seemed to have an odd fetish for watching me squirm.

I spent the rest of my Saturday hunched over books in Bridwell Library. I cracked every source I could find on angels and demons and heaven and hell, including the ponderous book of Enoch. The second heaven, Anael's territory, is apparently where the demons are kept. The very ones that raped those women. After this particularly heinous act of rebellion, God exterminated the population by pouring forty days' worth of water on the anthill. I guess He decided just to start over.

I got the feeling, reading it all, that I'd stumbled onto some secret keyhole I wasn't supposed to know about. Something straight out of an Indiana Jones movie. Something, as anyone who has watched Harrison Ford run from the boulder knows, is best left undisturbed. Poke your key into that lock and all hell can break loose.

At the end of the day, though, I'd made peace with the fact that, no matter how much I knew, I'd probably never understand the whole of it. The hard truth is, as much as the theologians would love to have you believe otherwise, the Bible is unclear about the entire matter.

One thing did stand out to me: all this mystical intrigue was just the thing to snare a girl like Drew Sturdivant. A girl wandering around lost without a soft place to land. I went back to the Hebrew that Eli had translated for me. "Daughter of Lot, lost and little." The Hebrew word for daughter is *bat*, of course. As in *bat mitzvah*. No wonder Eli had laughed at me for forgetting it. I'd attended his daughter's *bat mitzvah* two years ago.

I turned to the account in Genesis. This is one of those stories I always forget about—and then when I read it again, I wish it were never in there in the first place. God can be so confounding sometimes.

Angels show up at Lot's house in Sodom to warn him they're about to torch the town because of all the sickos living there. By all accounts, Sodom was every drunken festival you can imagine—Mardi Gras and New Year's Eve and Carnival, every day, all day long. In Vegas. Without the Elvis suits. But the celebrants weren't happy at all or even celebratory. Just sordid and foul-breathed and violent, not to mention sexually predatory.

So all the men in town turn up at Lot's door and demand he send out his houseguests to be raped by the masses. Nice. Lot, to his credit, refuses, but then, not to his credit, offers up his two virgin daughters instead. Real nice. The angels intervene, bar the door, and take the family out the back to safety. The town burns, Lot's wife looks over her shoulder, and the rest is history.

The part I'd forgotten about is that the daughters take a turn for the worse at this point. They look around, see no likely breeder stock, and then decide to get Dad soused and have a go with him instead. Real, real nice.

My psychologist mind always wanders into people's heads when I hear stories like this, not to find them an excuse, but to understand what could have gone so terribly wrong. Was Lot just a moron or had he perhaps been locked in a closet and tortured as a small child? And what about those daughters? How had they lost their way? With a father like that, growing up where rape is the town sport, was their outcome inevitable—some tragic version of predestination?

If I put myself there, behind their eyes, they seemed like Drew to me. Hopeless. Alone. Little. Lost.

Drew Sturdivant's family had been willing to offer her up, not once but twice. Brigid had started the whole mess when she'd abandoned her eight-year-old daughter at the Jesus commune. And then Drew's adoptive parents had turned around and offered her up again, marrying her off to a drippy, middle-aged insurance salesman type with a comb-over, when she was still a child herself (though admittedly a cranky one). Drew finished the job, turning even farther south after that, offering herself up on the altar at Caligula in a way that could only demean her.

Daughter of Lot, lost and little. And angry. So, so angry.

I had a clear picture of her now, in her room, with the pink walls and the gray chiffon curtains, spray-painting her life story on her headboard. Standing there in some renegade outfit she'd made herself, her crimson hair sticking straight out, her combat boots laced, ready for a fight.

But a fight, I believe, she knew she was bound to lose.

28

~

Melissa is the only rabbit I know (as though I know any other rabbits) who will play fetch. Which she does, endlessly. Her mouth doesn't open real wide, since of course she's a rodent, but she'd found a spool of thread—one of those little ones they sell in airports—and brought that to me a couple of hundred times, chasing after it as I rolled it away. After she'd entertained us both with this game for almost an entire hour on Sunday morning, she sat on my feet and calmly munched an apple (dead, raw, organic) while I read the paper. She was turning out to be good company.

I tucked her into her hutch, gathered my gear, and headed out to the SMU pool (indoor again). I swam a mile, and then did some lunges and squats to resurrect my Thigh Recovery Program. I'd forgotten about it in all the fuss. I wanted to be at my physical, mental, and spiritual peak by the time I arrived at the pokey that afternoon for my visit with Gordon Pryne.

Every fourth Sunday at my church is devoted entirely to singing, so the spiritual peak part was no problem. The service that morning was a lung-buster. I was dripping with the Holy Spirit by the time I got out of there.

I'm starting to get comfortable with jails, which worries me. So when I entered the Lew Sterrett Justice Center in downtown Dallas, I knew what to do. The procedure is all about suspicion. Guilty until proven innocent. Show your ID to prove you're actually you. Allow your personal effects to be examined to prove you're not smuggling anything in. Pass through a metal detector to prove you're not packing. Give your name to the receptionist and show your ID again—as though you could somehow have transformed into someone else during that ten-foot walk down the linoleum. And finally, wait for your escort because you cannot possibly be trusted to wander around unobserved.

The whole thing happens under the cold stare of armed guards who study you like you're about to hijack the place. And who can blame them, with what the world's come to? Suspicion is our one remaining buttress against the forces of evil among us. The human ones, anyway. That's a sad fact.

Enrique Martinez met me in the holding area and walked me into the bowels of Lew Sterrett. I couldn't help but notice how deep-set his brown eyes were, and the ambling, easy way he walked as he led the way. He looked good from behind in those jeans he was wearing.

The visitor room is just like all the other rooms in correctional facilities. Drab, damaged, and stinky, like an old banana. It's one long, divided space, with bulletproof glass running down the middle to segregate the land of the free from home of the captured. Tables run along the window line, with little booth-walls dividing the spaces. Chairs are lined up in front of speakers that allow for communication across the divide. Martinez motioned me to a booth and pulled out a chair for me.

Pryne came into the room on the other side of the glass, shackled at the hands and feet. He shuffled and limped, supported almost entirely by two guards who held him by the arms and slid him along between them on stocking feet.

Crystal meth is like anti-Botox. It ages you like no amount of Dust-Bowl hardship can. The mug-shot photo I'd seen of Pryne had been taken less than six years before, after the Chavez rape.

He'd looked his age then, maybe even a few years younger. The man who sat down in the chair opposite me looked seventy, at least. His face was scabbed and pocked, his eyes yellowed and hollow, and the dark circles under his eyes ran halfway down cheeks that had cracked and dried up like the floor of a dead riverbed. The wild brown hair was matted and filthy. I could smell his stink through the speaker-hole.

Without looking at me, he picked up the phone.

I picked mine up and waited, wishing I'd brought along some hand-sanitizer gel.

He mumbled through the line, his voice scratchy, like he hadn't used it in a while. "Will you tell them to leave me alone?" His expression was sheepish, obsequious. It was hard to believe this was the same man who had lunged at the mirror and howled at me in the interrogation room.

"Tell who? The police?"

His hands shook violently, his face screwed up, and he began coughing and heaving, doubling himself over his knees for a minute.

The coughing stopped and he asked it again. "Will you tell them to leave me alone?"

"I don't understand what you're asking me, Mr. Pryne."

"They're watching me," he said. "All the time." He yawned, showing me a mouthful of brown, rotting teeth. "They won't let me sleep."

"Who?" I asked. "Who is watching you?"

"They got eyes on me. Inside my head."

If I hadn't seen what I'd seen on that interrogation video, I'd have talked to him a second, patronized him just enough to assure him I'd deliver his message to the intruders in his head, and then walked down the hall and asked the sergeant on duty to take him to a Parkland shrink for evaluation. In another setting, he would have been just a run-of-the-mill psychotic drug addict who needed a script for 500 milligrams of Seroquel and seventy-two hours of observation.

As it was, I said, "Do you know who they are?"

"You know who they are," he spat. "I don't care to know. Don't matter no more. Not to me." He called me a name I won't repeat.

"Mr. Pryne," I said firmly, reflexively whipping out a set of well-oiled clinical skills, "if you want me to help you, you'll need to speak to me respectfully."

He ducked his head like a beaten animal and wiped his nose on his sleeve. "No offense."

"I don't know who they are," I said. "I'm sorry."

"You're a liar," he said quietly.

Martinez started to interject, but I held up a hand to stop him.

"What makes you think I'm lying?" I asked.

"I know all about you. Liar. Lyin' scheming…" There was that word again. "Everyone knows how women lie. Trying to trap you and trick you and keep you down. Thinkin' they're better'n you."

"Mr. Pryne, I thought we agreed you would speak to me respectfully. One more outburst and I walk out of here and never come back. Understood?"

He ducked his head again and shuddered.

"What makes you think I know who they are?" I asked.

"You was at the lake, wasn't you?"

"What lake?"

"The lake. Where the spirits are."

I felt the room get cold. I looked over at Martinez, whose eyebrows had come together, his expression sharp, alert. His hand had moved to his holster.

"I don't know what you're talking about, Mr. Pryne," I said.

"You're a liar," he said again.

He was right, of course. I knew exactly what he was talking about.

"What do they want with you, Mr. Pryne? Why won't they leave you alone?"

"You tell me. You're the one knows 'em."

"I don't know any spirits, Mr. Pryne."

He cursed at me and spat at the window, aiming a big wad of contempt right at my face.

I pushed back my chair and stood up. "I told you I'd leave, Mr. Pryne. I meant it."

I picked up my bag and motioned for Martinez to follow me.

Pryne started screaming. "Don't you walk away from me, you…" I sighed, wishing he'd choose another word. "You think you're better'n me?" he yelled. "That I ain't worth saving? I never killed nobody! Ask the rats! They'll tell you. Ask the rats!"

He stood up and screamed obscenities at me until the guards on his side of the world caught him from behind, slamming his face down on the tabletop to subdue him. He was still screaming when we walked out of the room, the eyes of the other visitors and prisoners following us silently as we left.

Neither of us said a word as we walked down the hall to the exit. It wasn't until we were standing outside in the cold sunshine that Martinez said, "Coffee?"

We walked around the block and found a coffeehouse. I ordered the largest possible serving of Earl Grey with cream and sugar. Martinez had a small coffee, black. Though it was cold outside, we both headed for a sidewalk table. I wanted to breathe some air and feel the sun on my face.

"You okay?" he asked after we sat down.

I nodded and took a sip of my tea. Too hot.

"You?"

He nodded. "Any idea what that was about?"

I shrugged. "What do you think?"

He shrugged back. "Beats me."

I took the top off my tea to let it cool, releasing a wisp of steam into the crisp afternoon.

I think we both knew that something was going on with Gordon Pryne. Something more than a psychotic break. I'd felt the evil in the room, that ominous and now alarmingly familiar feeling I get when Peter Terry comes around. I suspected Martinez had felt it too. He's sensitive that way like I am. But I sure didn't want to be the one to bring it up.

Martinez saved me the trouble.

"You feel the room get cold?"

I nodded.

"Like Jackson and McKnight said."

"And Yaya," I said.

"God rest her soul." He crossed himself. "Same thing happened when I saw him yesterday."

"The room got cold?"

He nodded. "Kept talking about someone watching him."

We waited for a bus to rumble past us.

"He's in terrible shape," I said.

"Yep."

"It's the meth," I said. "Dries people up from the inside."

"Wicked drug. No doubt about that." He took a drink of his coffee and looked up. Jet contrails had crisscrossed a big *X* in the bright blue sky over the city.

"Who do you think's watching him?" he asked finally. He leveled his eyes at me. "He seems to think you know."

I looked back at him. "I'm not sure."

"But you have a theory."

My turn to nod. "I do."

"Want to let me in on it?"

"Do you have a copy of the tape at your office?"

"The interrogation tape? Sure."

I scooted my chair back and stood up. "Let's go."

~ ~ ~

One perk of the job is that chaplains get real offices, not just cubicles. For privacy, I guess. Martinez's office is not unlike mine. He has more books than he knows what to do with. His desk is tidy, the pending business of the day stacked in neat little piles. His coffeemaker is a spotless stainless steel number, extra coffee cups sitting beside it, along with a variety of sweeteners. The coffee cups were clean and unstained, unlike every other vessel I'd seen in this building. A crucifix hung on one wall. Photographs of children were everywhere, a dozen or so little versions of himself, framed and propped up where he could see them. Three kids appeared as a group more often than any of the others—two beautiful dark-skinned, brown-eyed boys, and a little pig-tailed girl, who was always between them. I wondered if any of the children were his. It hadn't occurred to me that he might be married. He didn't wear a ring.

He reached onto one of his shelves and pulled out the tape, then walked me down the hall to a conference room and shut the door behind us. He put the tape in and turned on the TV.

I picked up the remote and fast-forwarded to the end, starting the video where the howling began, letting it roll with the sound off. We sat back and watched again as Jackson and Martinez backed away from Pryne, who threw himself against his chains and collapsed. We waited a few more minutes as the officers scrambled to get the situation under control.

"We're almost there," I said.

We watched together as Pryne was strapped to the gurney and rolled out of the room.

And then the screen went black.

"What happened?" I said.

"I guess that's the end."

"No, there was more. The tape rolled for another ten minutes or so. What happened to the rest of it?"

"They probably stopped the copy as Pryne left the room. The interview was over at that point. Why?"

I shook my head. "It doesn't matter. I thought I'd seen something at the end of the video."

"Want me to call A-V and see if they still have the original?"

"That would be great."

He stepped out and made the phone call, returning a minute later with a fresh cup of coffee. I was still nursing my tea.

"No dice. They erased it already."

I sighed. It was probably just as well.

"What happened at the lake?" he asked.

I looked at him, trying to decide whether to trust him. Not that he wasn't a trustworthy person—he didn't have that vibe about him at all. I mean, whether to trust him with my own vulnerability. Whether to expose the weird reality I'd found myself in the middle of or, alternatively, to lie through my teeth and maintain some reasonable façade of normalcy.

I opted for a toned down version of the truth, telling him about the day two summers ago when I'd met Peter Terry at Barton Springs in Austin, and about selected bits of the chaos that had followed.

"You think this guy's the one watching Gordon Pryne?" Martinez asked me.

"Put it this way," I said. "I think Gordon Pryne thinks Peter Terry is watching him. And somehow Gordon Pryne got wind that I've met him."

He took a sip of his coffee. "This is some creepy stuff."

I nodded. "And where's Yaya when we need her?"

He smiled. "Talking to St. Jude. I told you."

"Well, she'd better talk fast," I said. "'Cause the way this is going, we're going to need the help."

An airplane roared overhead. As we watched the plane bank

to the right over downtown, I noticed the contrails had faded above us and the X had dissipated into the afternoon sky.

"What did you say he's in charge of?" I asked.

"Lost causes."

I raised my paper cup and we toasted. "To St. Jude."

29

~

David Shykovsky had graduated summa cum laude from Sugar Pie School, so even though he wasn't speaking to me, he'd done his homework assignment and checked on the autopsies of Drew's father and husband. By the time I left Martinez, David had left me a message on my work line and faxed over the reports. I called to thank him, but of course he didn't pick up. I drove over to the office to get the pages off the fax machine before anyone else saw them. No need to let my colleagues in on the drama du jour. I had enough reputation problems already.

I fixed a cup of tea and let myself into my office and sat down at my desk. I reached over to my bookshelf and flipped on the stereo, letting the sound of Vivaldi into the room. Listening to classical music was a new affectation for me, and one I'm a little iffy about. Mainly because I sometimes worry I'm starting to get stodgy. Teaching at a university is a bad enough influence on me. Scholars are not fun-loving, if you get my drift. Everyone is just so serious and self-important. As if our work is actually crucial to anyone's existence but our own. As though we're discovering how to make fuel from orange peels or inventing air conditioning in a can or saving the Giant Panda. Well, there are probably academics somewhere doing things like that, but nobody in my department, that's for sure.

Classical music and university life—either one of them, if

you're not careful—can, I believe, be the death of an otherwise vital, interesting personality. While you're not paying attention, they eat away at your citizenship in the culture, one snobby little bite at a time. Pretty soon I'd be hosting poetry readings and using *bird* as a verb, if I didn't watch out. I'd already tanked my social life, which had been on a slow dive since I'd signed up for graduate school a couple of presidential administrations ago.

I reached back and flipped the station until I heard a boot-scooting Bruce Robison song that made me want to go dancing. Much better. I snapped my desk light on and spread the papers out in front of me, reading every word of each report.

When the events were considered separately, both men had died unremarkable deaths. Both were involved in one-car accidents, late at night, while driving alone. Toxicology on both men was negative. Neither had been using alcohol or any other drug that might impair their ability to function. Neither man had any history of brain injury or seizures. Both had perfect night vision.

David had also managed to scare up police reports from the accidents, both of which took place on the same two-lane road outside of Vidor, Texas, which is a dinky speck of a town in East Texas, not far from the Jesus commune. Vidor, as its one claim to infamy, is reportedly one of the last remaining cesspools of Klan activity in Texas. This fact, though repugnant in a gut-level, visceral way, did not seem relevant to matters at hand. Except that, to me, Vidor has always seemed a dark place. I'm sure there are many fine people there, but as is usually the case, the icky ones are the ones everyone talks about.

Both men had immaculate driving records. Neither had been speeding at the time of their accidents. Both cars had left skid marks suggesting a sudden swerve off the road and into a tree. The reports speculated they'd fallen asleep while driving or perhaps swerved to miss an animal. Both reports reached the same conclusion. Cause of death: multiple organ trauma.

Manner of death: automobile accident, single car.

The men, of course, had much more in common than the circumstances of their deaths. Both were related to Drew Sturdivant. And to Brigid, her fruity mother who worked as a psychic in Louisiana and never answered her phone. Of course, as far as I knew, the men had never met one another. Drew's father had died years before Drew even met her husband.

I skimmed the reports again, thinking I'd just run up against a dead end. It had been a wild hunch, anyway.

And then I saw the time of death. Both men had died at 3:30 a.m., according to broken dashboard clocks. 3:30 a.m. exactly. Over nine years apart. On the same road. Three thirty is Peter Terry Hour at my house. That's when he likes to show up and crack open my sanity and watch it spill out all over the floor, just for the fun of it.

This could be a coincidence, I guess. And for a less paranoid person under less surreal circumstances, that would be the logical conclusion here. But I am indeed paranoid. And this was no ordinary situation. It was spooky as hell, so to speak. And getting spookier by the minute.

I tapped my pen on the paper and tried to think.

"You look as though you're engrossed in something of great importance," a voice said.

I turned to see Harold Lansing standing in my doorway. Harold is a colleague of mine. He specializes in developmental psychology, so he spends a lot of time with little kids. He's always wearing Kermit the Frog neckties and bright yellow shoelaces, anything to set the kids at ease. He's got stuffed animals and Tootsie Rolls in his office and usually walks around with a kazoo in his pocket, just in case. He's into the kids way more than he's into the research, which makes his work much more quirky and interesting than most of my colleagues'.

I like Harold a lot. He's a bright spot in an otherwise deadly dull department. He's also the head of my academic committee. Which means Harold is currently the prime target of my campaign to get John Mulvaney removed from said committee.

I promptly hopped up and ushered Harold into my office, clearing off a chair for him.

"Cup of tea, Harold?"

He shook his head no and sat down. "Save the genuflect, Dylan."

My heart sank. "You talked to Helene."

"I did."

"And?"

"She suggested we give Mulvaney the boot."

"And?"

"And I agree, but it's really not possible."

"Oh, come on, Harold. Anything's possible if you just believe."

"Nice try, Dylan, but I'm fresh out of fairy dust. The only person who can get John Mulvaney removed from your committee is John Mulvaney. He'd have to excuse himself."

"That's the rule?"

"It's more than a rule. It's the way it is."

"But why? It doesn't make any sense. John Mulvaney couldn't evaluate the work of a seven-year-old—"

"Dog. I know."

"Then what's the point of having him evaluate me?"

"It's university policy, Dylan. Three-year reviews are done by the tenured faculty of the department. Period. Everyone is subject to the same rules. If we had the unfettered right to kick idiots off committees, the body count would outnumber the survivors, my dear. We've got people on committees that can't part their own hair, much less evaluate anything more complicated than a drivethrough menu."

"I'm sunk."

"You could…" he hesitated.

"What? Could what?"

"You could try to get Mulvaney to write a letter stating that he's not in a position to evaluate you. That might work. It's a softer approach."

"He'd never agree to it."

"You'd have to sell it."

"What do you mean?"

"The way to a man's heart is through his ego." He sat back in the chair and crossed his legs. "Make him feel important."

"You want me to inflate that already gargantuan ego? He's liable to pop. Think of the mess."

"Think about it. John's work is experimental. Yours is obviously clinical. Appeal to that. Make him think he'd be lowering himself to evaluate work that's done with real people. Better yet, make him think he can't spare the time. He loves to think he's busy." Harold cackled. "You'll have to break your rule and call him Dr. Mulvaney, though. You know how he is about that."

"I'm starting to feel faint."

Harold laughed and stood up. "And ask Helene to bake the man a pie. Just in case the other avenue to a man's heart is through the stomach, as the saying goes."

"That's actually a good idea. I saw him in the mall the other day eating with two hands. It was disgusting."

"Better make it a cobbler, then. They're bigger. Helene's got a great blueberry number. And don't forget the ice cream." He chuckled again and walked out.

I put in a quick call to Helene, who agreed to show up with a cobbler tomorrow morning, true champion that she is. I wrote myself a note to pick up a gallon of Blue Bell.

My conspiracy strategy in place, I turned off the radio and looked again at the pile of notes in front of me, not sure where to begin. Did I even want to go down this road? What did two car accidents in East Texas have to do with Drew Sturdivant's murder, anyway?

I pawed through my notes and found Brigid's number again. It was worth one more try.

Jesus must have decided to cut me a break, because Brigid answered on the first ring. "Serenity," she said.

"Pardon?"

"Serenity," she said again.

"Uh, okay. Serenity. Right back atcha." I cleared my throat. "I'm looking for someone named Brigid?"

"I am Brigid," she said regally, though she had a twang in her accent you could drive a tractor through.

"Oh, hey. I'm glad I caught you. I'm Dylan Foster. I called you a couple of times."

"I know who you are," she said.

"Great. You got my messages, then."

"I have received no messages."

"I'm sorry, I thought you said—"

"Not of the kind you are referring to."

"What other kind is there?"

"How may I be of help to you, my child?"

"Uh, okay. I guess we can start with that. I'm looking into the murder of your daughter."

"We're all daughters of the earth, Miss Foster."

"Right. But I'm talking about your own, personal daughter. You do have a daughter named Drew Sturdivant. Right?"

"Why do you ask?"

"Well, see, it's just that I saw this letter you wrote her and I was wondering what you meant when you said you needed time to think it over. What did you need to think over?"

I thought I heard her take a quick breath. "You saw the letter?" she said.

"I have it right here in front of me."

Her voice stiffened. "I don't recall writing anyone named Drew any letters."

"But you just said—"

"I'm sorry. I don't know what you're referring to."

"She tracked you down a couple of years ago. After you abandoned her in East Texas with your sister when she was just a helpless little kid? Right after her dad was killed? Your husband? The one that died in a car accident at 3:30 a.m. on Stringer Road? Right outside of Vidor, Texas? You do remember that, don't you?"

She hung up.

Even as the words flew out of the gate, I knew they were a mistake. I'd tried to lasso them before they got away. I really had. But my unruly tongue, along with my temper, is one of my Top Ten Terrible Traits. I have about a 30 percent success rate, I figure.

I dialed her again.

"I'm very sorry," I said when she picked up the phone. "Thank you for taking my call."

"Miss Foster, I'm afraid you have me confused with someone else."

I'd gotten this woman's phone number out of the book. Maybe she was just a run-of-the-mill scam psychic that worked under the name Brigid. Maybe there were lots of psychics named Brigid. I decided to try a curve ball, since I was pitching a losing game so far.

"Must be my mistake. I'm very sorry to disturb you. It's just that, well, see I must have gotten the wrong Brigid. Someone gave me your number. You don't know anything about Anael watches, do you? I mean, Drew, the girl I'm talking about, had a poster in her room for that brand of watches. I thought she'd gotten it from you."

Silence.

"Brigid?"

"Could you spell it?"

"A-N-A-E-L."

The line went dead.

I dialed again. She picked up, but hung up quickly without saying anything.

I dialed again. She didn't pick up this time. Neither did her answering machine. I decided to let it ring. Indefinitely. Now that I knew I had the right Brigid, I was prepared to wait until hell froze over for an answer. Me and ol' Adlai Stevenson. Sometimes when you're facing down the enemy, you just have to fold your arms and wait it out.

It only took a hundred rings or so.

"This is harassment," she said.

"This is important."

"Miss Foster, why won't you just leave me alone?"

"Your daughter is dead, Brigid. She was nineteen years old and someone killed her with an ax. Don't you care what happened to her?"

"I thought they caught the guy."

Ah. Base hit.

"They've arrested someone. A man named Gordon Pryne. Do you know him?"

"No."

"Who is Anael?"

Silence.

"Brigid?"

"I thought you said it was a brand of watches."

"You and I both know it isn't a brand of watches."

"Who told you about Anael?"

"Drew did. Indirectly."

"I didn't know Drew knew about Anael."

"Do you know what that means? 'Anael watches'?"

"The Watchers are watching. Always watching." She made a

little choking sound, and then sniffed loudly. It sounded to me like she was crying.

"Brigid? Stay with me here, okay? Who is Anael?"

She didn't answer.

"Do you know anything about her father's death?" I asked. "And her husband's? It seems like there were a lot of coincidences—"

"Drew's father was a terrible man," she snapped. "And that husband of hers was just disgusting. Absolutely disgusting. She never should have married that man."

"I didn't get the impression she had much choice."

"It was those Jesus people. They made her."

"The ones you left her with," I reminded her.

"I didn't think it would be like that. I thought she'd be safe."

"From what?"

She didn't say anything.

"From what, Brigid? The Watchers? Anael?"

"The Watchers are always watching," she said.

"I know. You told me that already. Is that who you wanted to save her from?"

"All I ever wanted was for her to be safe."

"Well, she wasn't. Do you know what happened in East Texas? On Stringer Road at 3:30 a.m.?"

"I believe they both fell asleep. Happens all the time," she said.

"On the same road? At exactly the same time of night? And they both happened to be related to Drew Sturdivant? And to you?"

"Possibly the supernatural was involved. Did you ever think of that, Miss Foster? That the universe may not be what it seems?"

"All the time."

"You can't pin that on me. I was nowhere near that road."

"I didn't suggest you were."

"Well you can't. I was nowhere near that road. I can prove it."

"Okay," I said. "Calm down. No one's suggesting you were involved."

"Besides, Drew's death is completely unrelated."

"How do you know that?"

"I just know. I do."

"Okay."

She was definitely crying now. "I'm asking you to leave me alone. I can't talk about any of this. I won't."

"Why? Is it dangerous?"

"Everything's dangerous."

And she hung up.

30

~

When I got home that night, my power was on and my water heater was working. Melissa was sleeping comfortably in her hutch, and there were no rats dying under my kitchen sink. If my answering machine light hadn't been on, it would have been a clean entry. I pushed the button and fished a pad and pen out of a drawer, waving away the stench of obligation I always feel when I see that stupid red light blinking at me.

My father had called again, livid that I'd be missing Kellee's baby shower in June. I'd seen it coming, of course, but this was a longer rant than I'd expected. I pushed replay and timed the message. Over three minutes. He was pretty mad. I should probably call him back.

Mending fences with my dad, a girl could get electrocuted. I just wasn't up to it at the moment. My life was scary enough already. I pushed "erase" and moved on.

The only other message was from Detective McKnight, who had returned my call and wanted me to call him back at my earliest convenience. I called him up on his cell phone, which turned out to be a big fat mistake.

"Detective, this is Dylan Foster. Returning your call?"

"All due respect, Dr. Foster, you want to tell me what exactly you were thinking? I mean, I'd really like to know. Just for my own personal knowledge."

"Pardon?"

"You can't just up and visit a suspect in a murder investigation. Not without authorization. Do you understand what we're trying to do here? I mean do you have any understanding at all of what you're messing around with? This is a murder investigation. You are not an investigator on this case. We have a dead girl and a solid suspect. We've got the suspect in custody. He already has a thing for you. I don't need you traipsing in there and—"

"Wait a minute, Detective. Slow down. I didn't just decide to go see him on a whim. It's not like I don't have anything better to do with my time. I had permission."

"Who authorized it?"

"Detective Martinez," I stammered. "I didn't know I was breaking a rule or anything. I'm sorry."

"Martinez authorized it?"

"Check the log. He signed me in."

"He should have checked with me first."

"Okay, fine. I understand that. Completely. Could you please take that up with him instead of yelling at me?"

"I will," he said. "At the first opportunity."

He was starting to calm down now. Maybe he'd just needed to let off some steam. I seem to be good at that—triggering the explosion. It's like a gift.

"Why did you want to see Pryne?" he asked.

"He asked for me. It wasn't the other way around, believe me."

"Oh." He cleared his throat. "I'm sorry I yelled at you. It's been a long day."

"It's okay. I should have told you. I didn't think about it, I guess. My mistake."

"It's okay. It's just that we're getting so close to nailing this guy. I don't want anything screwing it up. No offense."

"Why? What happened?"

"PES has preliminaries."

"PES? I forgot what that is."

"Physical Evidence Section. Forensics. Fibers on the body are consistent with fibers on a jacket we took from Pryne's apartment. Denim and fleece."

"You think he had the jacket on when he killed her?"

"Possibly."

"Was it bloody?"

"No."

"Had it recently been washed?"

"No."

"That doesn't make sense."

"It will. When we know the whole story, it will all make sense. It always does. Probably he had something on over it. An overcoat or something. There are still some fibers we haven't accounted for."

"But you haven't found the overcoat."

"We will."

"What about the gloves?"

"We'll find those too."

Another optimist. Where do these people get it? I'd like to try a bottle, please.

"What about time of death?" I asked. "Any news on that?"

"Between 6:30 and 7:30."

"How do you know?"

"He was seen with the complainant at 6:30. And the ax showed up on your doorway at 7:30. According to your statement. He made a drug buy at the Circle Inn at 8:25."

"The Circle Inn? That dump on Northwest Highway?"

"Rent-by-the-hour, day, or week. A real pigsty. Pryne's residence at the time of the murder."

"Didn't he go to see Maria Chavez at 5:30?"

"Yeah. Busy night."

"How far is it from the Circle Inn to Critter Cars?"

"Two-point-seven miles."

"Does he have a car?"

"No."

"How'd he get there and back so fast?"

"Must have caught a ride. We're looking into that."

"He must've had a car to get from Critter Cars to my house. How far is that?"

"Five-point-four miles. Driver must be the guy he's working with. We've got some leads."

"More drug dealers?"

"You doubting our case, Dr. Foster? You know something I don't?"

"There are just some things that don't fit for me."

"Such as?"

"Such as the fact that he put Drew's body in the trunk of a car."

"So? He didn't want anyone to find it until morning. Bought himself a little time."

"But he never does that. He didn't conceal evidence in any of his other crimes. He just blows in, ruins someone's life, and then leaves. Why the sudden concern for secrecy?"

"Maybe he didn't want to go back to prison. He's an escaped convict. Anyone spots him, he's in a van on his way back to Huntsville in twenty-four hours. Murder like this? He's looking at the death penalty. With his record."

"He's not exactly the kind of guy that thinks that far ahead, detective. Especially if he was on a meth high. Is that what he bought at the Circle Inn?"

"What are you saying? That he didn't do it? All our evidence points to him. Everything."

"Okay. Go back to the car lot. How'd he get the body past the dog? The dog comes at seven, right?"

"How do you know about the dog?"

"I talked to Kay Basieri."

McKnight swore under his breath. "Who else have you talked to?"

"Brigid."

"Brigid who?"

"Drew's mother. She doesn't use a last name."

"Drew's mother's name is Alison."

"Alison Sturdivant is her aunt. Her mother's name is Brigid. She lives in Louisiana. She's a psychic."

"The Sturdivants aren't her real parents?"

"Didn't they tell you that?"

"They wouldn't see me," McKnight said. "They said they didn't have a daughter. Insisted that their only daughter had died two years ago."

"When Drew divorced the husband, right? It's called shunning. They shunned her. It's a Jesus commune thing. Isn't that sick?"

"What, exactly, have you been doing, Dr. Foster? That you know more about this investigation than I do?"

"I just...asked around," I said, suddenly realizing I'd gotten myself into trouble again.

"Well, could you stop it, please? And leave the investigating to the investigators in this case? I mean, we are professionals. We've done this before. Once or twice. For crying out loud."

"Don't you want to know what she said?"

"Brigid? No, I don't. I'll talk to her myself."

"Do you want her phone number?"

"I do not. I think I can find a phone number without your help."

"You might want to look into the car accidents."

He swore again. "What car accidents?"

"Drew's ex-husband and her father both died in single-car accidents on the same road in East Texas. At 3:30 a.m."

"The same day?"

"No. Nine years apart. I don't think they even knew each other."

"Well, what's it got to do with anything, then? It's just a coincidence."

"I don't think so. Brigid sounded really suspicious when I asked her about it."

I heard him dig around on his desk, swearing again. "Okay," he said finally. "What's her number?"

I told him. "She probably won't answer the phone, though."

"Why not?"

"I sort of made her mad."

Swearing again. "What did you go and do that for?"

"It was an accident. I lost my temper. A little bit."

"Terrific."

"Yeah, I know. It's one of my worst qualities. Top ten, for sure. Why don't you just have someone pay her a visit? I bet you'd find out more in person anyway."

"Thanks for the advice," he said. "Anything else I should know?"

"I think Drew was into angel worship."

"What's that got to do with anything?"

"I don't know. I just think it's important."

"That's all the stuff on her headboard, right?"

"Yeah."

"What language is that?"

"Hebrew."

"Did you find out anything about Anael watches?"

"Anael is the angel of the second heaven. He's in charge of Fridays."

More swearing.

I kept going. "He's one of the Watchers in the book of Enoch. 'Watches' is a verb, not a noun. I thought it was a brand of watches, too."

McKnight sighed. "Can you write it all down and e-mail it to me? Save me the aggravation?"

"Sure," I said. "How much detail do you want?"

"Summarize."

"Okay. I'll have it for you tomorrow. What about the boy-friend? What's-his-name. Finn. Did you talk to him yet?"

"He's clean. Solid alibi. No priors."

"Anything interesting in the autopsy?" I asked.

He paused. "Nothing of note." Another pause, and I noticed, a rapid subject change. "What did Pryne want?"

"He wanted me to get the spirits to stop watching him."

McKnight chuckled. "Did you do it?"

"Not yet. I'm working on it, though."

"Right. Let me know when you've got that done, will ya? I'll see you get a commendation or something. Man's a nutcase."

"Detective, can I ask you something?"

"Sure."

"Do you think he did it? Really? Bottom line?"

"Yes. Absolutely no question in my mind."

"How can you be so certain?"

"Nine times out of ten the most obvious answer is the right one."

"The Occam rule."

"What's that?"

"Occam's Razor, it's called. Occam was a thirteenth-century philosopher. French, maybe. I forget. He developed this idea that in complex situations, barring the supernatural and the incredible, the simplest explanation is usually true."

"Well, he's right. I just didn't know it had a name. The evidence is lining up, Dr. Foster. It always does. Especially in a case like this, where the complainant knew the killer."

"That reminds me, detective. I keep forgetting to ask—was Drew sexually assaulted before she was killed?"

"Nope."

I thanked him for his time, apologized again for intruding on his case, and we said our good-byes.

I hadn't realized until that phone call how much information I'd gathered. McKnight was right. I'd been poking my nose around where I had no business doing so. Naturally, I had no intention of stopping now.

I'd promised McKnight a summary of my findings. I typed them up, all nice and neat, leaving out all references to Peter Terry, and printed an extra copy for myself. I made myself a to-do list for the next day. I called David one more time. Once again he didn't pick up.

I left him another contrite message, then started to get ready for bed. I wanted to make it an early night. I needed the rest.

I got undressed and started the bath water, then took off the necklace David had given me for my birthday. I fingered the moonstone, thinking about how thoughtful he'd been to go to all the trouble to find this necklace for me.

I'd mentioned to him once, months ago, that I liked moonstones. I love the opaque white—translucent without being transparent.

He'd known, of course, about the other necklace I have that was made by Rosa Guevera. The one I'd gotten that day at Barton Springs. To take the trouble to track down a moonstone necklace by the same designer—it was such a David thing to do. So thoroughly thoughtful and sweet. David's extra-mileness knocks me over sometimes.

I hated that I'd made him mad. I hated that I'd neglected him even the teeniest little bit. He deserved better. I didn't blame him for being tired of dealing with me. I was pretty tired of dealing with me too.

I turned the stone over and looked at the workmanship. I'd probably never meet Rosa Guevera, but I felt like I knew her. And

I could feel the connection with my mother when I wore Rosa's jewelry. My mother had given Rosa her start. And this is what I had to show for it.

I ran my finger along the silver back of the stone and felt the ridges of Rosa's mark: *RG,* with a little symbol next to it.

I squinted and flipped on the nightstand light, holding the necklace close to the bulb. For the first time, I noticed the symbol next to Rosa's initials.

It was an ankh.

31

~

I was up early and standing at the door in the cold when they unlocked Bridwell Library the next day. I wasn't sure how Rosa Guevera fit in, but it didn't take much time to connect the ankh to the rest of the story. The ankh is an ancient Egyptian glyph for magical protection. And according to angelic lore, it was also Anael's symbol. Whether this meant he flew around with one around his neck or what, I had no idea. Eli had said something about Anael's association with the Anakim—the Wearers of Necklaces. And now there it was, in plain black and white.

With Anael in charge of the demon pit, I could only guess that Drew had somehow begun to call on Anael, in some way that felt comforting to her, to protect her from the Peter Terrys of the world. Whether she'd met Peter Terry personally, I still didn't know. But the girl had enough inner demons to colonize a small village in hell, so I figured it was likely their paths had crossed at some point.

I felt myself slipping into another fit of sadness for her, but shook myself out of it quickly. Mondays are teaching days for me. Like it or not, I had no choice but to drill a hole through my pre-occupation with Drew's fate and pay attention to more immediate matters.

I packed up my stuff, shouldering my resolve as I slung my book bag onto my back and trudged through the cold to the other end of campus. I spent the rest of the morning with my office door closed, prepping for class and returning work-related phone calls and e-mails for the first time in almost a week. Lunch was quick—a cheeseburger from Jack's (milkmaid thighs be damned)—followed by a few student appointments.

My class was lively that afternoon, the debate sharp and stimulating. I felt grounded by the time I left, like I'd stepped back into reality from the other side of that stupid magnifying mirror. It was good to be behind my eyes again, inside my own skin, if even for a few hours.

I stopped by Helene's office after class.

"It's over there," she said, pointing.

She'd brought the cobbler in an insulated Tupperware thing that zips around a rectangular lidded pan. Leave it to Helene to have the good gear.

I picked up the cobbler. "It's still warm."

"You're welcome," she said.

I unzipped the cover and tipped the lid. The smell was intoxicating. Rich and buttery.

She looked up at me over her glasses. "It won't work unless you stuff your lousy attitude into that big leather bag of yours. You know that, don't you? Without that, it's just dough and fruit."

I sighed. "The man brings out the worst in me. He truly does. Every time I look at him, I'm just overcome with hostility."

"Well, try and contain yourself this one time. It's in your own best interest."

"I will. Believe me. I'm going over there right now." I turned to leave. "And Helene?"

"What?"

"Thanks."

"Go."

I made a quick trip to the grocery store across the street for a half-gallon of Blue Bell Country Vanilla ice cream, the pièce de résistance. Then gathered it all up and made the trek across the campus to the clinic.

I took a breath and knocked on John's office door.

I knew by now what to expect. There was the startled scoot of the chair, the scrambling and shuffling of papers, and the plodding walk across the room. He opened the door a crack.

I pasted a reasonably genuine smile on my face. "Hi," I said, as sweetly as I could manage.

John studied me dully, his face flushed and sweaty.

"Hello, Dr. Foster."

"Hi," I said again.

I'd decided that leaving out the nomenclature entirely would avoid the Dr. Mulvaney situation.

"I was wondering if you had a minute. I know you're busy." (I pictured Harold cheering me on.) "But I'd like to talk to you for a second. If you can break away from your work." I held up the cobbler. "I brought snacks."

He eyed me suspiciously. "What snacks?"

"Cobbler," I said triumphantly. "With Blue Bell ice cream."

"Just a minute." He closed the door in my face.

I put my ear to the door and listened while he shuffled around again. John acts as though his research is top-secret, Nobel-caliber stuff. I think he really believes he's doing something important in the universe with his little rat-maze experiments.

He cracked the door again. "Okay." He held out his hand for the cobbler. I think he actually meant to take the dish and leave me in the hallway empty-handed, if you can believe that.

I clutched the cobbler and took a little step backward. "I thought we could sit down for a minute. If you're free."

"I'm busy."

"I know. I'm really sorry. It'll just take a minute."

He looked at the Tupperware longingly.

"Helene made it. It's, uh…" I searched my memory, "some sort of blueberry situation, I believe."

He looked back inside his office, then back at me. He was weakening. I could feel it.

I then heard myself jabbering like a set of wind-up teeth. "Boy, I need a break like you wouldn't believe. Don't you? Man, oh man. I worked like a mad woman today. Academic life is really hard, don't you think? People don't understand the work-load, I tell ya. They think we just sit around all the time and teach a class here and there when we get around to it. But it's tough. Overworked and underpaid. Yep, that's us." I smiled again. I tried to make this one seem more sincere.

He hesitated, then stepped back and opened the door all the way.

I followed him over to his desk and started to put the cobbler down. John walked past me and left the office, the door standing open behind him. I stood there, mute, and watched him go. The man had the social savvy of a dead lizard. On his good days.

I pushed some papers out of the way and set the cobbler and ice cream down while I waited for him to come back.

It was freezing in his office, as usual. I walked over to Ozzie and Harriet and looked inside. The rats were curled up together in a ball. They looked up at me and sniffed, their little pink noses twitching. I shuddered, remembering my last encounter with a rat.

"Sorry, you guys," I said out loud. "It was nothing personal."

I walked the rows, past mice and rats until I got to a cage with a rabbit in it.

I leaned in over the top. "Hi, sweetie. How ya doing? Do you know my friend Melissa?"

The rabbit hopped over to me and stood on its back legs. It was a beautiful velvety gray, lop-eared and soft. I checked the tag on the aquarium.

"Hi, Eeyore," I cooed. "What's he got you doing? Nothing hard, I hope. Are you learning the maze?" I reached in and scratched its ears.

"They're not pets." John's voice came from the doorway.

I pulled my hand back quickly and turned around. "Sorry, John. It's just that someone gave me a—" I stopped myself as I saw the "John" register. Strike one.

"You'll screw up my research if you treat them like pets," he said in his thick monotone. "They don't need any affection."

"Aw, c'mon. Everyone needs affection. Don't you think?"

"That's a myth," he said. "A myth that propagates sentimentality. Animals need attachment only in the earliest stages of life. When they are unable to meet their own physical needs."

"What about Ozzie and Harriet over there?" I pointed. "They look pretty affectionate to me."

"They're a mating pair. Otherwise, they'd be in separate pens."

"Great names, by the way. Ozzie and Harriet. I used to love that show."

"I didn't name them. Someone else did."

"Oh." I resisted the urge to call him a heartless twit and instead said, a little too brightly, "How's the research coming, anyway?"

John stood there with his hands in his pockets and launched into a monologue about rodent brain activity and repetitious behaviors. I tried to look interested, but truly, it was impossible. As I tuned him out and watched his lips move, the droning of his words clunking along without me, I felt a little sorry for the rodents. They had to listen to it all day. They probably lived for the maze. At least when they were running for the cheese, there was something to look forward to.

Still talking, he eventually made his way over to the desk and removed something from his pocket. It was a large spoon, which I assumed he'd just retrieved from the kitchen. He opened up the cobbler, pried the lid off the ice cream, and then started eating, alternating bites, straight out of the containers, his face stuffed full, his mouth still chewing as he took each new bite.

"S'good," he said, through a mouthful of goo.

I took a step toward the door. Committee or no committee, I couldn't watch this massacre without losing my stomach entirely. Already I was doomed to spending the remainder of my life without blueberry cobbler. I felt myself starting to gag.

"Well, I should be going," I choked out.

"I tht ywntd ttlk abt smthg," he mumbled.

"It can wait," I said, still backing up. "I'll call you tomorrow. Okay, Joh…uh, I mean…yeah, okay. See you tomorrow. Thanks a lot."

I fled the office, pulling the door shut behind me and leaning against it to collect myself. I took a few breaths, trying to settle my stomach.

Marci was gone for the day by now. When my head had stopped spinning, I walked over to her desk and wrote John a chirpy "thanks for the great visit, hope you enjoyed the cobbler" note, then stuck it in his box and left, grateful for the cold air that hit my face as I stepped out of the building into the night.

My truck was parked across the campus near my office. As I started my walk up the tree-lined center avenue, hands in my pockets, my cell phone rang. I checked the number. It was David.

"I'm so glad you called," I said breathlessly.

"Hello, Dylan."

"You only call me Dylan when you're mad."

"Hurt, would be more accurate. I'm not great at mad."

"I'd rather you get mad and speak up than keep up the radio silence. If you'd talk to me, at least then I'd know how to respond."

"I don't like having to point out the obvious, Dylan."

"What's obvious? Point it out."

"Who's the guy?"

"What guy?"

"The one at your house at ten at night. Remember him?"

"Martinez? Nobody. He's a cop. He was dropping something by my house. You completely misinterpreted the situation."

There was a long silence. "I don't want to talk about this," he said.

"We have to eventually."

"Actually, we don't. That's the beauty of being an adult. It's one of life's big bonuses. We can just walk away from the whole thing and never talk about it at all. Ever."

"I don't want to do that."

"I do."

"Then why did you call if you don't want to talk about it?"

"Just passing along some news. I talked to Linda Fortenberry again today."

"And?"

"The baby was probably the boyfriend's. Blood types match, anyway. DNA will take a while."

"That makes sense, I guess. Thanks for telling me."

"Sure."

Another long pause.

"Talk to you later," he said.

"Come on, David. Don't do this. Can't we just—?"

"I need some time. I'll call you." He hung up.

I threw my phone in my purse. The night was crisp. Dallas's polluted air seemed less noxious than usual, and the stars were as bright as city stars can be, high above the copper-roofed dome of Dallas Hall. Live oak trees hugged in the view like a picture frame and the thin, remaining layer of snow crunched under my feet. I felt for a minute like I was walking inside one of those snow globes, when all the white is settled on the bottom. Everything is still and serene, right up until the moment someone picks it up and shakes it, unleashing the storm.

I stepped into the parking lot and kicked a remnant of ice off my boot.

I started my truck and flipped on the dome light, then fished in my bag for my notebook and paged through until I found the address I wanted. Now was as good a time as any. I had nothing better to do.

I pulled off the campus and eased my truck onto Daniel Avenue and into the traffic. Arlington was about twenty-five minutes from here. If the conversation was quick, as I expected it to be, I could make it there and back and be home to play with Melissa by nine.

32

~

I pulled onto Patrick Finnigan's street and pulled over a few blocks away from his house.

I cut the headlights and made myself think about Drew Sturdivant, picturing her driving down this street on a dark night, on her way to see the boy that was no man and not much of a boyfriend either. I tried to put myself in her place for a few minutes. I wanted to see Finn through her eyes, not through any preconceived notions I had. I was hoping the view would clear for me, that my perspective would widen enough to see what I was looking for.

Obvious answers are so distracting sometimes.

I found myself wishing, once again, that I'd bought that gun Detective McKnight had recommended. Who knows if I'd have the guts to use it? Still, I felt naked and unprepared. If Drew's boyfriend was what I thought he was, I'd have felt better packing a .38.

My phone rang, startling me and quickening my heartbeat. I said hello without looking at the number, hoping for David, but of course it wasn't him. It was my little friend Christine Zocci. Christine has the best Jesus radar of anyone I know. She practically sings with the angels. She always seems to know when I need to hear a friendly voice.

"Hey, Punkin," I said brightly.

"My mommy said I could call you if I wanted to."

"I'm glad she did, sweetie. What are you guys doing up there? About to have supper?"

"They're having macaroni."

"They are? What are you having?"

"I don't like macaroni."

"I didn't know that."

"I used to like it, but I don't anymore."

"Oh. Well, things change, don't they?"

"Did you use your lunchbox today?" she asked.

"I didn't use it today, but I used it Friday. Everybody was jealous."

"Why didn't you use it today?"

"I didn't take my lunch today. Did you?"

"Uh-huh," she said. "I had carrots, apples, and Fritos. I like Fritos."

"I like Fritos, too."

"And Cheetos," she said.

"Puffy or hard?"

"Hard," she said, as if it were the most obvious thing in the world. "The puffy ones are yucky."

"Hey, guess what?" I asked.

"What?"

"I got a bunny rabbit."

Christine squealed. "You did? What's its name?"

"Melissa. She has red hair like I do."

"Does she have long ears?"

"Yes."

"And a fluffy tail?"

"A big, fluffy tail and great big feet. Her ears are real long and soft."

"Where did you get her?"

Hm. It seemed inappropriate to explain to a five-year-old that

I'd gotten my bunny from a murdered girl. "A friend of mine gave her to me."

"Does she like carrots?"

"She does. And apples. Just like you."

"I only like crunchy food."

"Is that why you don't like macaroni?"

"It's not crunchy. Mommy wants to talk to you." The phone clattered as she dropped it and ran off to do something more interesting.

"Dylan?"

"Hey, Liz. Christine cracks me up. What's with the crunchy food?"

"She started that a few weeks ago. Her entire diet consists of carrots, apples, and Fritos."

"And Cheetos."

"Right. She just added those. I can't get her to eat anything else."

"How long will this last?"

"She seems committed. Hasn't eaten one Spaghetti-O since the first of the year."

"It's not a New Year's resolution, is it?"

"I hope not. She's five years old." She covered the phone and yelled at the boys to leave the cat alone, she doesn't want a haircut. And could they please get out of the dryer, it was time for supper. "My kids are so weird. Do you think that's me?"

"What about, like, hot dogs and French fries?"

"Not crunchy. Believe me, I've tried it all." She covered the phone. "What, honey?" I heard her say.

Then back to me. "Christine wants to know if you said you're sorry."

"To who?"

"She didn't say. She just...hang on a second."

Christine came back on the phone.

"What is it, Punkin?"

"Miss Dylan, when you hurt someone's feelings, you just need to say 'Oopsie, I'm sorry.' And then give them a kiss."

"Really? That's all there is to it?"

"Uh-huh."

"Okay. I'll try that."

And then she was gone again. Liz came back on the phone.

"Did you get that?" she asked.

I laughed. "What a simple formula. If only I'd known all this time. Think of the trouble I could've avoided. Ask her how she knows I need to say I'm sorry to someone."

Liz covered the phone and shouted the question. "Her angel told her," she said to me.

"Earl? Is he still the one?"

"There's only one, Dylan. It's always been Earl."

"Well, tell her I'll try it. Earl always knows."

"Maybe I can get him to talk her into eating like a normal person again."

"It's worth a try. He's the only one with any influence."

We talked a few minutes more. It calmed me down and reminded me that I had more to live for than a redheaded bunny rabbit and a boyfriend who wouldn't speak to me. The Zoccis were as close to family as I was getting lately, especially since my own family had begun to implode.

I said my good-byes, gathered my courage, tossed out a quick prayer for luck, and finished the short drive to Finn's house. I parked in the driveway and rang the doorbell.

I stood there a few minutes in the dark. The porch light snapped on and I could feel someone looking at me through the peephole. I tried to look nonthreatening.

The door swung open. A skinny young man of maybe twenty-five was standing there in baggy khakis that bunched up around his sneakers. His T-shirt said, "Rehab is for Quitters."

His long, black hair was pulled into a tidy ponytail.

"Hey," he said.

I waved. "Hi. Sorry to bother you. I'm Dylan Foster. I'm a friend of Drew's."

He squinted at me. "Dylan who?"

"Foster."

"I never heard of you before."

"I hadn't seen her in a while."

He stared at me without saying anything.

"Can I come in?" I asked. "I'd like to talk to you for a minute."

"Sure." He backed away from the door and let me walk past him into the plain, little house.

"Want some Ramen noodles? I was just about to eat."

"No, thanks. I'll only be a minute anyway. I don't want to interrupt your supper. I probably should've called first."

"It's okay."

He led me into a small living room, which was dominated by a huge, new, flat-screen television set. The only furniture in the room was a sagging couch, a coffee table, and a big brown recliner—the kind my parents had when they were still happily married. Before Watergate. It was that old.

Sparse as it was, the room was neat. There was no guy-litter lying around. None of the beer cans or newspapers I'd expected. The carpet was old but clean. There were no rings of sticky residue on the coffee table. I didn't smell cigarette smoke or dirty laundry. In fact, the place smelled faintly of Pine Sol. A magazine rack by the recliner held a few magazines. The one in front was *Rolling Stone*. The current issue.

I sat on the edge of the recliner. Finn took the couch.

"How did you know Drew?" he asked.

"It's kind of a long story," I said. "I'm a college professor." I figured that might suggest enough of a connection to satisfy him.

"I miss her," he said matter-of-factly.

"How long had you guys been seeing each other?"

"A few months. She was kind of screwed up, but she was a really nice kid." He looked down at his hands. "I miss her."

"What do you mean, screwed up?"

"Kinda mad all the time? And sorta…like, unpredictable."

"How?"

"She was all up and down. Happy one minute. All mad the next. Sometimes, she'd just start crying for no reason."

"Had she always been like that? Did she ever say?"

He nodded. "Since she was little. Up and down. Like a roller coaster." He laughed. "She didn't even like roller coasters. I didn't mind too much, though. She never really got mad at me."

"Did she ever say whether she'd been to a doctor for her mood swings? Had anyone ever diagnosed bipolar disorder? Anything like that?"

"You mean like a shrink or something? Her parents don't believe in medicine. They're real…" He looked around the room as if searching for the word. "Conservative," he said at last.

"Bob and Alison, you mean?"

"You know them?"

I shook my head. "I've never met them. But I heard they were like that."

"Kinda mean too. Drew had some pretty bad stories."

"Such as?"

"Like one time? They had this ol' dog and it got out of the yard one time and came back and had puppies under their back porch. And her dad found 'em and got mad. And while he was gone, her mom tried to drown the puppies. She put 'em in a pillowcase and threw 'em into the pond behind their trailer. Drew swam out there and got 'em. She got all but one, I think she said. She was real good with animals." He smiled. "She took a beating for that, she said. But it was worth it. She didn't mind a beating if it was worth it."

"You never hit her, did you?"

He looked up, startled. "I'd never hit Drew. I'd never hit no one. I'm not like that."

"I'm sorry, I didn't mean to be insulting. It's just that—"

"No offense, but I'd never do anything like that. The police asked me the same thing and I told them too. I didn't kill her, if that's what you're asking next. They got the guy that did it."

"I know," I said.

I looked at him, with his weak, watery eyes, his skinny white arms. He had a tattoo that wrapped around his wrist like a bracelet. He was nerdy and odd, but strangely likeable. I could see what Sharlotta meant. A boy and not a man. And not much of a boyfriend. He didn't seem like the sort of date who would exactly take charge of an evening or remember your birthday. But he seemed completely harmless.

I'd come over here thinking he'd done it. That he'd panicked about becoming a father and had killed her on impulse and then tried to cover it up. He just made so much more sense as a suspect to me than Gordon Pryne did. I figured meeting him would clear it up for me. One way or another.

"Did she ever mention any nightmares to you? Anything recent?"

"Drew had a lot of nightmares. When she ever slept. She wasn't a real good sleeper."

"Anything about a scary-looking bald guy, all white and bony?"

"You mean Peter Terry?"

The words slammed into my ears and just about knocked me over. I'd never heard anyone else mention Peter Terry by name. Not without hearing it from me first.

"What did she tell you about Peter Terry?"

"I never knew if she made him up or not. She had such a good imagination. She was real creative."

"I know."

"She dreamed about him a lot, though. She told me about it a couple of times."

"What did she say?"

"Just that she always woke up real scared."

"Did she mention a lake?"

He shook his head. "It was always the same thing. He was standing in the middle of the road at night. And then she'd hear tires squealing and somebody would start screaming and then she'd wake up."

I felt my skin go cold suddenly. "Who was in the car?"

"She never said."

I paused as the image sank in.

"How was Drew in the weeks before she died?" I asked. "Did she seem worried about anything?"

"She was always worried about something. She worked real hard in school." He paused. "She worked nights. That was one reason she didn't sleep too much, I think."

"You know where she worked."

"That dance place?" He shook his head. "I never liked it, but she said it was pretty good money. She was gonna stop after Christmas. She was saving up for a car."

"What kind?"

"Anything with tires."

I didn't ask about the baby. I had a pretty strong sense he didn't know. I figured the police would tell him soon enough.

I stood up. "I'm sorry I bothered you. I'll let you get to your Ramen noodles."

"Where'd you say you teach?" He stood and extended his hand.

"SMU," I said, without thinking. I'd meant to leave him with the impression I'd met Drew at El Centro.

"What do you teach?"

I picked up my bag and keys and started for the door. No sense lying now. "Psychology," I said.

His face lit up. "You know Dr. Mulvaney?"

"John Mulvaney?"

He nodded. "He's kinda weird, isn't he? He's not that bad, though, if you don't expect too much."

"How do you know Dr. Mulvaney?" I asked, noting that it didn't seem to bother me to use the title when he wasn't around to hear it.

"I supply his lab."

"Pardon?"

"His lab."

"I don't understand."

"C'm'ere, I'll show you." I followed him through the kitchen and into the back yard. The house sat on a double lot, one in front of the other. The back lot was rimmed by a ten-foot privacy fence that concealed a double-wide trailer. I followed him up the steps.

The trailer had no walls inside—just rows of tables and a sink at one end. Lights were strung from the ceiling to shine into the aquariums that sat atop the tables. I recognized the smell of cedar shavings, and the tinny squeak of little exercise wheels. I peered into one of the aquariums. Rats.

I looked up at Finn. "You raise rats?"

He nodded. "And mice. Any kind of rodent, really. They're all pretty much the same."

A light went on in my head. "You gave Drew a rabbit."

He nodded. "Melissa. Here's her litter-mate." He walked me over to another row. Inside the hutch was a little red bunny. "I kept this one. She didn't want me to sell it."

"What do you sell them for?"

He shrugged. "Oh, for research. Like Dr. Mulvaney does. It's real important for science and stuff like that. Or maybe to pet stores. Sometimes people buy them for their snakes."

"You'd feed that sweet bunny to a snake?"

He grinned. "Drew wouldn't let me sell it. She didn't want Melissa's sister getting eaten. I can't really blame her. She's a pretty nice rabbit. Sharlotta's got Melissa now. I might go over there and get her. This one's a little lonesome."

"Sharlotta gave her to me," I said, a little alarmed at the thought of losing her. "I sort of adopted her."

He smiled. "You did?"

"Do you mind if I keep her? I'm kind of attached to her already."

"Sure, you can keep her. I bet Drew would like that. She got real attached sometimes."

"Did John—Dr. Mulvaney ever meet Drew?" I asked.

He nodded. "Couple of weeks ago. She was over when he came to get a couple of breeders."

"Ozzie and Harriet."

He lit up. "Yeah! That's a real old TV show. I'd never heard of it before. Drew liked to name 'em all. She got too attached."

I extended my hand. "Thanks for your time, Finn. It was really nice to meet you. I'm glad you and Drew were friends."

"I miss her." He walked me to the front door. "Tell Dr. Mulvaney hi for me."

I shook his hand again. "I sure will."

33

~

I was pretty sure I'd figured out how to short sheet the devil. I could smell the truth. And it smelled just like cedar shavings. The truth's location, however, posed a particularly vexing problem. It was on the SMU campus. Inside the clinic building. Just on the other side of John Mulvaney's locked office door.

I'd let myself into the clinic against Helene's orders once before. And I'd enjoyed a few unauthorized visits into the archived case files over the years. But snooping around uninvited in a colleague's office—that was another matter entirely. I'd claim shooting rights if anyone did that to me. More than that, it was just the sort of activity that would not only enrage my review committee, but could get me and my milkmaid thighs hauled off to the Dean's office quicker than you can say "mandatory suspension without pay."

I suppose I should have called Jackson and McKnight and let them handle it. Or maybe Martinez. But honestly, the thought didn't even occur to me. Sometimes my impatience blinds me to simple, commonsense realities. It's another one of my Top Ten Terrible Traits. One I intended to start working on real soon. Right after I finished breaking into John Mulvaney's office.

The clinic building was dark, locked up for the night. I let myself in with my key, turned off the alarm system, and then locked the door and reset the alarm behind me. Marci is (quite appropriately) paranoid about people snooping through her desk, so she locks it up before she leaves at night and takes the only set of keys with her. Inside her desk, though, was the master key to the office. I had to get in there or I was a duck out of luck.

I looked through the stuff on her desk, eyeing the kitty-cat pencils and Garfield sticky notes, trying to remember what I'd seen in movies about jimmying locks. I tried a couple of paper clips first. That trick doesn't work, just so you know. I tried a nail file. I thought about trying a bobby pin I found on the floor, like in that movie *Misery*, but of course, I couldn't bring myself to pick it up. The thought of touching, even vicariously, Marci's nest of greasy grey hair was too much for me. I finally scored with a letter opener. It was just the right shape and size to slide into the keyhole, and with a gentle turn, achieved the click I was waiting for. The drawer slid open. I grabbed the key, shut the drawer and locked it, replaced the letter opener, and walked down the hall to John's office.

I knocked first, just to be sure, and then let myself in, shutting and locking the door behind me. I closed the blinds. No need to announce my criminal and unethical behavior to the whole campus. The place was lit with a bluish light, just enough to permit a thorough snoop.

The light came from a few aquariums that had been fitted with fluorescents. I guess John was subjecting those poor rats to sleep deprivation experiments or something. Funny how I'd developed so much empathy for them.

I started with John's desk, which revealed far more about the man than I could tolerate without a fresh bottle of Mylanta and some club soda. It took a few tries to crack his computer password, but eventually I remembered the Wisconsin sticker on his Honda (I'd forgotten he drove a Honda) and came up with Bucky Badger, the Wisconsin mascot, which opened John's sick inner world right up to me.

The desktop image on John's computer was my first clue. It was one of those dance photos they take at school events. The ones you wish your parents would just throw away. It's photos like this that remind most of us we should never run for office or become movie stars, to hedge against the off chance they'll surface in a magazine someday.

High school John was pimply and lumpy, his pale blue tux tight and his expression tighter. His pants were too short. His socks were white and his shoes were brown. Thick glasses sat askew on his stubby nose, and he held his date's hand awkwardly, smiling at the camera as though he'd just been caught pilfering his mother's panty drawer.

His date was equally homely, with a greasy brown Dorothy Hamill hairdo, a long yellow dress that looked like it had come from the costume room on the *Little House on the Prairie* set, and the same thick glasses. Her stiff, crooked smile revealed a mouthful of braces. They were a sad pair. And they both knew it.

The fact that this shy, pseudo-event remained significant to John after all these years seemed pitiful to me. It was probably his one date ever. And I was guessing he still looked at this photograph as the single thin shred of evidence of his citizenship in a club whose doors remained, all these years later, stubbornly closed to him.

John's computer screen faces the window and is angled away from the door. I'd never noticed before, but now that I thought about it, John always managed to stand between the screen and whoever was in his office, making sure no one could see what was on there. As I wound my way through his Internet files, I found out why.

John's computer was infested with pornography, mostly photographs and short film clips of women in humiliating sexual situations and men enjoying their misery. They weren't violent images, per se, just angry.

The images suggested to me a psychology of isolation, which I knew mirrored John's psyche with disturbing accuracy.

We'd had an entire seminar about pornography in graduate school. It was one of the more noxious courses in the long, rather unpleasant crucible of my graduate education, to be sure, but it had served to desensitize me to images like this. Though I found them disgusting, I muscled myself into a clinical mindset, stuck them in a mental file with John Mulvaney's name on it, and moved on.

The rest of his computer files were interesting for one reason and one reason only. They became chaotic and disorganized the Monday after Drew's murder. Up until that moment, John had kept immaculate records. That made sense, given his straight-line, scientific approach to life. John could turn an afternoon walk down the campus into a dizzying maze of procedural events without even realizing he was doing it. In fact, he was completely incapable of experiencing anything else about the journey—trees, sky, familiar faces. That his rigid, linear behavior had decompensated entirely after Drew's murder was telling, I thought.

I poked around some more, going through desk drawers systematically, top to bottom. I found nothing of note until I got to the bottom right-hand drawer. The locked one.

His keys were hidden in a cup full of pens on his desk. I fished them out and opened it up. It was like Halloween in there. Sugar Babies, Milk Duds, Three Musketeers, Hershey's chocolate in every possible permutation, Starburst, Sweet Tarts, Skittles. The drawer was a cyclone of disarray. Opened bags of candy were stored on top of dozens of empty wrappers, as though he were saving trophies or something. Some of the wrappers looked like they'd been licked clean.

I thought back to the day I'd run into him at the mall. I realized now that he had been on a massive food binge. It's a pattern my eating disordered patients are painfully familiar with. Usually it begins with a triggering event of some kind, which leads to extreme emotional discomfort.

Whatever had triggered John that day, and whatever feelings had tripped him up, he'd apparently found them intolerable and had resorted to comforting himself with an absurd amount of food. He'd been working on a load of cookies, a milkshake, and a gargantuan soft drink when I saw him. And that might have been just the wind-up. I've known binge eaters who could pack in three times that amount in one sitting.

It's an excruciating way to live, this secret life of self-immolation.

Standing there, sorting through the detritus of John's sordid little world, I felt a surge of pity for him. And sadness. Plain, ordinary sadness. My sympathy didn't extend so far as to excuse what he'd done, of course, but now that I'd seen John in cross-section, the ugly middle actually humanized him for me. I could see the bars, so to speak, of the cage he'd been living in. Candy bars, certainly. And strip bars, I suspected. Both served to cushion the blow of his solitary, pathetic life.

I locked up his desk and put everything back the way I'd found it. I snuggled Eeyore the bunny on my way out. Then I locked the place up, put Marci's key back in her desk, which I locked with the letter opener, and headed home. I called Detective McKnight on the way. He picked up immediately.

"Great news," he said, before I got a chance to tell him mine.

"What?"

"Gordon Pryne confessed."

"He what? That's impossible!"

"Two hours ago. Broke down bawling and admitted everything."

"That's impossible," I said again.

"Come again?"

"I don't think he did it."

"All due respect, Dr. Foster—"

"It's impossible. It doesn't fit. Pryne is a serial sexual offender, Detective. Why didn't he rape her before he killed her? And why did he hide her body? He's never that careful. Nothing about this crime fits Gordon Pryne's personality."

"Except the fact that he did it. Call me crazy, but that seems like a pretty good personality fit to me."

I told him what I'd found out about John Mulvaney.

"You seriously want me to consider a guy with no record, no history of violence, a respectable job as a professional in the community, and a tie to the victim that is tenuous at best? On the basis of Internet porn and some messy files? When I have a suspect who just signed a confession? All due respect, Dr. Foster—"

"Pryne is innocent, Detective. I'm positive he didn't do it."

"Tell that to Gordon Pryne," he said. "He seems to think he did."

And he hung up.

34

~

Gordon Pryne himself had shouted the clue at me, amidst ugly invectives and proclamations of innocence—all of which I'd roundly dismissed at the time. *Ask the rats*, he'd yelled. *Ask the rats*. I'd let the remark pass, of course, without seeing it for what it was. But the rats had taken me straight to John Mulvaney's office. I knew I'd been led there. By whom, I wasn't sure. Peter Terry, perhaps. I was certain now that he'd been in on this thing from the beginning.

I tossed in my bed most of the night, listening to the rats behind my walls, thinking about John Mulvaney. John's legendary social ineptitude had doomed him to a life without human companionship. He'd settled instead for a spurious form of stimulation that involved the humiliation of women—not uncommon for social misfits like him, who tend to blame women for their own stunning inability to relate to the opposite sex. I'd seen hints of that the year before when John had gotten so angry at me for having no interest in him socially.

If John's frustration were ever to escalate to the point of violence, I was certain it would be quick but gory, just as Drew's murder had been. A single blow to kill quickly and avoid the fight. And multiple blows following, indicating panic, rage—all sorts of complicated, powerful emotions, which he would be unable or unwilling to contain once the dam had broken.

Even the ax made sense. John would have chosen a weapon like that. They're common as dirt. If Helene owns one, just about everyone does, I was betting. Maybe he'd left the ax on my porch in a panic—not to implicate me, but get rid of it while drawing me into his drama. Or maybe to frighten me. The stalker note I'd received was a taunt, obviously. A jab to remind me he was out there. Watching.

It did dawn on me briefly that I could be jumping to a conclusion. Perhaps John had been connected to the murder, but had not actually committed it. It was possible he had witnessed it, I decided. But if so, why hadn't he come forward? What motivation would he have to keep silent?

I got up, put on my bathrobe and fluffy slippers, and let Melissa out of her hutch. It was three thirty—time to get up anyway. I'd surely hear from Peter Terry soon, with all the activity going on. He loves this kind of stuff.

I paced the kitchen and put the kettle on for tea, pausing to stare at Drew's photo on the refrigerator as I reached for a carton of milk.

"What's the answer?" I said out loud.

She looked back at me silently, her eight-year-old self freckled and wan, with her shaggy hairdo and her crooked smile.

I dug through my notebooks until I found Brigid's photo and stuck it on the refrigerator next to Drew's. The daughter was an unblemished, more confident version of the mother, a version of woman that I suspected Brigid had never been and could never hope to be. Perhaps Drew's anger, rooted in that free-spirited third-grader, had saved her, ultimately, from the strange, half-truth fate Brigid seemed to have found, lying to herself and anyone who would pay her to tell them what they wanted to hear. Drew had a hard life, but she had lived it on her terms. Defiant until the end. Small consolation.

I shut the refrigerator and squinted at the photos. The water began to boil on the other side of the kitchen. I tuned out the whistle of the kettle and focused on the pictures.

Drew's eyes were green, her hair a messy black fringe of neglect over eyes that seemed somehow aware of her destiny. She was the lost girl, collar askew, hating every moment of being photographed. Submitting to it out of…what? Not fear, certainly. Condescension, perhaps. Had she known that there was no winning? Had the odds, stacked so ominously against her, somehow impressed her, even in that tender, ignorant moment before it all came slamming down around her feet?

Melissa scratched at my ankle urgently, as if to nudge me toward the stove to quiet the kettle, which was screaming now for attention.

My feet stayed rooted by the refrigerator door, my eyes locked on to Drew Sturdivant's.

"What's the answer?" I asked again.

As my eyes moved back to Brigid's photo, the steam popped the top off the kettle and the whistle fell silent. I walked across the kitchen, turned off the stove, and poured the boiling water into the sink. I picked Melissa up and tucked her into her hutch with some raw, organic carrots, got dressed, and grabbed my keys.

If I hurried, I could make it to Shreveport by sunrise.

35

~

Brigid was clearly not a morning person. Normally, I find this to be a reassuring quality in the people I meet. I do not trust morning people. They are far too enthusiastic for me. But after several minutes of standing in the cold on Brigid's doorstep, pounding on her door with a blue fist, I was ready to make an exception. At least in the dead middle of winter on a frigid Saturday as the sun was rising.

Someone chained the door from the inside. It budged, an inch, and a woman with blowsy white hair with black roots fixed a groggy eye on me.

I tried to look respectable. "Hi. I'm Dylan Foster."

She slammed the door.

I knocked again.

"Go away!" she shouted.

"Not until you talk to me."

"I'll call the police!"

"Aw, come on, Brigid! I came all this way."

"I'm dialing!"

"I'll tell them about the car accidents on Stringer Road."

She cracked the door again. I found myself staring at that same eye, nowhere near groggy now.

"I had nothing to do with those car accidents on Stringer

Road. You cannot pin that on me, young lady."

"Yes, but you know who did."

She squinted at me. "You get off my porch or I will call the police." She said police like two words. Pole-lease.

"I'm not going until you talk to me. I just need five minutes."

"You get off my porch. I'm not going to say it again."

"Brigid, your daughter is dead. Are you going to talk to me or what?"

"I've got nothing to do with that."

She slammed the door again.

I pulled my cell phone out of my purse and dialed Brigid's number. I could hear the phone ringing inside the house.

"I am not answering that!" she shouted through the door.

"I'm not leaving until you talk to me."

"I'm calling the police."

"Five minutes, Brigid. That's all I want. I drove all this way. Please."

I heard some stomping around, a loud and somewhat alarming metallic click, and then she flung the door open. Brigid was standing there in her bathrobe, pointing a shotgun at me.

I jumped back and stuck my hands in the air. "Brigid, calm down. I just want to have a conversation."

"You get off my porch and get in that ugly truck of yours and go right back where you came from."

I smiled stiffly. "No need to insult the truck," I said, hoping the levity would settle her down, which it did not.

I squared my shoulders and tried to act like I wasn't intimidated by the double-barrel 12-gauge that had been shoved in my face. Though truthfully I couldn't be positive that I hadn't just peed in my pants.

"Five minutes. And then I'll leave."

"No."

"I need to know about Peter Terry."

I thought I saw a flinch, but she kept her voice steady. "I never heard of Peter Terry."

"I don't believe you."

She lowered the gun and glared at me. "You tell me why I should talk to you."

"I'm trying to find out who killed your daughter."

"They caught the guy that did it."

"They caught the wrong guy."

She looked at me for another long minute, then turned to walk into the house. I put my hands down and followed her inside. I could barely walk, my knees felt so weak.

I guess I should have called first.

She led me into the kitchen, pointed me toward a dirty, beige, vinyl dinette set, twisted the dial on an egg timer, and then leveled the gun at me again.

"Five minutes," she said.

"Can you put the gun down?"

"I will not." She motioned me to sit, which of course I did, even though I could tell the woman owned no effective cleaning products of any kind.

"Tell me about Peter Terry," I said.

"I don't know anything about Peter Terry."

"Come on, Brigid. I've only got five minutes here. Work with me. Is Peter Terry one of the Watchers?"

"All I know is he's a spirit from the other world. Like the others. Watching all the time."

"That must be annoying," I said, trying again to be funny.

"You have no idea what you're messing with, young lady. If you did, you'd turn right around and go back home where you belong."

"What about Anael? Who is he?"

"He told me he was Drew's guardian angel."

"He spoke to you directly?"

"When she was a baby." She shrugged. "They're all the same to me. Liars. I don't trust any of them. Not anymore."

"How did you meet Peter Terry?"

She paused, looking at me suspiciously over the gun barrel. "I channeled him," she said at last.

"Channeled him? What does that mean?"

"It means I lit some candles and did a reading one day for a customer and there he was."

"When was this?"

"January 10, 1986. A Friday."

"Why do you remember the date so well?"

"Day I met my late husband. He walked up to me on the dance floor like he'd known me all my life. Bought me a beer and just started talking and smiling and charming me into believing he wasn't the two-timing, no-good, gambling, whoring drunk he turned out to be."

She started talking and waving her hands around, pointing the gun every which way. I tried not to flinch every time she swung it in my direction. She was lost in her story, though, so eventually I settled down and watched her tell it.

I could see traces of Drew's angry beauty in her face, but it was almost unrecognizable, Brigid's faded features showing the hard wear of a person twice her age. She was a pale, pocked, used-up broomstick of a woman in a thinned out bathrobe, badly bleached hair sticking out everywhere, and yellowy nicotine stains on her fingertips.

Her kitchen was a wreck. Days' worth of dishes were piled in the sink. Tacky knickknacks covered every possible square inch of shelf and wall space. An opened carton of Marlboros was spilled onto the countertop, among cans of tuna and various bags of junk food. As though someone had dumped the groceries out of the sack and gone outside for a smoke without bothering to put anything away. About two weeks ago.

"I always blamed Peter Terry for bringing that loser into my life," she was saying.

"How long were you married?"

"Nine years, two months, and three days. Right up to the minute he slammed his Chevy into that tree on Stringer Road."

She set the gun down and reached for a pack of Marlboros, tapping the pack before she ripped it open. She dug in a few drawers until she came up with a book of matches, then lit the cigarette and took a long drag.

I tried to look relaxed and keep my eyes off the gun.

She smoked for a minute. I waited impatiently as the egg timer ticked. "That wasn't my fault," she said at last. "You can't pin it on me. I wasn't anywhere near that road. And I've never talked about it once, to anybody."

"Except Drew."

"That's right. She knew."

"What happened, Brigid?"

She looked at me and kept smoking.

The egg timer dinged.

"Time's up," she said.

"Brigid."

She kept smoking, though thankfully she left the shotgun where it was.

"I asked Peter Terry for a little help. That's all. A favor."

"And what happened?"

"King was dead by mornin'."

"Why'd you take Drew to the Jesus commune?"

"I thought she'd be safe there. From Peter Terry and his kind. My sister and her husband, they're real religious. I thought she'd be better off." She pushed the hair out of her eyes and looked at me, her eyes watery now.

"Yeah, that didn't work out too well, did it? And Drew's husband?"

She shook her head and smoked, dabbing her finger at the corner of her eye. "What do they call that? A coincidence? Yeah, that's it. A coincidence."

"Did you talk to Peter Terry about him too?"

Her hands were shaking. "He shouldn't have hurt my baby girl. That's all I've got to say about that."

"How well do you know Peter Terry?"

"Well enough to wish I'd never met him." She looked at me. "What's your story?"

"I met him last year. At a spring-pool in Austin, Texas. And he knew my mother, I think."

"Lucky you."

She nodded and motioned me to follow her, which I did, into a tiny, cluttered room with a window-unit air conditioner, a sink with a neck-hole in it, and one of those old beauty shop chairs with the hair dryer attached.

"I do hair," she said, as she leaned over in a corner and pawed through stacks of papers and books. She came up with a photo album, flipped the pages, and handed the book to me, pointing with a yellow-stained finger.

"I threw all the rest away. I only kept this one because Drew was in it."

It was a photo of Brigid and a slim, good-looking man in pressed Wranglers, pointy-toed cowboy boots, and a white Stetson. I could see how he'd be a charmer. He had that rakish ain't-I-a-stinker look about him. Drew had clearly gotten her good looks and her fighting spirit from him. He and Brigid were each holding the hand of a poodle-girl version of Drew. She wore a stiff pink dress, white gloves, and a bonnet. Her anklets were little explosions of white lace. No wonder she'd taken to making her own clothes. The three of them stood in front of a commercial garage with a sign on it that said, "The Tire King—New and Used Tires, Retreads and Repairs. King Sturdivant, proprietor. Since 1979."

"Easter Sunday," Brigid said. "Two days before he died. His parents took that picture." She tapped the photo. "Named their only child King. What does that tell you? They thought that man set the world to spinning. He could spit on 'em both between the eyes and they'd a thanked him for it."

"May I?" I asked.

"Have at it."

I flipped back to the beginning and began paging through photos from Brigid's childhood. I got to the junior high years and stopped cold. I recognized the crooked smile, the thick glasses, the bad skin.

I looked up at Brigid and studied her face again. "Where did you grow up?"

"Just south of here. Till tenth grade. My dad moved us to Beaumont when the oil business took off. He did refinery work."

I flipped another page and pointed at the school dance photo.

"Tenth grade," she said. "Nicest boy I ever knew in my whole life. Shy. And nothing to look at. Sweet as a cupcake, though, and sweeter than that to me." She shook her head. "I coulda married him if my daddy hadn't moved us. I'da been a lot better off, I tell you that much." She tapped the photo. "He went off to college. Someplace north. He was older than me. I married King right after that. I was sixteen. Thought I knew everything there was to know." She shook her head.

"Did Drew ever meet him?"

"I never saw him again after he left for college." She looked up at me. "He's a genius, you know. He's a doctor now. Dr. Mulvaney. Don't that sound nice? I coulda been a doctor's wife." She took another drag on her cigarette and stumped it out in the sink. "I'da turned out different if I'd married him. Instead of that rattrap loser King Sturdivant."

"Brigid, could I borrow this photo?"

She looked at me sideways, her crooked mouth frowning down. "I'll want it back."

"Absolutely."

She pulled it out of the album and handed it to me.

I took the photo, thanked her for her time, and left before she had a chance to pick up the shotgun again.

I called McKnight from the road and woke him up.

"Drew Sturdivant knew John Mulvaney," I said.

McKnight swore. "Haven't we already had this conversation?"

"He was her mother's junior high boyfriend. I have a picture of the two of them together. I'm holding it in my hand. John has the exact same one on his computer at work."

McKnight swore again. "I'm listening."

"Can't you just check it out? Check the fingerprint on the note? Check his trunk? Something?"

"I'll have to get a warrant for the trunk," he said. "That'll take a little time. I can ask him to voluntarily submit a fingerprint."

"Great. Do that."

"I'll go over there today. You got an address for him?"

"Just an office address. But it's Saturday."

"I realize that, Dr. Foster. No home address?"

"No."

"How do you know about the picture on his computer?"

"I saw it in his office yesterday." I left out the part about breaking in. "He uses it as a screen saver."

"You're not there now?"

"I'm in the car. On my way back from Shreveport. I went to see Brigid. I just came from her house."

"It's not even eight in the morning."

"Yeah, she wasn't too happy about that part."

"She say anything about those car accidents?"

I thought about telling him, but couldn't imagine what the point would be. Peter Terry had gotten away with two more killings. There was nothing I could do about that now.

"She just said she wasn't there. She said it was probably a coincidence."

"Didn't I tell you that?"

"Will you call me after you talk to John Mulvaney?"

"Why not? You already ruined my day."

36

~

I drove the rest of the way back to Dallas squinting in the bright, cold sunshine, my head throbbing. Three cups of coffee and a dose of Extra Strength Bayer later, my head was still spinning, the swirl of thoughts almost nauseating me as the stripes on the road rushed under my truck.

I headed straight for the campus when I got back to town and went for a swim, hoping to clear my head. I needed to keep moving. I was looking, I guess, for the comfort—that false sense of progress—that forward movement can provide.

McKnight had left me a message by the time I got out of the pool. John Mulvaney had refused to submit a fingerprint.

I dialed McKnight.

"What did he say?" I asked.

"Threatened to call his lawyer, accused me of invading his privacy, violating his constitutional rights. Stuff like that. Lame, white-collar, intellectual horse manure."

"Did you tell him why you wanted the fingerprint? You didn't mention the note, did you? Or me?"

"Dr. Foster, you seem to be under the impression that I recently fell off the back end of a cattle truck. Of course I didn't mention the note. Or you. I am not a complete imbecile."

"Sorry. What are you going to do now?"

"Get a warrant. Man's got something to hide. That's obvious."

"So you think he did it? I'm right, aren't I?"

"I didn't say that. Did I say that? I said the man had something to hide. That's all."

"What does Jackson think?"

"Jackson would think I was nuts if he knew I was listening to you."

"You haven't told him any of this?"

"Detective Jackson has been a homicide detective for fifteen years. We have evidence. We have opportunity. We have a pattern of priors. And we have a confession. He's not looking for anything else."

"So you're just doing me a favor?"

"I'm trying to close this case, Dr. Foster. That's my only concern here. Gordon Pryne confessed, for crying out loud. The evidence fits. He did it. But I would like to know how that ax ended up on your porch. On the off chance John Mulvaney knows something about that or is connected to this crime in some way, I am willing to get to the bottom of that. I'm tying up loose ends. That's all."

"Thank you."

"Don't thank me. I'm doing my job. And it's a hard enough job without any more help from you."

"Okay, sorry. When will you get the warrant?"

"If I have a chance, I'll go down to the jail this afternoon and get the magistrate on duty to sign it. Otherwise, it'll have to wait until Monday."

"Oh. Why?"

"I'm off tomorrow."

I waited.

"Not that it's any of your business," he said at last.

"Oh. Sorry."

"John Mulvaney is not going anywhere between now and Monday. Neither is Gordon Pryne."

"Neither is Drew Sturdivant."

"That's right, Dr. Foster. Drew Sturdivant is staying right where she is. Nothing we do between now and Monday will change that. Why don't you try to relax or something? Take in a movie."

"I can't. Not until I know what happened."

"No offense, Dr. Foster, but I really don't consider that to be my problem."

By this time, I'd grown accustomed to people hanging up on me. I no longer took it personally.

I threw my phone in my purse, showered, and got myself warmed up and dried off. I felt better knowing that McKnight was at least willing to get a warrant. I was still edgy, though, and steered my truck over to the clinic, unwilling to leave well enough alone. Some people never learn.

Saturdays are busy clinic days, but I doubted there would be much traffic before noon, given the sleeping patterns of our clientele.

Sure enough, only one of the offices was in use, muffled conversation coming through the closed door. I checked the clock. I should have at least ten minutes, depending on whether the session was running on the hour or the half hour.

I worked quickly, unlocking Marci's desk with the letter opener and letting myself into the top drawer. I grabbed the key and shut the drawer. I intended to be in and out quickly, the key locked back in the drawer within a minute or two.

John Mulvaney and I have one thing in common—other than the fact that neither of us can stand him. We both hate to return phone calls. I had a hunch there was a pile of message slips somewhere on his desk. I let myself into his office and locked the door behind me.

I found the messages stacked neatly on his desk, underneath a colossal paperweight shaped like a big wedge of cheese. I thumbed through the slips and found it immediately. A message to John Mulvaney from Drew Sturdivant, dated two days before she died. I squinted to read the writing in the dim light. It must have been one of Marci's depressed days. I could make out only the names and "iend of her other's." I pawed through the rest of the slips but found nothing significant. I tapped the stack back into place and stuck the paperweight on top, folding Drew's message carefully into my pocket.

I would have slipped out of the office in quiet triumph if I hadn't heard a sound that made my blood freeze up right then and there. Someone had shoved a key in the lock.

I crouched behind the desk as the door slid open and John's heavy footsteps thudded into the room. I heard him shut and lock the door.

Screaming seemed a bad idea. I clamped my hand over my mouth and tried to track his footsteps instead.

He headed first toward the lit aquariums on the table at the other end of the room. He ran some water and walked among the rows, filling water bottles, I guessed, and dumping food pellets into stainless steel bowls. A few of the exercise wheels started to spin. Then he started for the desk. I ducked underneath and slid as far back as I could against the wood in the leg-hole.

I'd never noticed John's feet before. They were stubby clubs sheathed in, of all things, Wolverines—those yellowy-tan work shoes with the steel toes that construction workers wear. New ones. I could smell the leather. I'd pictured oxfords. With frayed laces and warped soles. Whatever his reasons for wearing the Wolverines, they looked to me like they could kick a hole through the side of a concrete bunker, and would certainly make quick work of me. I flattened myself against the inside of the desk, my eyes on John's feet and my ears pricked, trying to make out what he was doing.

John stood by the desk for a minute, shuffling things around. He opened the blinds, then grabbed the chair and sat. There was a quick shove of the chair toward me as he scooted forward. His foot stopped an inch or so short of my thigh. I sat there, trying not to breathe, thinking that possibly my Thigh Recovery Program had saved my life.

I heard a whir as he turned the computer on, and the thunk of the paperweight over my head as he moved it to look through the messages. Then swearing. He tore through his drawers, finally unlocking the candy-stash drawer and dumping a bunch of the wrappers onto the floor in a frenzy. If he got down on the floor to go through them, I was sunk. He'd see me for sure. I closed my eyes.

A minute of silence and then a violent groan as he shoved the chair backward.

I heard him pacing the room. There were sounds I couldn't identify. Shuffling. Stomping. My guess was he was tearing his office apart looking for that message—which, I surmised, he'd come to his office on a Saturday morning to get. The phone call from McKnight had surely triggered the search.

I sat underneath his desk and listened as he continued to ransack his office. The racket somehow made it easier to breathe. I took long, even breaths and tried to slow my pulse and calm myself down. Eventually, the door jerked open and John walked out. I didn't hear the door click behind him.

I peeked my head out from behind the desk and listened for footsteps. I tiptoed over to the door and looked through the crack, then made a run back for the desk as I saw John walking back down the hall toward his office.

I ducked back underneath the desk. John walked straight to the desk and sat down, scooting his chair all the way in, hitting me this time with both feet.

He ducked his head down and stared at me.

"Hi, John." I smiled stiffly. "It was unlocked."

"What was?"

"Your office."

He moved with surprising agility and strength, grabbing me by the hair with both hands, then dragging me out from underneath the desk. I shrieked and clutched his wrists, trying to pry his hands off my hair. He let go, shoving me against his desk. Pens scattered everywhere. Message slips went flying. Before I knew it, he'd stalked across the room, slammed the office door shut, and turned on me again. I found myself face to face with the rage, the angry animal strength, that Drew Sturdivant must have encountered in her last moments.

The feeling that surged through me at that moment was primal. A raw panic, unlike anything I've felt before or since. I felt claustrophobic. My chest began to cramp. My arms went numb. I couldn't breathe. It was all I could do not to double over and cry and beg for mercy.

"What are you doing in my office?" he asked quietly.

"John, I—"

"Answer me."

"John, calm down."

He pointed at the floor. "Pick those up."

I looked down at the message slips, scattered everywhere.

"Okay." I knelt down and gathered them up, careful to keep an eye on the paperweight in his hand. "Calm down, okay?"

John snatched the stack out of my hand and thumbed through them. He looked at me. "Give it back."

I stood up slowly and took a step backward. "Give what back?"

He picked up the paperweight and raised his arm to hit me. "I want it back. Now."

I edged away, cornering myself against the aquariums, and put my hands out defensively.

"John. Calm down. You're not going to hit me. We both know that."

He lunged for me then, swinging the paperweight at my head. I ducked, shoving the table backward and toppling the entire row of aquariums. Glass shattered. Rodents began to scatter around the room.

John lunged for me again. I crawled on my hands and knees over the broken glass, scrambling to get away from him. Blood began to show through my jeans. I had a vague notion that I was in pain. And an almost clinical realization that I was bleeding.

John grabbed my hair again and yanked me backward. Another table toppled. Mice and rats—surely gleeful at their unexpected bounty of luck—surged from the wreckage. Cedar shavings were everywhere.

John threw me against his desk again and took a step backward, his chest heaving.

He was shaking now, his face reddening.

"Give it back."

"John, Marci has a copy. Those message pads are in duplicate. She keeps them, like, forever. It's clinic policy. It's probably locked up somewhere right now."

He hesitated, glancing at the door, then looked back at me.

"John, think about it. You won't get away with it. Be smart."

His face twisted with rage. He lunged forward and tackled me, knocking me flat on the desk. He put his hands around my throat, the weight of that potato-sack body trapping me underneath him.

I tried to pry his hands off my neck. My vision started to darken at the edges and I was beginning to get dizzy for lack of air.

I pulled at his hands, managing to loosen a couple of fingers. I could smell his breath, feel the damp heat of his body against mine.

"I'll kill you," he said. "I will. Give it back."

I gritted my teeth and kneed him in the groin. He let go of my throat and doubled over. I backed away, gasping for air, and leaned against the wall, my head spinning. I didn't have the stamina to run. John sank to the floor, still squeezing his legs together in pain.

He moaned softly. I put my hand to my throat and closed my eyes. The room was strangely silent—the buzzing of the fluorescents and the scuttle of rodents suddenly deafening.

"I didn't do anything," he said at last.

I drew a deep, rattling breath and opened my eyes, batting my eyelids as my vision began to clear. "Let's just…settle down, okay? We've both got to settle down here."

The door swung open then, and a stooped, uniformed janitor stepped into the room. He was coal-black and ancient, his features rough and rutted like an ironwood tree.

"I saw a mouse," was all he said. "It crawled out under the door." He stood calmly, looking first at John and then at me, his eyes catching mine with a little twinkle.

"John," I said. "Look where we are." I gestured toward the janitor. "What are you going to do? Kill us both? You've got to stop this. It's over."

John stared dully at the janitor for a moment, then back at me, a look of resignation in his eyes. "I knew her mother. That's all."

"Brigid."

His eyebrows came together. "Carol. Carol Anne Stevenson. We went to homecoming."

"Right. Carol. I met her. She really liked you a lot. She told me that, John."

"You talked to her?"

"I went to her house this morning."

"You did?"

"She lives in Shreveport. She really liked you a lot. She told me. She showed me the picture of homecoming."

"I guess she recognized me."

"Drew?"

He nodded. "That must be why she called. Because she recognized me."

"At Finn's house. Right?"

John nodded. "And at that place where she…"

"Worked? You saw her where she worked? At Caligula?"

He wiped his nose on his sleeve and looked at the janitor again, who looked back at him, his shriveled face serene, unruffled. John looked down at the floor. His shoulders started to shake and tears dripped off his face and onto the linoleum.

"John, hey," I said. "Lots of men go to…those places. I mean, it's not the Middle Ages. No one's going to burn you at the stake or anything. Did she see you?" I asked. "At Caligula?"

"That's why she called me."

"You're sure she saw you? Did you talk to her?"

He nodded. "On the phone. Later."

"She called you and you called her back."

He nodded. "She was going to blackmail me."

"She said that? She used the word blackmail?"

"All I did was call her back. I never should have called her back. She wanted me to meet her. To talk."

"Did she tell you why, though, John?"

"She wanted to blackmail me."

I was still light-headed. I sank to the floor, my back to the wall, and sighed. "John, I don't think she was blackmailing you. She wasn't that sort of person. When did you see her at Caligula?"

"Thursday night."

"You saw her on Thursday night? You're sure?"

"That's why she called. She saw me. She recognized me."

"John, she called you before that. Thursday afternoon."

He sniffed loudly and looked up at me.

"What?"

"The message is dated Thursday. Not Friday." I reached into my pocket and produced the message, holding it up to show him.

It was smeared with the blood from my fingers. "See? The twelfth, 2:08 p.m. Maybe you got it on Friday. But the message came in on Thursday afternoon. Marci's very good about that."

He nodded in mute agreement. Marci's accuracy was indeed legendary.

"Did you ever go to Caligula before?"

He shook his head. "I never go to the same place twice."

"Really? Are there that many to choose from?"

He nodded.

I sighed again. The truth was getting uglier by the minute. "Did you meet with her?"

He nodded.

"Saturday night?" I asked.

He nodded.

"You met her in the alley, didn't you? Behind the car place."

"The pawn shop. Next door."

"And that was when she asked you for money?"

He nodded. "I got so mad." He started to cry again, huge, long drippy tears.

"And the ax?"

"I had it in my trunk. In case…"

The fight went out of us both then. At that moment, I felt like I might never live again. Not like a normal person. Not like I used to.

John groaned. I watched the arrogance deflate, the defensiveness wither. He looked up at me, meeting my eyes, for once, his face soggy, sorry. "I didn't mean it. I just got so mad."

"John, we have to call the police and tell them what happened."

I looked up at the janitor, who nodded and left.

John shuddered and kept crying.

"John, did you know she was pregnant? Did you give her a chance to tell you that?"

His blue eyes widened. They were bloodshot and sodden, his lumpy cheeks sticky, grimy.

"She was? It wasn't mine."

"I know that, John. She was probably going to ask you for help. Her whole life, her mother has told her you were the nicest person she's ever met. She needed help. That's all. She wouldn't have blackmailed you. She just needed some money."

John's shoulders started to heave. He balled himself up like a child, his head on his knees, and sobbed.

"I didn't know," he kept saying.

"I know you didn't."

"I just got so mad."

I heard a door open. I limped to the doorway as Helene emerged from the office at the end of the hall. I motioned for her to come. She stepped into John's office, her eyes sweeping around the room taking it all in, and listened as I explained the situation. As I talked, she walked to the sink, grabbed some paper towels and clamped them over the cuts on my hands. I'd forgotten that I was bleeding.

As the clinic began to buzz with weekend activity, campus security escorted two DPD cops into the clinic, along with a couple of paramedics. Helene sat with me in the hallway while the paramedics bandaged my hands and my knees and the cops secured the scene. The cuts were painful now. My neck throbbed.

Helene turned to me and sighed. "Well, I guess you got him off your committee."

"Not funny, Helene."

"You're right. I shouldn't have said that. But he wasn't the person we thought he was, was he?"

"No. He wasn't."

McKnight and Jackson showed up then. They stood and shook their heads as I told them what happened. I wasn't sure if it was anger or disbelief I saw on their faces—both, I guess.

"You're lucky he didn't kill you," McKnight said to me.

"I know."

"You're going to need stitches," Jackson said, pointing at my injuries. "I told you not to be a hero."

"I know."

"We'll need to talk to the janitor," Jackson said. He turned to the security guard. "Where is he?"

The guard shrugged. "Never saw a janitor."

"Isn't he the one that called you?" McKnight asked.

"It was some lady from Chicago. She said her kid was upset and wanted us to check the clinic. We got here right when the cops arrived."

Jackson asked me for a description of the janitor. I gave it to him, knowing they'd never find him.

Earl, Christine Zocci's angel, had intervened on my behalf once before. He'd been dressed as a hotel porter that time, not a janitor. But his ancient face, black as the night sea and just as old, had worn the same winsome, wise expression. I'd recognized him the instant I laid eyes on him.

Two uniformed cops led a weeping John Mulvaney out of his office. Students and staff lined up in the hallways, mouths open, as the detectives walked John down the hall in handcuffs. Helene and I followed them outside, the crowd from the clinic trailing behind us.

I thought I'd seen some terrible things. Heard some terrible stories. But as we all stood there, blinking in the cold daylight, and watched John Mulvaney duck, still bawling like a child, into the backseat of a squad car, I knew I'd hit a new bottom. It was truly the saddest sight I've ever seen.

A search of John Mulvaney's property turned up a pair of leather gloves (wool-lined), a pair of coveralls, a denim jacket with a fleece lining, and a pair of Wolverines, size 10—all stained with Drew Sturdivant's blood and hidden in a garbage bag in John's garage. Traces of Drew's blood were found on the gas and brake pedals of John's Honda. (They always forget about the pedals, Jackson had said.) The carpet in his trunk smelled as though it had recently been cleaned. And the fingerprint, of course, turned out to be his.

I still didn't understand why John had so deliberately drawn me into the carnage. Until McKnight sent a squad car for me late Sunday afternoon. "I think you should see this," he said.

I walked into John Mulvaney's living room and looked around. The floors and walls were bare, the furniture stiff and unwelcoming. There were no lamps, only an old overhead fixture, which had become a burial ground for moths and gnats. The only touch of personality came from several picture frames, arranged at angles around the room. I walked over to the mantle, picked one up, and gasped, then looked more closely at the rest. All the photos were of me.

As we walked through the house, the rooms became more bizarre and disordered. Books, newspapers, and magazines teetered in stacks. Dirty dishes were piled in the sink. Dark lumps of clothing lay in heaps on the floor. A plant lay overturned and dying. And everywhere, there were photos of me.

Snapshots were taped to the cabinets in his kitchen and poster-size shots were pinned to the walls of his bedroom. Framed photos punctuated the shelves of his study. All the photos had been taken without my knowledge, of course. At different times of day. In every possible state of dress. Some, it seemed, had been taken from quite a distance. In many of them, I recognized the rooms of my house in the background.

One photo taped to the wall in his study—a close-up of me smiling and talking to David at an outdoor cafe at night—was pocked with holes. He'd been using it as a dartboard.

His study housed a Macintosh computer stocked with photo-imaging software, along with what looked to be a very expensive color laser printer. His desk was littered with digital photography equipment. McKnight scrolled through the images in his cameras. More images of me.

"Stop," I said finally. "I don't want to see any more."

McKnight put the camera down.

"I guess he had a thing for you," Jackson said.

"How flattering," I said.

"These pictures," McKnight said, "they could be of anyone. You know that, don't you? You're just…the object of his obsession. Object being the key word here."

"I know. It's not about me. He doesn't know me."

"No, he doesn't," Jackson said. "He couldn't possibly."

I turned to McKnight. "Still believe in the Occam rule?"

"How does it go again?"

"In complex situations, barring the supernatural, the simplest solution is usually the right one."

He shrugged. "Sure. But sometimes the simplest explanation isn't the obvious one. I'll give you that."

I stepped past the dartboard and back into the living room, McKnight following along silently behind me. "You can't bar the supernatural," I said at last.

"Come again?"

"'Barring the supernatural, the simplest explanation is usually the right one.' That's the rule. But you can't bar the supernatural."

"Take a look around, Dr. Foster. This ain't the supernatural. This is just plain sick."

"What do you make of the evil you saw in that interview room? You saw it, Detective. You felt it. It was as real as the two of us standing here now."

He nodded. "Yep. I did."

"There's more to this than simple deviance and violence. We ran across…something dark, something very dark in that interview room."

He nodded.

"That's all I'm saying," I said. "Sometimes there's more to a situation than you can see with your eyes."

I said my good-byes and walked out of John Mulvaney's twisted little world and out into the crisp afternoon. The sun had begun its slide behind the leaves, pinking the sky and lighting the houses around me in a bright, golden wash of light. The bare branches of the trees seemed sharp, lined out against the wash of color in hard relief. The scene was so artful, so vivid, it seemed almost ordained, like a photograph.

But I'd had enough of photographs for one day. I got in my truck and drove to my house, my back to the sunset, switching my headlights on in the dimming winter light, my eyes fixed firmly on the road ahead.

I never got the chance to ask Gordon Pryne why he confessed to a crime he didn't commit. Martinez saw him a couple of times before they shipped him back to Huntsville. Jackson and McKnight blamed it on the meth. And barring the supernatural, I suppose that made sense. But from what I knew about Peter Terry, and about the battle Gordon Pryne was clearly losing for his mind and for his soul, I suspected he'd been put up to it.

Peter Terry is a liar, a cheat, and a thief. He'd steal what was left of Gordon Pryne just for the sheer entertainment of it. He enjoys waste, I believe. He preys on the lost and broken while they're standing at the brink, and then lures them over the edge to an ugly demise. To waste a soul, to trick a human being—the invaluable bearer of divine image—into despair and self-abnegation, this, for him, would be the consummate victory in his strange, twisted game. A losing game for his side, ultimately. I was certain he knew that. But clearly he intended to rack up as many points as possible before the buzzer.

I hoped that sometime, during her years at the Jesus commune, Drew Sturdivant had heard about love instead of judgment. I wanted to believe that someone had mentioned to her, even once, that God, unlike any other father she'd known in her short, impoverished life, is magnanimous with His love. That He dips from a bottomless well of regard and would fill even her dirty, chipped cup generously and without blame.

I hoped she'd heard somewhere along the way that love is not something that must be earned. That grace is not a merit-based system. And that there are no grades to be won or lost.

I doubted she had. Her report cards were proof enough of that. The paucity of this truth in Drew's life was, to me, the final tragedy of her brief time on this hard, surly earth.

I met Maria Chavez that night for supper, and invited Detective Martinez along at the last minute. The three of us went to a little Italian place with outside heaters and a roaring brick pizza oven and sat outside, tossing our winter coats aside in the warmth of the enclosed patio.

I sat across the table, my injuries throbbing, but feeling safe for the first time in weeks. I watched the two of them laugh and talk in Spanish about their Yayas and wondered to myself what sort of help Maria Chavez really needed. What had that dying homeless woman meant that night in the E.R.? Maria was a survivor. Anyone could see that. And she was, clearly, the perfect mother for her son, chosen, it seemed, for that purpose.

But her son, born of violence into serenity and love—what of him? Was Nicholas, sweet, wild-haired Nicholas, really as fatherless as he seemed? Had Peter Terry been there that day too? With Gordon Pryne? In Gordon Pryne?

I studied Martinez, so strong and quiet and wise, and wondered what a father—a spiritual man, a man of God, a man of strength and integrity—what could a man like that add to Nicholas's life?

"Dylan," someone said.

I came back to the table. "Hm?"

"We're being so rude! We're leaving you out of the conversation entirely," Maria said. She turned to Martinez. "No more Spanish tonight."

Martinez nodded. *"Si, no mas Español."*

"No, it's okay," I said. "You guys are hysterical. I don't feel left out. I just wish I had a Yaya, that's all. Anyone know where I can get one?"

We sat laughing and talking and eating pizza and drinking wine late into the night, the company warming me as much as the fire did. It was the first time in a while that I could remember smiling. The first time I could remember feeling anything other than afraid. Or alone.

I missed David, of course. He still hadn't called. Eventually, I knew he'd come around, at least to end it politely. It wasn't in his nature to leave things unresolved.

I hoped, though, that sometime soon I'd get the chance to talk to him. And to give him a kiss. And to say, quite sincerely, that I was sorry.

That, after all, is what is required in matters such as this. A little angel had told me so.